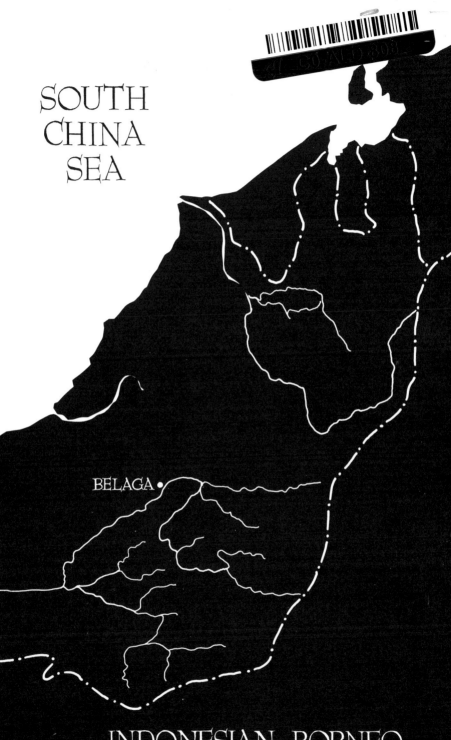

SOUTH
CHINA
SEA

BELAGA •

INDONESIAN BORNEO

THE DAY NOTHING HAPPENED

TERENCE CLARKE

THE DAY NOTHING HAPPENED

TERENCE CLARKE

Mercury House, Incorporated
San Francisco

This is a work of fiction. Names, characters, places, and incidents either are the product of the author's imagination or are used fictitiously. Any resemblance to actual events, locales, or persons, living or dead, is entirely coincidental.

The author wishes to thank the editors of *The Yale Review,* who published, in slightly different form, "The Red."

Copyright © 1988 by Terence Clarke

Published in the United States by
Mercury House
San Francisco, California

Distributed to the trade by
Kampmann & Company, Inc.
New York, New York

Mercury House and colophon are registered trademarks
of Mercury House, Incorporated

Manufactured in the United States of America

Library of Congress Cataloging-in-Publication Data
Clarke, Terence.
  The day nothing happened / Terence Clarke.
    p. cm.
  ISBN 0–916515–36–2 : $16.95
  1. Borneo—Fiction.   I. Title.
PS3553.L338D3   1988
813'.54—dc19   87–28747
                                                              CIP

For Cathleen

Contents

Author's Note   ix

1 / The Red   1

2 / Apai   21

3 / The Wee Manok   47

4 / The Champion   66

5 / The Truth   84

6 / The Lost D.O.   99

7 / A Rite of Passion   117

8 / The Well   136

9 / The Wo Family   156

10 / The Day Nothing Happened   179

11 / A Posthumous Gift   193

12 / The King   205

Author's Note

On August 31, 1957, the Malayan peninsula received its independence from Great Britain. In 1963, the island city of Singapore and the British Borneo colonies of Sabah and Sarawak became independent and were added to Malaya, despite the fact that the Borneo territories are separated from Malaya by several hundred miles of the South China Sea. The new nation was given the name Malaysia.

Sarawak immediately faced a military onslaught known as *konfrontasi,* or the "Crush-Malaysia campaign," launched as a guerrilla war by President Sukarno of neighboring Indonesia, who hoped to draw attention from internal problems plaguing his faltering government. For a period of about five years, owing to the war, Sarawak contained an unusual selection of peoples. First there were those who had always been there: ancient animist tribal groups, the most numerous of which were the Ibans; the indigenous Muslim Malays; Chinese and Indians. Then there were British and Australian troops who were helping the new government defend itself against the *konfrontasi.* Finally, there was a large civil service manned by British ex-colonialists, newly powerful Malay officials, and a few American State Department representatives.

Dan Collins was one of those Americans.

Yes, I have seen a little of the Eastern seas; but what I remember best is my first voyage there. You fellows know there are those voyages that seem ordered for the illustration of life, that might stand for a symbol of existence. You fight, work, sweat, nearly kill yourself, sometimes do kill yourself, trying to accomplish something — and you can't. Not from any fault of yours. You simply can do nothing, neither great nor little — not a thing in the world.

JOSEPH CONRAD

1 / The Red

"This is your house, Tuan."

Lubang gestured toward the shack. One corner of it sagged on a broken stilt. The tin roof shone miraculously above the shack's dirty rattan walls, bits of which fell away like leaves. Through a torn strip in the front door, a red rooster poked its head, pecking at a bit of offal on the porch. Several dozen chickens perched on the roof.

"How can that be?" Collins asked in Iban.

"Something wrong, Tuan?"

"Yes. The chickens are wrong," the American said.

Lubang stepped toward the shack, waving a hand in the air.

"These chickens live somewhere else," he said. "They just come here to spend the day."

The two men climbed the wooden stairs to the porch. The floorboards were dappled with white smears, covered with them, like chalk. There was a small, rusted lock on the latch, but the hasp had fallen away and the door was ajar. Lubang pushed it open as far as he could. Set askew, the door scraped against the floorboards. There were cobwebs everywhere. A bat flew past Collins's head and fled reluctantly into the sun out over the Skrang River. Collins ducked, and in the process dirtied his shirt against the rattan wall. He was too big for the room anyway, which had been made to Iban dimensions. He put a hand to his hair, which was black and quite curly, to brush away the dust that had settled on it when he had entered the room. In his white

1

shirt, gray British shorts, and sandals, Collins appeared enormous and baggy. The room was filled with chickens. The smell of their leavings, their loose feathers, and the airless coop they had made of the shack overwhelmed the American. He placed his hand over his nose. The chickens bobbed and jerked as they surveyed the intruders. Their clucking cluttered the air like laughter.

Collins strode from the room. He told Lubang he wished to speak with Tuan McGregor, who was in charge of Skrang Scheme. They hurried down the steps and climbed into Collins's Land Rover. He turned a quick circle through some mud, raising a cheer from the group of Ibans who watched from the porch of the adjoining longhouse, which Lubang pointed out as his own.

"These people will respect you, Tuan," he said as the Land Rover sped down the mud track. "Because I am their headman."

"Well," McGregor said a moment later, "it's the best I can do. My wife and I would put you up, but we haven't the room, you see."

McGregor leaned far back in his chair and laced his fingers behind his head. He was an angular man with red elbows and cheeks. He was well known up and down the rivers for his mastery of the Iban language, a tuan pandai, a wise man. The Ibans at Skrang, refugees from Malaysia's war with Indonesia, revered him. This had caused problems with some of the British with whom he worked, who disapproved of his success and, more particularly, of his Iban wife and half-breed son. McGregor's eyebrows protruded unevenly, red and gray wings that fluttered beneath a crag of red hair.

"Just declare war on them. They'll be gone in a day or two. The chicken is a coward, you know."

McGregor smiled, a half-painful expression that underscored his indifference to Collins's problem. Collins felt affronted.

"But this isn't what the people in Kuching told me would be here," he said. "I'm with the State Department. I'm supposed to have housing. I've been in Sarawak two years, McGregor. Engineer, Agency for International Development, all of it, and I've never been treated like this. They sent me out here to build your roads and you put me up in a chicken coop."

"Aye, laddie," McGregor replied.

Collins drove back the quarter mile to his shanty. He could see it from the main road, set apart from the longhouses the government had set up for the Ibans. There were still many chickens on the roof, little puffs of white that blended with the clouds. He drove past a group of longhouses, blockish rattan slabs thrown up in the middle of enormous fields. The buildings were intended to imitate the traditional Iban village but seemed more like exotic project-housing. There were no trees, and heat surged from the orange ground. Collins's shack looked over the river, directly opposite Lubang's longhouse.

Collins planned to make some overture to the inhabitants of the longhouse, to inquire about the chickens. This time of day, only women and children were on the porch. Collins parked his Land Rover and walked down the path the length of the building.

The women wore simple sarongs, which they wrapped about themselves and cinched above their breasts. They were short people with rough features. Teeth were missing, their arms were scratched and bruised from hard work. The women's feet had no grace at all, and their calves were muscular and globed like hard melons. The children had a softer look, due simply to their youth, Collins thought. All of them had decaying teeth, fallen apart from lack of care and a ruinous diet. One small boy was dotted with open sores and sat apart from his mother. He appeared exhausted. A girl several doors down was covered with scratched pocks. Many others were quite beautiful, Collins observed. Their skin remained smooth and dark, unravaged by the sun and the early aging that would afflict them later on. All along the porch, there was laughter as Collins passed.

When they encountered white people, the Ibans spoke with a floating, satirical jab that made each utterance sound like an insult. As he had grown fluent in their language, Collins had learned the humor of such exchange. He and several women prattled at each other now, the strong undertone of laughter present in everything they said. Yes, we know who owns the chickens, Tuan. We own them. No, there's nothing we can do. Chickens are chickens. They go where they wish.

He shrugged and smiled, but he was getting nowhere. Chagrined, he returned to his house.

He spent the afternoon sweeping it out, doing repairs on the larger rents in the leaf walls, and swabbing the floor with river water and soap. He had to break periodically to fight off the chickens. After the shack was straightened up, he unloaded his Land Rover. He had brought few possessions from Kuching, and it took him only three trips to bring them all into his house. After the first, he had to shoo away a rooster from the front seat of the Land Rover. It was a large, red bird that pecked at the cover of his tennis racket. The rooster squawked aggressively and tripped through the air toward the longhouse. Collins rolled up the Land Rover's windows. He pulled out his workboxes and engineering tools, a duffel bag containing his clothes, and a trunk carrying a variety of canned and packaged foods. All these he carefully arranged in a corner of his shack.

Collins broke out his mosquito net and hung it from the ridgepole, then went to the Land Rover for his mattress. As he climbed the stairs once more, he noticed the approach of three Ibans, one of whom was Lubang, the tallest of the group and evidently the oldest. The headman's dark blue tattoos were partially hidden beneath the short sleeves of a white sport shirt. His graying hair floated in wisps above the deeply lined face. The others deferred to Lubang and followed him in a line. Collins could tell they had dressed for the occasion. One man actually wore a blue pin-striped suit, soiled from years of occasional wear and the ravages of heat and mold. His bare feet, like those of all the men, were caked with red mud. His companion wore a traditional loincloth and a blue, Japanese T-shirt.

Lubang cradled a shotgun in his right arm. It had a single barrel and a stock with ragged, peeling varnish. Several rough gouges crisscrossed the butt. The barrel was dotted with rust.

"Welcome to Skrang Scheme," Lubang said, an utterance repeated quietly by both companions. Lubang had taken on a stiff manner, and in a formal gesture he held out the shotgun before him. "We're honored by your presence here, Tuan, and we thank you for helping the Iban people."

The others looked on silently. Collins, embarrassed by his awkward position, dropped the mattress to the stairs and held it there with a foot as Lubang extended the shotgun toward him.

"We hope you will accept this gift. Tuan Huntington, who was District Officer upriver some years ago, gave it to us when he returned to White Man's Land."

The gift touched Collins. He realized the delegation of Ibans was a very important matter. He mumbled a thank-you, and then offered stronger, more affirmative thanks.

"He said," Lubang continued, "that when someone came from White Man's Land who was kind, who would help the Iban, who could speak our language, we must pass this on to him."

He handed the gun to Collins, then reached into the pocket of his shorts for a box of shells.

"He said such a person would help us. A great deal."

Lubang handed the shells to Collins. The American, distracted a moment by the passage of a dozen chickens beneath his house, thanked the men finally and shook the hand of each. For a moment he wondered what Lubang meant by his remark about help. Wasn't he here to help already?

"I'm honored," Collins replied. "Very honored."

Lubang and the others took Collins's hand and pumped it awkwardly. They said nothing else and turned away in silence, leaving Collins with the shotgun in his hands, somewhat embarrassed that he had had so little to say to them. They returned to the longhouse. Collins picked up the mattress again, rolled it around the shotgun, and continued up the stairs.

He was confronted by the rooster, perched on the railing just outside his door. It was not a large bird, and it had a burgundy chest. Its crown sparkled on the top of its head. The Red, Collins named it. A gorgeous bird, he thought, though he swore as it defecated on his porch.

He shouted at the rooster, which, startled, burst into the air. Collins entered the room and threw his mattress on the bedstead. He came back onto the porch with his bucket of water and cleared away the dollop of excrement. The Red nosed about beneath the house, then came out into the sun. He pecked at some rice grains beneath the left fender of Collins's truck and disappeared again beneath the building.

Collins had come to Skrang Scheme to build the roads the government had planned for the rubber plantation there. After his first full workday on the plantation, he was exhausted as he entered the shack. He found his packaged food had been destroyed by the chickens. Powdered soup littered the floor and his luggage. The box of sugar was shredded. Paper lay in bits everywhere, and he surprised three of the birds inside his mosquito netting. The Red, trying to escape, tore away the support twine, and the netting collapsed on his bed.

The next morning Collins carefully lowered the wooden shutter on each window and locked the door. He placed the broom and his single chair upside down before the door to block any intruders. When he arrived home late in the afternoon, his shack resembled a small ship, birds everywhere in the rigging, lining the decks. A group of Iban children helped him scatter the chickens. They shooed them from the porch, then ran beneath the shack to scatter them further. Many of the birds flew back onto the porch, where Collins attacked them with his broom. The birds on the roof he could not reach, so that the ones who fluttered away did so of their own volition. Throughout Collins's defensive action, which was accompanied by laughter from Lubang's longhouse, The Red stood his ground. He hurried from the children's gleeful shouts, taunting Collins all the way. Collins concentrated his anger on The Red and pursued him for several minutes. If I can intimidate this one, he thought, I can control them all. He realized the foolishness of this and retreated again to his house, which was still crowded with laughing children.

That evening, The Red ascended the stairs and jumped up to the railing. Collins sat reading on his chair at the far end of the porch. The Red did not seem to notice his presence. He clucked and muttered, scratched himself, pecked at the roof-support to his left. Collins told him to go away. The bird ignored him, and

Collins began to shout. The chicken simply moved a few feet away. His head bristled, individual feathers shining in the warm light. Collins felt an unwarranted rage roiling in his gut. He stared at his book but could not read. Finally he threw the book squarely at The Red. It turned about over the rooster's head and fell noisily to the mud below.

The next morning McGregor ascended the stairs like a sergeant major. He tested the railings and admired the sturdiness of the fluttery walls. Collins offered him a seat on a wooden box.

"You've not done so badly here, Mr. Collins."

"Thanks. I've had a few problems, as you know. If it weren't for the damned chickens . . . and their owners . . . it wouldn't be half bad."

"Yes, well, you can't push these Ibans too far."

Collins nodded agreement.

"I introduced those chickens to them, you know," McGregor said.

"You did!" Collins sat down on the edge of the bed.

"Yes, it was a coup for me, as a matter of fact," McGregor continued. "There was a 4-H program set up in Simanggang by a few Americans. Your Peace Corps, I believe. They came up here offering us chickens for free. And the equipment to raise them."

McGregor leaned on his knees.

"You know, the Ibans have always raised chickens," he continued.

Collins sighed, awaiting a place to interrupt.

"And their birds were always so scrawny. Bones hung with twine, not much else . . ."

"Mr. McGregor!"

"But these! You know the Americans are bloody geniuses, aren't they? These are firm, full-bodied, wee birds. We're rather proud of them, Mr. Collins. Without them, these people would need more help, more food given to them by the government, more everything."

McGregor stood and walked out onto the porch. Against the line of trees that bordered the opposite bank of the river, his profile seemed transparent. The line of his nose faded into the bright light. He placed a green denim cap on his head and turned to the stairway.

"All this is by way of a suggestion, Mr. Collins."

The American closed the door behind him and followed McGregor down the stairs.

"A well-intended suggestion," McGregor continued.

Collins tightened his lips.

"So what is it?" he asked.

"Forget about the chickens and get on with your work."

Collins grunted unhappily.

"I'm sorry about this," McGregor continued. "But you're being frivolous about a matter of some importance to them. So, as you Americans would say, lay off!"

McGregor continued down the stairs and moved slowly around the end of the longhouse. He was greeted immediately by a burst of laughter from the women. He waved at them and stopped to talk a moment with several children — small, muddy urchins who gathered about him. He resembled an alabaster statuette, the porcelain ruined by an unkempt red beard. Collins resented McGregor's advice, though it made sense to him. It was only that its kindness was so bothersome. Collins feared now that he was simply discounting the Ibans and their chickens, something that offended his sense of professionalism. But to hell with professionalism, he thought. He decided his attitudes were just plain unkind and that he had become an unfeeling intruder.

The trouble was they were driving him nuts. He tried following McGregor's advice, but he could not sit by while, daily, the chickens soiled his house. Every day it took an hour to clean their shit from his porch. Having turned his trunk into a kind of food container, he was dismayed to find it covered with feathers and excrement each afternoon. Collins felt like a drowning case, washed over by waves of clucking chickens. One morning he took extra measures to secure his room. He mended the smallest tears in the walls and placed new latches on the shutters. For five days after that he successfully kept them out. On the sixth day he arrived home to find chickens perched everywhere inside, as though the house were a lecture hall. He attacked them with his broom.

All his efforts went for nothing, as the chickens scattered unharmed from Collins's house. He sat down on his top step and dropped the broom in his lap. In the distance The Red scurried about a field with several other chickens. The flock rushed back and forth in deference to his chattered instructions. The Red had taken on a kind of dictator's importance, and Collins identified the bird as the spirit that drove the chickens against him.

Collins built a trap. It was a variation of the stick-and-box invention he had used as a seven-year-old to try to catch rabbits. That technique had never worked, but Collins considered his failure then to be due to inexperience, to youth.

Now Collins imagined The Red as he pecked toward the box, lost his way, and meandered about the porch jabbing at the rice Collins had left out as bait. He would spot the little piece of canned fish attached to the stick and pick at it until the stick gave way. Collins imagined his feathers, a claw perhaps, sticking out from beneath the box, the vivid muffled squawks, and the rattling of the box itself.

He took special care with the box. He planned to leave the device on the porch, primed, while he was at work. The box had to be heavy enough to withstand The Red's justifiably feverish attempt to escape. At the Scheme store Collins was delighted when the Chinese behind the counter showed him a small, metal trunk that had been used as a seat for the past few years.

"This one, Tuan," the Chinese said. "Carry big stuff."

Collins gave the man his money and carried the trunk to the shack.

Before leaving the next morning, he set up the trap. The chickens were clucking beneath his house, awaiting his departure. Collins walked slowly down his stairway and greeted the women already working on the longhouse porch. He chatted with them a few minutes about the heavy rains, how the mud affected his Land Rover. Climbing into the front seat, he drove more slowly than usual up the dirt track. Collins was very excited, yet aware that he could easily reveal his excitement to the chickens. So the Land Rover passed slowly through the Scheme, Collins's arm waving at the children from the open window.

Arriving home that evening, he saw there had been no attempt at the fish. It remained on the stick, covered with white ants. The rice, on the other hand, had been cleaned away entirely, and The Red sat on the far end of the porch, indifferent to Collins's grumbling. Collins sprang the trap himself, an action that sent The Red and several others fluttering away to the protection of the longhouse. Collins then walked angrily to the river for a bath.

He prepared a curry for himself that evening and saved a morsel of it for the trap. He arose quite early the next morning, set the trap carefully beneath The Red's favorite railing, and left.

Again there was no result. When he returned, chickens were everywhere, and he threw dirt clods at them to scatter them from his porch. Collins felt so foolish doing this that he attempted it noiselessly. But several children heard the racket and joined him, searching for small clods of mud and tossing them fecklessly onto Collins's porch.

The sun had set when he returned from work the next night, and he approached the shack slowly. He expected no change in the trap, and when his headlights fell across the porch, he was certain none had occurred. A half dozen chickens lined the railing before his front door. Several others pecked about beneath the house, riveted by the light like small statues between the stilts. Collins revved the engine and the chickens scattered. He got out of the Land Rover, leaving the lights on and making sure all the windows were tightly closed. He climbed the stairs, intent on finding his Coleman lantern. When he reached the porch, hardly paying attention, he suddenly halted. The trap had been sprung.

He wanted to lift the trunk right away to make sure The Red was inside. But there could be no question of it. Collins had set the trap for The Red. The Red had not appeared among those chickens that had frozen in his headlights. It had to be him. Collins feared, though, that if he lifted the trunk too quickly, The Red would get away.

A coup de grace was necessary. He saw no feathers. No telltale claw. But Collins did hear rough scratching, and the trunk shivered a moment in the glare of light on the porch.

He entered his room, fired his Coleman lantern, and looked about for a weapon. The toolbox contained a tire iron, but he decided a broader surface was necessary—something that would crush the rooster irrevocably. He stepped over to his luggage in the corner. Holding the lantern above his head, Collins saw the familiar worn grip of his tennis racket, a Slazenger Challenge No. 1. He unzipped the cover and tossed it aside. Hurrying to the porch, he placed the lantern on the boards and prepared himself for the confrontation.

He moved the trunk a few inches. From within came a feverish scratching, some hollow knockings and squeaks, then silence. Collins raised the tennis racket above his head and steadied himself. He was partially dazzled by the headlights. The glare threw harsh shadows across the porch. One side of the trunk gleamed in the light, the others disappeared in darkness. Collins's hands and arms gave off a metallic glare. The hair on his arms resembled wires. He reached for the trunk, took hold of the handle in his fingers, and pulled it up.

A black river rat, crusted with mud, ran from the trunk. When it encountered Collins's foot, it turned up his calf, then scrambled across his instep, screaming with fear. Collins cried out and jumped aside. His tennis racket fell through the air and ricocheted down the steps, where it landed among several scattering chickens.

Collins's heart was in chaos. He leaned against the railing to calm himself. He heard noises from the longhouse, the sound of several people running toward his shack. The chickens disappeared, clucking, into the distance. Lubang, followed by several others, appeared before the Land Rover. They formed brightly outlined silhouettes, a confusion of arms and legs.

"OK, Tuan?" Lubang shouted.

Collins spoke, though there was a nervous tremor in his voice he could barely control. He felt only the rat, groping at his foot.

"I'm all right," he said. "There was a rat here, a rat . . . He surprised me, that's all."

"Yes, Tuan. Rats everywhere," Lubang replied, "Not much we can do. You get rid of one rat, right away you've got ten others."

The crowd assented. Collins picked up the lantern and shoved the trap into a corner of the porch. When he reached the bottom of the stairs, Lubang handed him the tennis racket. In the distance a hen skittered about, lost in the dark.

At dawn, he was awakened by the call of a rooster. He reached out and fingered his mosquito net, pushing it aside a few inches to look out the window at the sky. Collins saw the tops of two coconut trees, bursts of foliage that changed color as the sun rose, from silhouette black to bright dusty green. On clear days the trees were motionless, and Collins could pretend he had a painting hung from his ragged wall. He lay on his bed, nodding sleepily as the sun rose and changed the light on the canvas. He dozed, dreamed, and lazily turned about, always aware of the view, always dismayed by it as the noise of the chickens rose through the light.

After several minutes he sat up and rubbed his eyes. He had barely slept. Memories of the rat had flashed through his mind all night, followed by drugged mutterings and epithets. Collins hated the impenetrable concern the Ibans had shown for him — impenetrable because they so obviously intended to do nothing about his troubles. Instead they gathered together to resist the interloper, to laugh at him, and to assist in driving him crazy without themselves being responsible for the outcome.

And you! he admonished himself. How can you be so distracted by such an idiotic situation? He got up and opened the door. The river had risen during the night, and Collins watched the children bathing on the bank far below. They reminded him of water lilies as their sarongs floated up to the surface beneath their arms. The children turned and swirled noisily in the brown water. He lay down again to read for a few minutes, but he could not focus on the pages. An embarrassed fury washed through him moment to moment. He felt his face flush. His eyes were painfully hot, as though filled with dust.

The Red hopped along Collins's porch past his door and fluttered up onto the railing. A petty, childish thing, Collins thought, to be affected so much by a goddamned chicken. He turned over, his back to the door, and continued reading.

The Red pecked and scratched. His occasional clucking seemed pleasant and communal, and that infuriated Collins. Another chicken dipped about the porch, nibbling at the grains of rice still left from the previous night. The Red chatted quietly, exchanging minor news interrupted by brief turns of excitement. Overhearing all this, Collins laid his book aside and quietly pushed away the mosquito net. He walked to the corner and rummaged among his things — the suitcase, the few technical books, the toolbox, and the slide rule. Lubang's shotgun lay along the base of the wall. Collins placed a shell in the barrel, sat down on the edge of his bed, leveled the gun at The Red, and blew him away.

All the chickens outside scattered, many of them bounding across the field toward the longhouses. For Collins, the noise was hilarious. But the deep, stormlike echo of the shotgun blast, making its way back from the hills across the river, grew louder and louder. It hovered over his shack a moment, then receded like dark rain. Collins heard shouts from the river, then Lubang and several others approached the house. He hurriedly put on his pants and propped the gun in a corner of the room. He walked onto the porch. There were several crushed feathers on the boards below the railing, though the force of the blast had pushed the rooster far into the field. The Red was barely recognizable — a pastiche of blood and feathers, entrails and bones sticking out at odd angles. The head was still intact. The rest was in complete ruin. When Lubang and the others arrived, they gathered about The Red, then looked up at Collins with surprise and, he realized, considerable resentment. He stared at them a moment, feeling falsely invincible from his high perch and amazed by what he had done.

"Collins," McGregor said as the American sat down in his office later. "This is a terrible thing."

"What's a chicken?" Collins shrugged.

McGregor spoke very precisely, his mouth so tight and thin lipped that it seemed mechanical.

"What do you think this is, Yank? Corregidor?"

"Of course I don't."

"Damned chicken means a lot to these people, you know."

"Where I live means a lot to me."

McGregor waved a hand before his chest.

"I know that. But the chickens would pass in time. They . . . tell me, do you know anything about chickens?"

"Too much, McGregor. I'm not the villain of this piece. If anyone is, you are. Lubang and his people are. Why can't they have some consideration for my needs?"

"Listen to me a moment. You've been there just a week. The chickens aren't used to you yet, that's all. They'll move on. Basically, they don't like human beings, you know."

"Shit all over us, don't they?"

McGregor did not speak for a moment. He seemed shocked by Collins's abrupt rudeness. "I'll continue on, if I may," he said. For a moment he did not look at Collins. There was distaste in his tone of voice, a wish that this moment would quickly pass away. "These people have been living at subsistence level for years. Forever! We've been able to do something to relieve that. Introduced them to diversified farming, although it's a valid question whether God himself in heaven could make anything grow here. Better pigs. And chickens, lad, chickens!"

Collins grunted and did not reply.

"By shooting that rooster, you've taken away a most valuable commodity."

"There are hundreds of them."

"It simply appears that way. The chickens decided to make your miserable wee shelter their home more than a year ago. And I'm sorry to tell you that you inhabit the roost of all the chickens for this part of the Scheme."

"That much I know."

"They may seem to be many, from your point of view, Collins. But they are few. One per family, sometimes two. And you did in the headman's only rooster."

McGregor's eyes descended mournfully toward the desk and he pursed his lips. He spoke with restraint.

"It gives me pain to say this, but you've made a grave error. Many errors, all in one. You've taken away potential food. You've imposed yourself on them in an overbearing way, to say the least. And you've insulted Lubang deeply, deeply."

Collins resisted the urge to leave the man's office without a reply. Unhappily, he feared McGregor was right.

"Well, what do you want me to do?" he asked.

McGregor's face opened up and he spread his hands before him.

"Come to the longhouse with me tonight. They want to get rid of you, you see. But I need you, Collins. I need your roads. They need them. So come with me and we'll see about an apology."

McGregor smiled and offered Collins his hand.

"It's a devilish, a ticklish matter, Collins. High diplomacy."

He smiled broadly, and Collins with reluctance took his hand.

The roof of the longhouse blotted out the stars, a black wedge shoved into the sky. The sound of their shoes in the drying mud put Collins on edge. The two men ascended the notched log that served as a stairway into one end of the house and entered the gloom of the porch.

A longhouse makes up an entire Iban village. This one had twenty-one rooms in a row, all opening onto a wide roofed porch. During the day women worked on the porch, stringing baskets, preparing food. Several doors connected that porch to another uncovered one, parallel to the first, which also served as a workplace. Each room housed a family, usually more than one generation, with separate mosquito nets for children, parents, and grandparents.

When Collins's eyes adjusted to the dim candlelight, he made out a group of Ibans at the far end of the covered porch, gathered about Lubang and a few other dignitaries from the Scheme. The floor was made of halved bamboo slats, which creaked and rattled as the two men walked its length. As they approached the meeting, Collins became quite nervous. His mind wandered away willfully from the moment at hand. He was unsure, peeved, feeling the need to argue.

The Ibans welcomed them. Lubang rose and gestured toward an empty straw mat opposite him. Between them lay an open packet of Rothman's cigarettes, an old Zippo lighter, a can of Chinese tobacco with a chewed English pipe, plus three metal cups and a large, green bottle of tuak, the local rice wine. Lubang poured wine into the cups and passed them to Collins and McGregor. It was a clear liquid with sediment of burnt rice at the bottom, an acrid drink that, taken in a single gulp, brought tears to Collins's eyes.

"Well, Tuan Collins and I have talked about the difficulty," McGregor addressed the Ibans. "He has told me of his sorrow for having killed your rooster, Lubang. He did not understand what he was doing."

"Yes, I want to apologize," Collins interjected. "I simply went amok for the moment."

His use of the Malay word was helpful. Running amok in Malay is something for which there is emotional justification. It is a passionate craziness. The Ibans mumbled assent, and Lubang poured a second glass of tuak for the American.

"I cannot explain, you see. It was something that possessed me."

"Yes, these things happen among our people," McGregor interrupted. He caught Collins by surprise. "In our country a man is overtaken from time to time, driven to strange acts by the haunted forces."

"What are you talking about?" Collins asked in English.

McGregor held up a hand and continued.

"A terrible thing like this can be explained," he said. "Such ghosts make it impossible to think, to act properly. A fearful event. A spirit enters into you . . ."

He placed his clenched hands on his stomach and raised them toward his chest.

"Climbs to your throat, into your head . . ."

"A strong ghost," Lubang muttered. "Dangerous."

"Yes, it is."

"McGregor, this is foolish," Collins said. His use of English had no effect on the Ibans. They seemed to conclude that the white men had to use their own language to speak properly of such odd events.

"Very dangerous," McGregor continued. "Who knows why it happens? It is a dark ghost, an invisible darkness. You can't control it. It comes for no reason."

A tide of mumbling swept through the Ibans. They discussed the haunted forces with real dismay. Collins heard a few references to similar types of possession in their own experience. He grew alarmed. When he protested again to McGregor, the Scotsman answered him in English.

"Don't worry. We'll have this matter in hand presently."

"But it isn't the truth!"

Lubang and the others whispered among themselves. The men turned guarded looks toward Collins. Their voices were muffled by their fear of being heard by him.

"These spirits," Lubang asked. "Do they last forever? Do they move from person to person?"

"Oh no," McGregor replied. "They are often benevolent. They can turn an act of evil into one for good."

"Jesus Christ!" Collins said.

"But they are difficult," McGregor continued. "Often they resist."

"What do you do?" Lubang asked. "Are there charms? Can they be dispelled?"

"No," McGregor replied. "The spirit lives in the heart. It acts on its own."

"No fetish to make it work? Do you dance? Are there festivals?"

"No!" Collins interrupted. "No fetishes. No such thing!"

"Difficult to believe." Lubang shook his head. "Strange ghosts that simply act when they want to. We believe we have more control over the haunted forces than that."

"Yes," McGregor said. "But all spirits act on their own. You've seen bad harvests. You've seen your best fighting cock lose."

"This is as you say," Lubang assented. "And I don't have a rooster. As much as we welcome Tuan Collins and respect his haunted forces, I don't have a rooster."

"I can change that!" Collins said hurriedly. He had been straining to bring a note of rationality to McGregor's preposterous claim. "I'll replace the rooster. And more!"

Lubang grunted, alarmed by Collins's sudden outburst. The Ibans remained silent.

"What more?" Lubang asked.

Caught up, Collins had no reply. He sat back ponderously, in need of time. He pushed his glass forward and waited for it to be filled. The Ibans were pensive, quietly alarmed. He feared McGregor's claims had marked him as a ghost himself, a harmful label that could render his presence in the Scheme useless.

"Surely we can think of something," Collins said.

"We are a poor house," Lubang replied. "Poor people, from far upriver."

He shook his head.

"We come from very, very far," he continued. "And we need food. You know, Tuan McGregor. You've seen us. Maybe his ghosts will treat us kindly."

"He's right," McGregor said in English.

"We need supplies," Lubang continued. "Food."

"Chickens," McGregor said.

"Yes. Chickens."

The two men turned toward Collins and waited. There was a brief silence, punctuated by the rooting about of animals beneath the porch. Collins sighed.

"How many?" he asked.

"Perhaps twenty-five?" Lubang muttered deferentially.

Collins lowered his eyes. A puddle of tuak on the mat reflected the dim yellow flames of the candles. A lone Rothman's remained in the packet. He searched the toes of his left foot. He coughed and glanced at McGregor.

"Twenty," he said.

"Plus the rooster," Lubang replied quickly.

Collins nodded in agreement.

"Good boy, Yank!" McGregor slapped his knee.

The Ibans began clapping. The women laughed, screeched, threw their arms toward Collins. He found himself surrounded by them, each wanting to shake his hand. He could not grasp them all, so that fingers and palms fumbled about his arms. The women examined his eyes and perused his white, hairy hands. From a distance, the children watched him with awe.

"It's only right," McGregor said. In the confusion he had to speak loudly to be heard. "Though it's too generous, Mr. Collins."

"Least I can do, McGregor, dammit."

"Oh, it's more than that, lad. These people remember acts of kindness. You know what happens with this sort of thing? You get celebrated. The people love you."

"Terrific."

"They do, they do. And when you pass up and down the longhouses, they compete for your attention. Compete for it! The Ibans don't forget an act of generosity."

"Well, I'm glad to do it."

"Good for you, Collins."

McGregor slapped Collins's knee and laughed out loud. It was a reticent sound, gleeful but harsh.

Lubang poured more tuak and waited as Collins and McGregor tossed the drink down. The Ibans laughed at Collins's grimace, then stood to shake his hand. He spoke with every person who passed before him, thanking each one for understanding his problem. After several minutes he excused himself and walked down the porch toward the exit and the notched log.

A vein of gratitude ran through the longhouse. McGregor spoke in a heartfelt way about this example of American generosity, how you could tell the kindness of a people by the sincerity of their actions. Look how well he speaks the language. Look at the ease of his generosity, how he asks nothing in return. The Ibans spoke all at once, a stampede of good feeling that reached a high point as Collins passed through the door far down the porch.

He hurried from the longhouse. An outburst of laughter came from inside. Collins struggled with the notion that the Ibans and McGregor were really celebrating his foolishness. The thought fluttered again into his mind despite his effort to get rid of it.

He made the turn toward his shack. He knew the chickens would be there, fastened to the railings around his porch. At first he merely heard them, a quiet clucking that belied their numbers. He switched on his flashlight and sprayed it across the roof. The chickens were frozen for the moment against the darkness. They appeared made of cardboard, messily painted by children. Their eyes were like pinholes in the splashed feathers.

Collins doused his light and trudged toward the shack. He noticed a movement near his Land Rover and retrieved the light from his shoulder bag. When he shined it on the truck, he saw a large rooster, yellow and brown, dipping and nodding from the steering wheel. Another smaller bird hopped quickly through the open window onto the seat. Two others rested on the back cushion of the driver's side. Both appeared to be asleep, and they were startled by Collins's light. Defeated, Collins climbed the stairs to his room, shut himself in, and went to bed.

2 / Apai

Panau shielded her face against the water. Hunkering on the floorboards of the longboat, she held herself steady with one hand on a gunnel. She pulled a ragged batik cloth about her shoulders for protection. Her husband, an Iban chieftain named Bada, stood in the back of the boat operating the outboard engine. Panau had taken this moment to speak privately with Collins, who sat next to her, his knapsack resting in his lap. She was crying.

"I don't know where my daughter Apai is, Tuan," she said. Her tears mixed with the spray. Gray hair stuck to her forehead in thick strands. "She's in Kuching. But Kuching is so far away, so big."

The boat moved down the left bank of the Skrang River beneath the trees. With the couple as guides, Collins had been visiting longhouses, explaining to the upriver Ibans why the Malaysian government was putting the Skrang Scheme rubber plantation on this part of the river. Collins had never met Apai. Once he had seen her children — two-year-old twin boys. They now lived with their father on the Rajang River more than a hundred miles away. The dissolution of Apai's marriage had infuriated her father, who had told her she was no longer welcome in the longhouse, and she had disappeared. No one had heard from her for a year.

"I'm so worried," Panau said. She pulled the cloth more tightly about her shoulders. "My husband won't let me speak about her. But she's my daughter, Tuan. Apai should be here with us. She can find a good husband. She can farm with us."

Collins studied Panau's face and her pinched, reddened eyes. She lowered her head against another wash of water over the bow. Collins touched Panau's hand where it clenched the wet cloth.

"Maybe I can help," he said. A meeting of AID personnel was coming up at the American consulate. Despite Panau's fears, Kuching was a small city. Collins could spend an extra day looking for Apai.

He worried though about what he could do for the girl if he did locate her. Bring her back out here? he thought. What if she doesn't want to come? The fact is her father will throw her out again. Collins felt he was the wrong person to be searching for her anyway. There was an expectation among the Ibans that if you were white you were English and therefore could do anything. And Collins was not English. He feared he had simply been typecast.

But what are you here to do, he wondered, if not that? Build roads? That's all? Mix cement? Collins grew quite angry with himself when, faced with a problem for which he had no solution, he fell back on regulations. Such problems almost never could be solved by logic. They always involved some colleague's emotional failure, for example, or a beleaguered, impossible wish that Collins could not understand. A regulation somewhere, he remembered — maybe no more than an admonition from one of his superiors — had said that officials like Collins were not to become mixed up in the host population's personal difficulties. He had always disliked the term "host population." It made the people sound like bugs on a dog.

But English or not, Collins was indeed viewed as a powerful figure by the Ibans. He *could* get things done for people, so much so that he was almost always asked to do so. Disaster, such as the poor, mulched rooster he had killed at Skrang, was one of the possible outcomes. His stubbornness there had created a scandal. Here, with Panau and her daughter, he feared he would go wrong the other way. Attempting to help, he might, in some way he could not foresee, reveal a secret or unearth an old betrayal that no one wanted to remember.

"Well, I'll be there next week," Collins said finally. "There's a chance I can find her."

Panau ducked her head and glanced quickly back at her husband, afraid he would see her crying.

"I'd be so grateful," she said. She wrapped herself in the cloth and sat back against the canvas-covered pile of slabbed rubber behind her. Her misery, so complete yet so guarded, welled up in her again, and she began weeping. Collins looked toward the riverbank. The trees grew like pillars up the shore, adorned with heavy mosses and vines. Broad-leafed plants and ferns filled the spaces between them. The air itself appeared so green and so dark that the fecundity of the forest seemed to give way to rot and water.

In Kuching Collins searched the bars on Rajah Brooke Road for Apai. Malaysia's war with Indonesia had filled Kuching with Malay, British, and Australian soldiers. Collins was not sure what he would tell Panau were he to find Apai in one of the bars. But he had nothing to go on in his search except the sad expectation that Apai could hardly have gone anywhere else.

Early in the evening he walked into Albert's NAAFI Lounge. The Beatles' raspy voices rose from the jukebox in a song about love forever. A British soldier jumped about to the music, sliding in his jackboots across the linoleum floor. He wore fatigues and a dirty T-shirt. A long, sheathed knife was attached to his belt. He was dancing with an Iban woman, quite small, whose back flexed and shone in the dim pink light. Her low-backed minidress, which was sequined and red, just covered her. Her eyes were expertly made up, giving her the look of one of the stars of the Malay movies that played in the theater across Rajah Brooke Road from the bar. Her bare legs knocked against the Briton's. She moved her tiny feet in flip-flops so deftly about the floor that they escaped his clumsy, happy shuffling altogether. She was a foot shorter than he, though when she laughed her voice was much louder than the Englishman's. It so spirited the soldier when she laughed that he picked her up and twirled her about to the music, causing her to laugh even more.

Collins sat at the bar and watched the couple's dance reflected in the mirror before him. The jukebox, which was a new British model, glowed at the end of the bar, making it the major source of light in Albert's NAAFI. The bar itself was a long formica counter, edged with metal runners, that was covered with small puddles of water. Albert Wang, the owner and bartender, stood at one end watching the dancers. Red paper lanterns hung like small pagodas from a runner along the top of the mirror. The black wire that ran between them was clotted with dust.

Collins was a favorite in the Kuching bars. He spoke the Iban language, something none of the British soldiers could do. It gave the women in the bars pleasure to make fun of the British, in Iban, for Collins's benefit. Few of the women understood the difference between Collins and the soldiers. He explained he was from the United States, and they understood it was a different country. But they couldn't imagine where it was or that it could be very far from the country of the principal white people — that is, England.

Members of a Liverpool regiment headquartered in Kuching, the soldiers spoke a language Collins himself could barely understand. Their accent tripped and surged, forcing him to listen carefully. There was grace in the accent though, in the way so many statements sounded like questions, in the lilt and irony of the tone of voice. Albert's NAAFI was a favorite hangout of the Liverpool soldiers, half a mile from their regimental quarters.

"Well, what do you think of her?" the soldier asked. As the record was changing, he had come to the bar for change for the jukebox. His elbow pushed along the bar in front of Collins's as he sprawled on the formica. The soldier was about thirty-five years old, and his white T-shirt was stained with sweat and, here and there, whiskey.

"Beautiful," Collins said. "Lovely skin."

"What's that?" The soldier sat up. "Say that again."

"I said she's very pretty."

"You're an American!"

"That's right," Collins replied. A large grin appeared on the soldier's face. He placed both hands on the bar. His short-cropped hair looked like a low hedge across his forehead.

"Never been to the States, Yank. Like to, though," he said. He extended a hand. "Name's Glendenning. Jimmy."

He turned around and spotted Albert at the far end of the bar. "Bring the Yank here a whiskey, Albert."

"Yes, Tuan."

"Me, as well."

"Yes, Tuan."

Albert looked beneath the bar for two glasses and brought up a bottle of Haig and Haig Pinch. His hands enveloped the glasses. As he walked along the bar, he appeared stooped, almost old, though he was only about thirty. His straight, black hair hung across his forehead.

"Bloody 'Tuan,'" Jimmy said as Albert took up his place again at the end of the bar. "I've only been out here a week, and I hear that all the time. What the hell does it mean?"

"Just a term of respect," Collins said. "Everyone uses it here. Except the Chinese."

Jimmy glanced at Albert a few seconds.

"But Albert's Chinese, isn't he?"

"Yes. He's making fun of you."

"Albert?" Jimmy turned back toward Collins. "Go on. He wouldn't make fun of the British Army, would he?"

Collins accepted the drink and toasted Jimmy. The American's face glowed in the light from the jukebox. His white, short-sleeved shirt had a pink sheen. The soldiers, those who could understand his accent, liked Collins because he avoided the American habit of self-glorification.

"What are you doing out here, then?" Jimmy asked.

"I work in the outback," Collins said. "I'm an engineer."

"Giving the British a hand," Jimmy said.

"No. I'm with the U.S. State Department. I'm working at the Skrang Scheme, building the road system there. Do you know it?"

"Nope. I'm headquartered here in Kuching, myself. Don't even know where that . . . what is it? Skrang? Don't even know where it is. I'm a mechanic. Work on the lorries."

Jimmy sat back on his stool and contemplated Collins a moment.

"CIA," he muttered.

"What's that?"

"Out here helping us out, isn't it?"

"Beg your pardon?"

"A bit of espionage."

"No, I . . . "

"Come on!" Jimmy said. He took up his glass and drank down most of the whiskey. "What was your name?" he asked.

"Dan Collins."

"Right, Dan. Why else would you be out here? You must be a spy."

Collins hung his head over his drink. A lot of AID people around the world *were* involved in intelligence. But Sarawak was crowded with counterinsurgency specialists from Britain, Australia, and New Zealand, all of them worried about the war with Indonesia. In addition, there were thousands of troops from those countries fighting against the Indonesians on behalf of the new Malaysian government. In view of all that, Collins's own activities were of little importance. Collins simply did what the Interior Ministry had hired him to do. For the moment that meant building several sections of gravel road in a government rubber plantation. The mud and the forest gave up little that was suspicious.

Jimmy leaned toward Collins. His breath smelled of cigarettes and curry.

"Not many Americans out here," he said. His voice was guarded. He looked over his shoulder. "With all this, the war and all . . . "

Jimmy took a packet of Players from his shirt pocket. The cigarette he pulled from the box sagged with humidity.

"I don't believe that about building roads, Dan," he said. Lighting the cigarette carefully, he hid the flame between two cupped hands. He leaned his shoulder next to Collins's. He did not look up. Red-skinned, with lumpy tattooed forearms and fat bulging from the sleeves of his T-shirt, Jimmy was happy with his conspiratorial discovery. "Come on, what are you really doing here?"

"Just now I'm looking for a woman."

"Like the rest of us," Jimmy said.

"No, she's a particular woman. She comes from the Skrang region. Her family are friends of mine."

A paper cup hit Jimmy in the back of the head. The woman, his dancing partner, broke into laughter.

"Apai's her name," Collins said.

Her voice rose up behind the two men as she shouted in Iban that the British were cheapskates, that they never paid for what the women gave them. The jukebox had started again, and she began dancing with one of the other soldiers.

"What'd she say?" Jimmy asked.

"That you look like a kind man," Collins said. He lied to avoid causing an argument between the couple. "That she would like to dance again soon."

"Well, that's all right by me, Yank."

Jimmy stood up.

"Of course she's out there with that idiot Steuben just now, but we can put a stop to that."

"Steuben?"

"Eighteen years old. Mathew Steuben. Thinks he owns the whole fuckin' world."

Jimmy stepped onto the dance floor, then looked back.

"Do you fancy getting something to eat later on, Dan? At the bus station. We can talk some more about this."

He turned away, then reached back to the bar to put out his cigarette.

"About the espionage, that is," he said.

"But there's nothing to it."

Jimmy laughed, then turned toward the dance floor.

"What did you say that woman's name was?" he asked.

"Apai," Collins said.

"Well," Jimmy replied. He pointed at the dancing couple. "I believe you've found her, mate."

"How so?"

"'Cause that's her name. Apai."

Jimmy walked out onto the dance floor and cut in on the soldier. A very young man with blonde hair, Steuben wore jeans and a short-sleeved sport shirt hanging outside his belt. He was not as large as Jimmy, who placed his hands on his hips and waited.

"I'm not going to give her up, Jimmy," Steuben laughed.

"Pack it in, mate," Jimmy said, pushing Steuben aside. Steuben stumbled and let go of Apai.

"My turn," Jimmy said.

"No," Apai shouted. "Mathew. I dance you!"

She stepped between the two men and took Steuben's hand. For the moment she had the look of an affronted debutante. She pouted. Steuben began dancing.

"You my boyfriend," Apai said. She placed her hand on the back of Steuben's neck, then stuck out her tongue at Jimmy.

"Fickle, aren't they?" Jimmy said as he sat down again next to Collins. He laughed. But Collins discerned Jimmy's real disappointment. His laugh faltered and he said nothing else. The two men simply watched Apai dance. Steuben, teenaged and unblemished, held on to her like a lover in a movie. His face hung over her shoulder and his right hand caressed her back. He clutched her as though he were desperate, grateful, for her attention. After a moment Jimmy took up his glass of whiskey. He did not sip from it. He and Collins simply watched her dance.

Collins remained at Albert's NAAFI the rest of the evening. From Albert he learned that Apai indeed had come from Skrang and that she had been in Kuching for about a year. He decided not to tell Apai who he was until he could have a moment alone with her. He worried she wouldn't want to talk with him at all if he just blurted it out. Delicacy was important. He did not want to frighten her.

He danced with her twice. Her hand on his neck, the press of her legs against his, the way, when she laughed, she pulled him closer — he found that he too was chagrined by her preference for Steuben. But Collins was disturbed as well by the nervousness in Apai's laughter and its strained hilarity. She alone of all the women seemed not to care that he could actually speak with her. Apai made him feel as though he were just another customer. A British customer at that, just another soldier. This intruded on his hope that his knowledge of Iban put him in a different class from the British, a more intimate one. Collins found that he liked Apai. Her eyes and her laughter were alike, bright yet tinged with a distracting sadness. The fact was, he liked her a great deal.

At midnight Collins joined Jimmy at the outdoor food stalls next to the bus station in downtown Kuching. Beneath a canvas pavilion about twenty makeshift kitchens had been set up for the night. Each chef cooked for a half dozen tables, all of which were out in the open beyond the pavilion. There was a territorial rigidity to the arrangement of the tables. A customer had to know which chef owned which tables in order to be sure where to sit. Jimmy led the way to Louie Foo's, where they were greeted by Louie's waiter.

"Got a place for us?" Jimmy asked, and the waiter hurried about setting an empty table with chopsticks, cracked porcelain cups, paper napkins, and a large pot of tea. "Two bottles of Tiger, mate. Big ones," Jimmy said.

Despite his gruff orders, Jimmy maintained an air of friendliness. He had talked all evening of how much he enjoyed Kuching, how he'd served in a lot of places in the world — Honduras, Aden, Hong Kong, "Northern Ireland, for Christ's sake" — and none had contained a town quite like it. Jimmy rhapsodized, through his laughter, about the women, the food, and the weather. He loved it all.

"And you know, Dan," he said as the waiter brought the drinks. "I might marry that woman I met tonight."

"Apai? What for?"

"Not many others like her, that's why."

Jimmy poured two glasses of beer. Light brown foam spilled over the rim of Collins's glass.

"I've been everywhere, seen everything. She's the best I've found, that's all," Jimmy said.

Sipping from his glass, Collins looked at the crowd in the square. The waiters carried trays with bowls of chicken soup, buckets of rice, pork, dim sum, and sweet pastries. Almost every table was occupied. Jimmy ordered rice and chicken, a hot-rice soup, and a plate of vegetables, plus two more bottles of Tiger Beer. When the first platter came, Jimmy served Collins.

"But I want you to do something for me, Dan."

Collins took up his chopsticks. The vegetables steamed into his face, and he stirred them about to cool them.

"I know you've a bit of background in espionage, see?" Jimmy said. He poured some vegetables over a large pile of rice in the middle of his plate. "I need some spying done."

"On Apai?"

"That's it. You know that little guy she was dancing with earlier."

"Yes."

"Mattie Steuben's his name."

"Yes, I . . . "

"Bloody Kraut."

"But he's from Liverpool, isn't he?"

"Yeh, we all are. But his parents are bloody Krauts, or his grandparents. I don't know."

Jimmy slurped some of the vegetables from his plate.

"Look, Dan, I know you can talk with Apai in her own language. The truth is, I want to know if Apai loves him or loves me."

"Jimmy, she's a prostitute."

"What, you don't think a woman like her is capable of love?"

"Of course. Certainly."

"Goddamned Americans, no sense of romance."

"No, it's just that . . . "

"I love that woman, and I want to take her back with me to England, see, after I'm done here."

"She doesn't speak any English."

"She'll learn. I'll teach her."

"Jimmy."

"I'll get a job in a garage somewhere. Easy, a man of my ability. Get a little house. Garden. Roses."

Jimmy took a piece of chicken into his hands and gnashed at it. Grease covered his lips and hands. For the rest of the conversation a large splotch of it remained on his chin.

"Have some kids," he said.

Collins picked up his plate and shoveled rice and vegetables into his mouth with his chopsticks.

"You Americans do have terrible manners," Jimmy grinned.

"Apai eats with her hands, Jimmy."

"I'll teach her to use a fork, then, won't I?"

Collins laid his plate back on the table and took up his glass of beer.

"Pardon me, Jimmy. It's just that there are serious problems, I think, when you ask one of these women to leave Sarawak and go off thousands of miles to some strange country. Apai, a prostitute, no family. And in Liverpool."

As Collins spoke, Jimmy looked off to the side. His lips turned down with chagrin.

"Well, what are you doing out here, then?" he said.

"What?"

"You're just as much a stranger out here. Americans? In Borneo? That's preposterous, Yank. Besides, I've been defending England and Her Majesty for seventeen years."

"So what?"

"There's not much happiness in the army, that's all. Not much . . . well, not much happiness."

He leaned over his plate and rested his chin on one hand. His fingers glistened with grease.

"I know blokes like us fall in love with women like Apai all the time. I know that. You see them everywhere back in England. Ruddy old men, unshaven, sitting about in the pubs, with their ruddy old Asiatic wives back home. Hello, love. Been watchin' the telly?"

He clasped his hands and leaned forward again. Steam rose past his face, and the noise of the crowd and the traffic about the square distracted him for the moment.

"But I'd like that, Dan," Jimmy said. His eyes were wide and sad. "Damned army," he muttered. "After so many years, it's just a waste of time."

Collins had found few women himself during the two years he had been in Sarawak. Always upcountry working, he'd hardly met any women at all. Or at least he had met none with whom he could begin anything. Collins suffered from being too attractive a man to the Ibans, a situation he found laughable and discouraging. The British were revered by the upriver Ibans, and he was assumed to be an Englishman himself. Young women were always available to him. But a liaison with an Iban girl would ruin her life, unless Collins agreed to marry her. Once having been approached by a Tuan, she would be of no interest to the Iban men, a melancholy fact, but a fact nonetheless. Collins did not want to inflict that sort of an end on anyone simply for his own gratification.

But the ideal he had fashioned for himself—as a solitary explorer working with the natives, off in the romantic jungle, the heat, the blue cooling rain—had finally worn off. What remained was its loneliness. Really, he *longed* to have one of the Iban women. That they would so happily accept him if he wished had eroded his self-righteousness. He suspected they laughed at him when they talked about him in the longhouses at night. Sitting on a longhouse porch, he would watch the headman's daughter approach with a pot of tea and a bowlful of the small fried fish the Chinese sold in the bazaar, and there would be desire in the glance she gave him. The situation was made worse by the wishes of the fathers to simply give their daughters to Collins. The girls were his if he wanted them. So his isolation appeared increasingly senseless to him. His confidence that he was, really, a better man for not giving into the fathers, or for that matter to the girls themselves, just made him a prig, and he hated that.

He could not imagine how it was for a man like Jimmy. Prostitutes were the same everywhere as far as the soldiers cared.

Particular languages, the way they dressed outside the bars and brothels, the foods the women cooked, how they really made love — these were so unknown to the British that they acted as though the women had no nationalities at all. Arabs, Ibans, Africans — they were all the same. The whores expressed themselves therefore in ways the British understood. Their language was coarse English, their dress was coarse English. To the soldiers the rest of the women's lives didn't matter.

But I think Jimmy really means it, Collins thought. There was, of all things, misery in the way the soldier surveyed the bowl of soup before him.

"Jimmy. Jimmy."

Apai's voice rose above the traffic noise. Jimmy looked about and saw her with Steuben, sitting down at another table several feet away.

"Shit. Look at her," Jimmy said. He glanced at Collins. "Damned prima donna, isn't she?"

He looked again over his shoulder. Apai's mouth was freshly made up with dark red lipstick. She had combed her hair and, quite black, it fell across her right shoulder over her breast. Her shoulders were tiny and smooth, with little substance. Apai's hands, held up against her cheeks as she spoke with Steuben, glittered in the semidarkness.

"Queen of England," Jimmy grumbled.

He took up his spoon and plunged it into the bowl of soup. Collins did the same, bringing the spoonful of soup close to his lips so that he could blow on it. Quite drunk, Steuben sat down. He seemed unaware of Jimmy's presence. He looked over a paper menu.

Then Apai stood and waved at Collins.

"Nobody loves me, Tuan Dan," she said in Iban. "No one loves me like you do."

Collins settled back in his chair. The spoon hovered over the soup bowl like a small balloon, dripping with yellow liquid.

"What'd she say, Dan?" Jimmy asked. "Was she talking about me?"

For the moment Collins could not speak.

"It's you, Tuan," Apai called to him. "I don't care for any of these others at all. It's you I love."

Many of the customers turned laughing to watch. Steuben pulled at Apai's hand, but she would not sit down. Finally he forced her and she pulled her hand away, swearing at him repeatedly in English. In a rage, Jimmy stood and walked across the square toward the couple.

"When you make love to me, Tuan Dan, it's like a spirit has taken me," Apai shouted. She laughed and pointed out Collins to the crowd. Several people stood up to watch. Mostly Chinese, they broke into laughter as Jimmy tripped over a chair. Getting up quickly, he headed for Steuben and knocked him to the cement. The two men sprawled on the ground, knocking down several more chairs. Collins stood and walked through the tables toward Apai. She held her fingers to her mouth, and her nails dug into her lower lip. She looked up into Collins's eyes.

"You see what they're like, Dan. Animals, these white men. Animals."

She pulled at a strand of hair, then touched his chest.

"No kindness. Not like you. We love you. We all love you."

Jimmy and Steuben groveled about in one another's arms. A Malay army Land Rover pulled to the curb and four soldiers jumped out. They rushed through the square, pushing people aside as they approached the two struggling men. They pulled Jimmy away. He turned against them, shouting. Steuben took Apai's hand and moved to the edge of the square.

"Go after her, Dan," Jimmy shouted. The Malays pulled him toward the Land Rover. "Don't let him take her away from me."

Romantic idiot, Collins thought. But with Apai's words stinging in his mind, Collins realized he was one himself. He followed Steuben and Apai from the square toward the wharves. When he crossed the street and started down Jesselton Road, he lost them in the darkness and the crowds.

Food stalls, set up on carts, lit the street. A gas lantern hung above each stall, so that the street appeared to be partitioned into small rooms of light, many people within each, into the distance. The steam and smoke rising from the woks enveloped the cooks in mist that turned muddy the moment it left the circle of glaring light. Customers sat on stools by the carts. Mostly workmen, they slurped their food from small porcelain bowls held close to their mouths. Their wooden chopsticks flickered in the smoke.

Collins looked into each of the bars and noodle shops on Jesselton Road. He waited on corners, looking for Apai. He sat at one of the stalls himself for half an hour, sipping a cup of tea and watching for her. Finally he stood up and turned down a side alley toward the wharf, where a few more stalls appeared faraway and watery against the river.

As the light and noise from Jesselton Road decreased, real darkness settled over the river. Collins knew he was pursuing Apai for himself, that Jimmy, dragged off to the barracks, was unaware of what was going on. But she doesn't need these men, he thought. She can become my girlfriend, my lover. He stopped for a moment on a corner. There was little noise, and the lights from the stalls now seemed playful, as though they illustrated little scenes, distant dioramas with mannequins. But then you'll be just like the soldiers, Collins thought, you and Jimmy fighting for Apai. He stepped from the curb.

The heat and the darkness became palpable, thick, like mud as Collins approached the river. The buildings on either side of the street rose up in black crags. Little activity stirred outside the Chinese hotels where the prostitutes took their customers. Two cargo boats were moored at the docks at the foot of the street. Squat and low, their silhouettes formed black curves against the black water. Most of the women from the bus station took their customers to the New Sincere Hotel, which was on a side street. Collins passed the last food stall, where the cook, seated on one of his stools, read a Chinese newspaper. A Royal Army Land Rover was parked in front of the New Sincere.

Collins entered the hotel.

A Chinese night clerk sat at a desk at the top of the first flight of stairs.

"Yes, John," he said in English. "You looking for room?"

The clerk took up a cup of tea.

"Almost time go home," he said.

Collins looked at his watch. It was a few minutes before two o'clock, curfew hour for the British soldiers.

"No. I'm looking for Apai."

"Apai? She here. Down there."

He pointed down the hall. Collins heard a couple arguing in English and Iban.

A British military policeman in fatigue pants and canvas boots came up the stairs. He carried a long billy club in his right hand. His white T-shirt was rolled up at the sleeves. He had wet black hair and blotched skin, and he was quite heavy.

"Let's see it," he said to the clerk.

The Chinese handed the soldier a list of the hotel's rooms. Collins remained standing at the desk. There was a crash in the room down the hall. When the soldier finished reading the names on the list, he attached it to a clipboard.

"Are you waitin' for a ride back to the barracks, then?" he asked Collins. "Or can I suggest you take a rickshaw?"

"No, I'm not one of your people," Collins replied. "I'm an American, Sergeant, Sergeant . . . "

"Smith."

Smith looked over the list once more. Apai screamed in Iban that she had no use for these British fools. A glass crashed against the wall, and the night clerk started up the hall.

"Stay here, you," Smith said.

"Big fight," the Chinese said. "I go see."

"I said don't move."

Complaining, the clerk sat down again at his desk.

"Let me see your papers," Smith said to Collins.

"Like I say, I'm an American. I'm here on my own business."

Smith laid the billy club on the desk and adjusted the sleeves of his T-shirt.

"Papers, I said."

"I don't understand what for."

"I want to see your picture, love."

Collins leaned against the wall and folded his arms.

"I like to kill you!" Apai shouted. Collins shook his head, gazing at the floor.

"I'm not going to give you my papers," he replied to Smith. "Moreover, I'm going to speak with your commander, Sergeant, because you don't have the right to . . . "

Smith's billy club smashed down on the night clerk's table.

"Let's see the fuckin' passport, Yank."

"No, dammit!"

Smith placed his hands on Collins's chest and backed him to the wall. Collins's head cracked against the cement.

"We don't get many of you Yanks here," Smith shouted. He crumpled Collins's shirt in his hand and shoved him against the wall once more. "You blokes don't belong here, see."

Collins quickly reached into his shoulder bag and took out the passport. Smith let go of him. His back against the pale gray wall, Collins glanced down the hallway. Bare light bulbs hung from the ceiling like soiled pears.

"Well, there's nothing here to be worried about, Yank." Smith handed the passport back to the American. His tightly shining eyes and gapped smile degraded Collins even more. Smith took up his billy club. "You stay here while I gather up my lads, and then you can have the whole fuckin' place to yourself."

Smith walked down the hall, beating once with his club on each door. There was shouting inside the rooms, women's voices. Several men came out, and one of them stumbled drunkenly against Smith. The sergeant took him by the shirt and pushed him against the wall, then sent him sprawling to the floor. At the end of the hall the last door on the left opened, and Matty Steuben came out, bare-chested and carrying his shirt. Apai was right behind him, shouting at him. Steuben's forehead was badly scratched. He seemed relieved to see Sergeant Smith. As he passed the sergeant in the hall, Apai threw a flip-flop at Steuben. The sandal skittered up the hall and stopped, on its side, near the desk.

"You pay," Apai screamed. "You pay."

"Time to go, lads," Smith said. Apai was dressed in a sarong cinched about her chest. Her arms were slight, bony, like sticks.

Though it was gathered in a rubber band, her hair flew about. Steuben hurried down the stairs.

"All yours," Smith said to Collins, and he walked down the stairs himself, his billy club swinging against one wall. Collins looked up the hall. Apai appeared garish, lurid beneath the light bulbs. After a moment she turned away, and Collins followed her.

"Wait a minute, John."

The night clerk looked up from the desk. He extended his hand.

"Twenty ringgit," he said, and Collins quickly paid.

Apai sat down on the edge of the cot. Her face was smudged with lipstick. She had been crying, and her eyes still welled with tears. She pulled a strand of hair down before her eyes and examined it. Her fingers were long and dark. Her feet did not reach the floor.

The walls of the room were of cement. A single wood-shuttered window looked out on the river, and a light bulb hung from a wire nailed across the ceiling. Collins took fifty ringgit from his wallet and placed the money on the table next to the bed. Apai glanced at the money but seemed not to care about it. Collins sat down on the cot next to her. He kissed her, but she did not respond. Collins caressed her waist. Apai turned away, then lay back on the cot. Her hair was crumpled on the pillow, like rags.

"I want to go home," she said in Iban.

"You don't want to be with me?" he asked. He touched the crumpled cloth of the sarong over her breast.

"Home!" Apai groaned. She sat up and gripped the edges of the mattress. She glared at Collins. "Don't you understand?"

Disgruntled, Collins moved away from her. He wanted her badly. But Apai was so anguished, for the moment barely able to speak, that Collins realized he had to leave her alone. He recalled her mother, weeping in the longboat, and suddenly felt ashamed of himself. Disappointed, he stood and walked toward the door.

"I'll get a trishaw," he said.

"No, Dan. I mean to Skrang, to the forest."

She brushed her hair back. She wore a long plastic necklace that resembled amber. One earring, made of blue plastic teardrops hanging from strands of fine chain, lay against her neck. She touched it, pushed it back, and played with it.

"I miss my children," she said. She stared across the room in a heated wander. Collins sat down on a chair next to the window.

"They're too small. It's not fair that he took them away from me."

"Apai," Collins said. "I've met them. I know them."

"My children?"

"Yes. And your parents."

Apai sat up and gathered her legs beneath her. Her eyes had a fluttery look of surprise. She appeared frightened, as though a damaging secret had been found out.

"How?" she asked.

"I've worked in upriver Skrang. I've been a guest in your longhouse."

Apai leaned her head against the wall next to the cot.

"Your mother is very worried about you," Collins said.

"They sent you to spy on me," Apai said.

"No. I'm just trying to help them out."

"They hate me. They threw me away."

She shivered with anger.

"They think I've betrayed them," Apai said. "But I did nothing wrong. Nothing."

"No, Apai. Wait."

"He divorced me," she shouted. She gripped the metal cot frame below the mattress. Her knuckles paled, but she held on to it as though otherwise she would fly away. "He got rid of me!"

"But how did that happen?" Collins asked.

Apai wrapped her arms about her waist and sat back against the wall.

"He didn't like me."

"But what did you do wrong?"

"Nothing. I had my children. I worked in the paddy. I did what women do."

Apai's costume necklace twisted about her neck. She gestured, the back of her hand like a cloth dusting a table.

"Who was your husband?"

"Makota, the son of Sadong, from Rumah Dor."

Apai said all this as though Collins would naturally recognize the names of the men and the longhouse.

"He was a lemambang," she replied. "He recited the incantations at the festivals."

The poetry, chants that sometimes lasted several days, could be recited only by someone of considerable prestige. Makota had been visited by the spirits. He was an important man. Collins imagined him in a loincloth, his hair to the middle of his back. His feet were wide and thick, crusted with mud. His mouth was red with betel juice.

"What could I do?" Apai said. "He said he didn't like me anymore. My family has little paddy, Tuan. I have many brothers and sisters. It was a disgrace."

"Where I'm from, women can defend themselves in a case like this."

For a moment Apai glared with disbelief at Collins.

"But don't you understand, Tuan? Don't you understand divorce? My husband threw me away. And my father threw me away, so I had to leave. They laugh at me."

She lay down and folded her arms, tightening them against her stomach. Her hair fell down over her eyes.

"And now, Tuan, I have to fuck the white men. Wishing my husband loved me. That my family loved me."

She held Collins's gaze several seconds. Her eyes glittered in the yellow light.

"Will you . . . will you help me?" she asked. Her voice was demanding and high.

"How?" Collins said.

"Find Makota for me, Tuan. Please. Find my husband and tell him I'm here. Tell him to bring me my children. They live on the Rajang, far up. Above the big rapids."

"But how can I, that far away?"

"You can. You found me."

"But I can't just search the forest. It's so many days' travel just to get there. And what if he's not there at all?"

"You came here."

"Please, Apai, I can't!"

"You searched me out. Why can't you help me?"

Collins moved to interrupt.

"I thought the white men loved me," Apai said.

"Oh, Apai," Collins replied, "some of them really do."

Apai glanced at him, then away. With the brief turning of her eyes, Collins felt suddenly hated.

"Get out of here," she said.

"Pardon me? I . . . "

"You and those others. Love . . . "

She turned her face toward the wall. Collins stood and approached the cot. He put his fingers on her shoulder.

"Apai."

She turned over quickly and grabbed Collins's hand. Pushing it away, she held on to it nonetheless, attempting to hurt him. Collins yanked his hand from hers, and the force of the movement pulled Apai from the cot to the floor. He stood over her a moment, amazed and penitent.

"You white fool," she shouted. She lay with her face on the floor. "Get out!"

"Please, I didn't mean . . . "

"Get out! Get out!"

The next day Apai did not come to Albert's NAAFI. Collins and Jimmy were both there in the afternoon, asking for her. None of the women had seen her.

Collins told Jimmy how he had searched for Apai and Steuben. He told him he had found them at the New Sincere.

"She *was* with him, then," Jimmy said.

"Yes. But they were arguing."

"Arguing!" A smile appeared on Jimmy's thick face. "About me?" he asked.

Collins shook his head. He avoided looking into Jimmy's eyes.

"No. He didn't want to pay her."

"And where'd she go after that?"

"I don't know, Jimmy. I was tired. I left."

"Didn't sleep with her?"

Again Collins shook his head.

"Right. I knew I could trust you, Yank."

The following morning Collins asked at the New Sincere, and the day clerk told him he had not seen her. Collins returned to Albert's NAAFI in the afternoon. Albert stood behind the bar. Jimmy was at a table with Steuben and three other soldiers. When Collins entered the bar, Jimmy left the others and joined him.

"I've found out something about Apai, Dan."

"You have?"

"She's left us for good, apparently. Wang there tells me she's gone to someplace called Battoo Toojo. Is that where she came from? Mum and Dad, that sort of thing?"

"Batu Tujoh," Collins replied. He laid his shoulder bag on the floor. "Albert, is that true?" he asked in Malay.

Albert nodded, his chin resting on his palm. He laid his newspaper on the bar.

"They took her there yesterday," he said. "Talk talk talk. But makes no sense."

Collins sighed, and Jimmy awaited a translation.

"What is it?" he asked.

"Batu Tujoh's a terrible place," Collins said.

"What is it?"

"A nuthouse. An asylum."

Jimmy turned around and leaned back against the bar. His face fell, and he cradled his bottle of beer between his hands.

"Mattie," he said.

Steuben stood and joined them at the bar.

"Bit of trouble with Apai," Jimmy continued.

Fine, light hairs grew from Steuben's cheeks. Only his hands, which were thick and lined with residual grease, looked like a grown man's. The tattoo of the Union Jack on his forearm seemed to Collins a phony assertion of worldly experience.

"She's been taken to hospital, apparently. That's what it is, eh, Dan? This Battoo whatever?"

"Yes. But it's only a compound of buildings. Nothing much. They just put the people away, really. Keep them out of sight."

Steuben shrugged. "Not much we can do about that, is there?" he said.

"We can go out to see her," Jimmy replied.

"Not me. You won't get me to go to a place like that."

"You don't even know what it's like," Jimmy said.

Steuben placed his beer bottle on the bar.

"I do too. The Yank here just told me, didn't he?"

Jimmy took up the bottle a moment and examined it. Steuben ordered another.

"But don't you have any feeling for her?" Jimmy asked. The question was sudden and tense. It was more of an accusation.

Steuben took the new beer from Albert and wiped condensation from the bottle with the palm of one hand.

"Of course I do. But she's a whore. What do you expect?"

He turned away and joined the others at the table. Jimmy, still holding the empty bottle, turned around and surveyed the bar. His shoulders hunched over the formica.

"That's the trouble with blokes like him, isn't it," he said finally. Anger creased the skin about his eyes. "Just fuckin' get rid of the women, don't they?"

"We can go out there this afternoon," Collins said.

"Yeh. Do we get a taxi?"

"We'll take a bus from the station. It's only seven miles out the main road."

"All right. I'll meet you at the station then. At three. I want to get cleaned up."

Jimmy turned toward the door. When he opened it, bright sunlight splashed his face.

"I'll want to look presentable, Dan," he said.

The gate at Batu Tujoh consisted of barbed wire suspended between two wooden poles. A cyclone fence surrounded the compound, five wooden buildings on pilings. From the bus shelter at the side of the road, Collins saw many women on the porches working at mending clothes and weaving baskets. Others hulled rice in the shade beneath one of the buildings. That the activities were so peaceful at first made the fence and the barbed gate appear unnecessary. From the corner of his eye, though, Collins noticed movement along the fence. Two women walked toward the gate, fingering the wire, raving. They paused at the gate to look out. One of the women had gray hair tied back in a bun, darkly splotched skin, and no teeth. The other, much younger, wore a ragged, cotton sarong cinched about her waist as though she were about to take a bath in the river. Barefoot and barebreasted, she carried an empty straw basket in one hand. Her hair was filthy and she appeared very angry. The women spoke Land Dayak, a dialect Collins did not understand. They looked out at him and muttered. He and Jimmy moved from beneath the shelter, and the women's eyes followed them. After a moment the women continued along the fence. The old woman led the younger one by the hand.

Collins and Jimmy approached the guardhouse. It was a tiny, open, thatched hut with an officer of the Sarawak Police standing inside. A Malay, he was dressed in a dark blue uniform with walking shorts and sunglasses.

"Yes, Tuan, may I help you?"

Collins brought out his passport and gave it to the officer.

"We're here to visit a patient. An Iban woman named Apai."

The soldier looked over Collins's passport and stepped out of the hut to unlock the gate. He motioned the men into the compound and handed Collins his papers.

"The office is straight on there in the middle building. Ask for Dr. Rahman, please."

The two men proceeded across the compound. It was so warm that the ground threw heat up into the air. Collins felt it through the soles of his sandals. Cleared of trees, the compound offered no relief from the heat at all.

"Dan."

Jimmy placed a hand on Collins's arm. He pointed across the compound to a single water tap in front of one of the buildings. Apai sat before it, her head leaned forward beneath the rush of water from the faucet. The water splashed over her shoulders and down her back. Her blue sarong clung to her. Apai's skin shone in the sunlight as she pulled at her hair over and over again.

The two men approached.

"Apai, we've come to see you," Collins said in Iban. "Are you feeling all right?"

She jerked at a strand of hair.

"No, no," she said in English. "Get 'way."

"Apai?"

She continued washing herself, shaking the water from her hair and letting it fall through her fingers to the mud. She stared at the water, which sparkled in the sun despite its silty color. She plunged her head into the flow, washed her arms in it, and leaned forward again to let the water cascade down her back.

A Malay walked down the steps of the nearest building. He was a slightly built man of about fifty with a round stomach that stretched the front of his white shirt. He wore a pair of dark brown pants, leather sandals, and dark-tinted sunglasses. He approached the two men nervously.

"What do you want?" he asked in English.

Jimmy glanced at him, then addressed Collins.

"Who's this, then?"

"My name is Rahman," the Malay said. "I'm the doctor. I'm in charge, and we don't like intruders."

"Excuse us, Doctor," Collins said. "It's just that we both know this woman, and we heard she'd been brought here. We don't want to bother you. We're friends of hers."

Rahman pursed his lips.

"You know she's a whore," he said.

"Of course," Collins replied, chagrined by Rahman's abrupt, disapproving tone. "But we're friends of hers. We're very worried about her."

"Worried, eh? Fucked her, and now you're worried about her."

"That's not true, mate," Jimmy said. "You don't have the right . . . "

"Wait, Jimmy," Collins interrupted. "Dr. Rahman, we're here simply because we know Apai, that's all. We don't mean any harm."

"I can't get over you bloody Englishmen," Rahman said. "You do such damage to these women and then expect in your shabby ways to make amends. You feel sorry for yourselves, but you don't care for them. You really have nothing to do with their problems. She's not gone mad because of you."

"Wait a minute, Doctor," Jimmy said. "What happened to her?"

"She's been mad for days, for months," Rahman said. "Many of these women are. Families hate them. They have nothing."

"Families!" Jimmy turned toward Collins. His voice seemed about to fail. "How did this happen?"

Swearing to himself, Collins sat down before Apai.

"Get 'way," she shouted. She tried dispelling him with water, fists of it in his face, then scrambled about to the opposite side of the pipe coming from the ground. Water spilled across her legs.

"But she'd be happy with me," Jimmy said after a moment. "In England."

His voice intruded on Collins's anger, and the American cursed himself again. He cursed his self-assured fluency in the language and his false sympathies. He recalled Panau and her tears, then thought how foolish he had been to believe he could do anything at all. But you believed it, Collins thought. Believed you could just step into this and solve it. The savior.

He took up a handful of the dirty water. He wanted to caress Apai's face. But all three men waited in silence as Apai bent down once more below the tap, her fingers clutching the pipe. The water scattered across her head into the mud.

3 / The Wee Manok

Collins, the American, did not like Craft, the Englishman. But he feared Craft liked him, that indeed he wanted to be friends.

"You see, old boy," Craft said as he leaned far over the table between them. He lowered his head and looked to the side, as though they were entering a mean-hearted conspiracy. "The reason we've got to do something about McGregor is his wife."

Craft's receding hair was very black, and his forehead was splotched with sunspots. At fifty-five, he still refused to wear a hat, though he worked most of the day outside. He touched the ends of his fingers together and studied them a moment.

"And he's Scotch as well, of course," he continued. "So he's suspect on two counts."

Collins remained seated and upright. He had just come in from the project and was steamy with perspiration, smudged everywhere with yellow mud. He hadn't even removed his hat, and his longish, black hair was squashed by the dirty straw.

"He sold his heritage marrying that woman," Craft said. He sat back into his chair with a broad, pained smile. "Though it's a goddamned sorry heritage, anyway."

Craft folded his arms. They were white and bony, covered with black hairs.

"Don't you agree?" he asked.

"I don't, Alec," Collins said. "He's the best man we've got here, you know, with respect to knowing the rubber. And the

Ibans love him. You can't imagine how fluent he is in their language."

"Bloody gargle, if you ask me."

Collins removed his hat and laid it on the table. He ran his fingers through his hair, trying to air out the gully of sweat that ringed his head. He pulled his shirt away from his chest, let it drop, then pulled it up again. The resultant breeze did nothing to refresh him, since the air inside Craft's office was warmer than that outside.

The one fan that worked struggled to push the air about. There was a larger fan, left broken by Craft's predecessor, an Englishman named Tracy who had returned with his family to Britain. The fan and several other items that had belonged to Tracy's small children—a pair of shoe skates, a cricket bat, a few pairs of pants, and some shirts—remained in the corner unused.

"What does it matter who he's married to?" Collins asked.

"It matters quite a bit if she's a savage," Craft said.

"But she isn't!"

"Balls."

"If you knew what you were talking about," Collins said, "you'd realize that no Iban is a savage."

Craft broke into laughter. "But they're headhunters!" he said.

"Not since they went after the Japanese at the end of the war."

"Well, *they* deserved it, of course."

"Alec," Collins grinned. "The Ibans have a very complex language, a mysterious religion, art, dance."

Craft stared at the table. He pursed his lips and his eyelids fluttered.

"The next thing you'll say," he continued, "is that we should send them all to bloody Oxford."

"Not at all. But even if she were a savage—well, you've met her, haven't you?"

"Yes. And their son. Speaking that patois—Scotch and Iban." Craft's shoulders wobbled, as though he had taken a chill. "It's worse than gargle," he said.

"But she's educated. She's a teacher."

Craft wrapped his fingers together and looked down again sadly. Collins thought he detected a smile beneath the Englishman's glowering survey of the tabletop.

"Well, I must say there's one thing you can depend on," Craft said.

"What's that?"

"You damned Yanks can't be trusted," he muttered.

There was a knock at the door to Craft's office and Tom McGregor came in.

"Hello, lads," he said. He removed his hat and dropped it onto a nail sticking out from the wall. "Sorry I'm late."

Dressed in a pair of British walking shorts and a white shirt, McGregor sat down at the end of the table. He laid out a narrow, three-ring binder and a manila folder, which he opened as soon as he lowered himself into his seat. McGregor was as overheated as the other men, but he maintained an appearance of winterish efficiency, ready for business. His shirt was dotted with splotches of sweat, yet it had not wilted as Craft's had, or grown sodden like Collins's. Also, his red hair was dry. His eyebrows, which were large and gray-red, moved up and down as he spoke, so much so that Collins was distracted by their comic jittering. But McGregor was essentially a serious man and had no intention of distracting anyone, so Collins kept his amusement to himself.

"I'd like to get back out to the project," Collins said. "We're trying to finish that grading job on the section of road by the river. Should have it done by this afternoon."

"Terrific," McGregor replied. His Edinburgh accent gave the word a noticeable trill, which seemed to disgruntle Craft. The Englishman glared into his hands. "Feather in your cap, Mr. Craft," McGregor said.

"Get on with it."

A breeze from the fan rolled up the edges of the papers in the folder. McGregor rearranged them and began his recitation of the expenditures of the Skrang Rubber Scheme, Ministry of the Interior, State of Sarawak, Malaysia, for the month of August 1965. Craft, his superior officer, said nothing, while Collins silently denounced the Englishman.

That afternoon Collins sat on the porch of his office, drinking a large bottle of Tiger Beer. The air was incredibly hot, and sweat oozed from Collins as he fanned himself with a magazine. The offices of the Scheme were in two separate wooden buildings across from one another, each with a covered porch.

Collins watched Craft, who sat at the desk in his office across the way. A pot of tea rested on his desktop. Craft was distracted every few moments by Ian Damu, McGregor's son, who stood in the doorway watching the Englishman work.

This was Ian Damu's habit. Despite his tiny stature, the seven-year-old boy resembled his father quite a bit. His body was angular, his joints thicker than his arms and legs. His head was topped by a red cowlick sticking up from a mat of disheveled black hair. Ian Damu's skin was quite different from his father's. McGregor's was bright, almost transparent, covered with freckles, while Ian Damu's was dark brown and very smooth. The boy's bare feet were spattered with dried mud. Like his father, he was usually laconic and glum, although he loved playing on Craft's porch. For some reason Craft made Ian Damu laugh. Maybe, Collins thought, it's a child's natural interest in something large and clumsy, in something entertaining. Collins knew that Ian Damu drove the Englishman to distraction.

The boy was followed everywhere, at a distance of three or four yards, by a large female cur. The yellow dog sneaked about, obsequious, fawning, in the hope that Ian Damu, or anyone, would give her a scrap of food. The dog concerned Collins because she appeared scattered and undependable, a victim of much mistreatment. One ear stuck up in the air, the other flopped down the side of her head. She was not mangy or diseased, though she was very thin. She actually sniveled whenever Craft chased her from his porch. She had large, hanging teats from many litters. She appeared to be near starving, and Collins understood that she followed the boy around because he fed her. Collins had nicknamed her Muttah.

Craft gestured to Ian Damu to get off the porch. The boy leaned against the doorjamb. He wore a T-shirt and a pair of ragged gray pants. He was sucking his thumb. Muttah stood on the porch a few feet away.

Craft gestured with his fingers, as though he were sweeping a dead insect from a table. His lips moved: "Go away, boy. Leave me alone." Ian Damu remained a moment, watching him, then turned around and sat down on the porch. He rolled a rubber ball against the wall and caught it when it came back to him. Craft listened a moment to the tapping of the ball against the wood, then leaned over his papers, his head resting on the palm of one hand.

"McGregor," Craft said the next afternoon at their meeting, "does your son have to play on my porch every day?"

"Of course not. Is there a problem?"

"Well, I come and go, and the boy, and that dog, get in the way."

"Aye. He's a wee manok, isn't he?"

The Iban word for chicken was an affectionate usage, commonly used for children.

"Yes, but he bothers me, that's all. Stares at me, you see. Thinks I'm a plaything. He, he . . . What's his name?"

"Ian Damu."

"What sort of name is that?"

"Scots and Iban. Properly reflects his heritage, that's the idea."

Craft glanced at Collins, who did not acknowledge the look.

"Well, it just isn't proper," Craft said.

"Why not?"

"I believe we must work during working hours and play at other times."

"Ian Damu plays all the time," Collins laughed.

"But *I* can't work. That's the problem, Collins. I'm a serious man. I can't run this Scheme while that boy laughs at me on my own porch."

McGregor's eyes remained on Craft. The Scot was considering a response, which Collins was certain would be unfriendly. McGregor's papers lay before him on an open folder. There were two piles, each one neat and orderly. McGregor had always kept his feelings about the Englishman to himself. Collins knew, though, there was a strain between them. McGregor had been living in Sarawak for twenty years, while Craft had arrived from Malaya only nine months ago, a holdover from the pre-Independence Malayan civil service. Craft was a good administrator, Collins felt, organized and direct. But a kind of poisonous sadness seemed to moil about within his heart. He believed he deserved more from the life he led, more authority, more dignity, more respect. But everything came up short. Craft kept accounts and filed papers, while McGregor managed the real purpose of the Scheme, helping the Ibans learn how to farm rubber. Even Collins had a better job—constructing the gravel roads in the Scheme—because of the grime and risk it entailed. Craft saw his own duties as everyday and adventureless. He therefore larded his suggestions with an insistence that he be treated properly, as a man of real, thoroughgoing, English importance.

"Not much I can do about that, Mr. Craft," McGregor said. "An Iban child has the run of the place, you know. Endearing habit they have, really."

"That boy is British."

McGregor made an effort to rearrange his papers.

"Yes, I suppose he is, partially."

"Your part, at least," Craft said.

McGregor closed the manila folder and looked coldly at Craft.

"My son has an Iban mother," he said. "Iban grandparents, cousins, uncles, aunts. He lives among them every day. He speaks their language as fluently as a seven-year-old can speak anything."

"Yes, quite. No need to . . . "

McGregor stood and took the manila folder under his arm.

"But your boy is not to play on my porch," Craft said.

"You should try to understand these people better, Mr. Craft."

"Rubbish, McGregor."

"They'll love you for it if you do."

McGregor stepped out from behind the table, put on his hat, and walked from the office.

The air in the building felt wrecked, as though it were unbreathable, in ruins. Collins did not speak as Craft stared at his hands. Craft's hair came away from the sides of his head like ragged wings. His skin was red, and a large dollop of sweat moved slowly down each side of his wattled neck, one of them dispersing finally into the wrinkles of his skin.

"I'm sorry, Collins," he said after a moment.

The American slumped in his chair. He took his own folder in his hands and gestured as if he were about to speak. But Craft abruptly stood and moved toward the door.

"Bit of a family argument you had to witness. I'm very sorry." His lips were turned down with dismay. He appeared hurt, but hurt by himself, by his own hateful anger. He went out of the office into the sun.

After work Collins walked to McGregor's house. The Scotsman and his family lived in a wooden building on pilings, which overlooked the Skrang River. The corrugated tin roof formed a shiny peak that glistened against the line of the forest beyond. The building was made of moss-ridden planks, ragged with the stresses of the seasons when one month the wood was sodden, the next month like tinder. The house had a porch on two sides with a plain board railing. A cache of tools lay in one corner of the porch. There were several large trays, used in rubber processing, and an assortment of hammers, braces, and shovels. A pile of canvas lay to one side. Splotched with dried mud, it hung partially off the end of the porch.

McGregor sat on the porch in the dusk sunlight, sipping a cup of tea. He was so thin that, when he crossed his legs, the toe of his upper foot reached the floor.

"Tom?" said Collins.

"Hello, Dan," the Scotsman said from the porch. "Come on up."

Collins's shirt had begun to dry out in the cooler evening air. The salt from his sweat gave the shirt a tacky, wooden texture. McGregor leaned through the doorway into the house.

"Sati. Collins is here," he said in Iban. "Will you make some more tea?"

Sati waved at Collins from the door. She was a teacher at the Scheme school. The one time Collins had visited her classroom, the children had been lounging about on the three tables in the room, wrestling on the dirt floor, making faces at Collins. Sati sat in a chair whispering for order. There had been a pleasant, threatened grin on her face.

Now she wiped her hands with a cloth and approached Collins, genuinely glad to see him.

"Do you want to have dinner?" she asked.

"Good idea," McGregor said in English. Sati brought cups and spoons out to the porch.

The sun shone directly on Collins's face when he sat down on the top step. McGregor stood behind him, his tea steaming in a large ceramic cup. The sun and the high clouds grew pink, then dark red-brown. Collins accepted a cup from Sati and held it in his hands as he watched the sun go down.

"Too bad about that business with Craft this morning," Collins said.

"Bloody unpleasant," McGregor replied.

"I know. But I'm hoping you'll . . . "

"You come to expect this sort of thing from the English," McGregor interrupted.

"You do?"

McGregor set his cup on the railing. The skin around his eyes resembled crumpled paper.

"These fellows . . . Craft, I mean . . . don't have the kinds of talents you and I have, Dan."

The sun touched the tops of the trees across the river.

"You and I are technocrats, aren't we? Isn't that the American word?"

"I suppose so," Collins replied.

"I know rubber. You know how to grade a road. But Craft, and others like him, the sort who manned the empire, they have no skills."

McGregor leaned on the railing and joined his hands.

"They couldn't affect things at home. And places like Sarawak appeared to them a source of riches, of adventure."

McGregor turned away from the sun.

"And self-esteem, Daniel, self-esteem."

He sat down on the stair next to Collins.

"It's very bad. What they can't get away with in Britain, they can wallow in out here. They can freely express their hatreds, you understand. And imagine! You think I'm disliked because I'm a Scot? I'm at least white, Daniel."

McGregor sipped his tea. The faces of the two men darkened more as the sun disappeared behind the trees.

"You have to be careful with these people," McGregor muttered.

"But you're not giving him any chance at all."

"The English are very ingratiating, Dan, but they are cold. They know how to manipulate you and they're heartless."

"That can't be true."

"I know I'm speaking out of turn," McGregor continued. "But I've been here since 1945, and I've known few of them who've taken the time to understand these Ibans. Very few."

McGregor lifted his teacup to his lips.

"None," he concluded.

Ian Damu would not leave Craft alone. He came up to the porch every day, and every day the confrontation was different.

Ian Damu frequently carried a small, leaf-wrapped packet of sweet rice around with him. It was a snack he shared with most people he met. Even Muttah was a recipient of his largesse, finishing off the rice when Ian Damu threw the sticky leaf away. He began bringing an extra packet to Craft, leaving it on the doorsill and pulling Muttah away as she struggled to get it for herself. The first few times Craft tried giving the packet back to the boy the following day. Finally Craft gave up because Ian Damu refused to take it. Craft took the rice home with him, though Collins suspected he just threw it away.

Now and then Ian Damu played football at the bottom of the steps, pushing the ball around, kicking it backward, chasing it. When Craft came out to stretch his legs one morning, Ian Damu asked him if he wanted to play.

"No," Craft replied. His arms stiffly at his sides, he returned to his office.

One day Ian Damu did not show up. In fact he stayed away four days in a row. On the second day Muttah groveled up the steps and peeked into Craft's office. The Englishman came out onto the porch, his fists clenched. Trapped, Muttah snapped at him, growling and frightening the Englishman. She ran back down the steps. That incident aside, Craft appeared relieved at the boy's absence. He looked out his door every few hours each day and smiled to find the boy still gone.

On the fourth day, though, Ian Damu was waiting for Craft when the Englishman came to work. As always, Collins had come to his office early to prepare for his day during the cool of the morning. He heard Craft trudge up the dirt track from his house. The Englishman carried a leather briefcase in one hand and a notepad in the other. He paused at the bottom of the stairs to read something from the pad. The morning light shone on Craft's back as the sun rose over the Scheme. He mounted the stairs, still reading. Ian Damu, who sat on the top step, moved to one side to let Craft pass, and the Englishman nearly stepped on him.

"For God's sake," Craft said. He proceeded to his office, muttering, reading. Ian Damu followed closely behind.

Collins suspected there was more to the boy's interest than simple entertainment. The child carefully observed Craft's rule that he was not to enter the office, and Craft continued telling him to go away. But after a while Ian Damu's obdurate, but civil, disobedience won him a permanent spot on Craft's porch. He reminded Collins of the Indian servant in movies about the British raj, sitting on the colonial porch pulling the cord to a fan. But Ian Damu was in no such reduced state. For example, he appeared late one afternoon dragging a small wooden crate up the dirt track. Collins guessed it had been used to transport supplies of some sort to McGregor. It was covered with Chinese characters, handwritten in grease pencil. He hefted the box up the stairs, showing, Collins thought, remarkable diligence for a seven-year-old. Craft came out of his office when he heard the rattle of the box against the stairs. He stood in the shade, his arms folded, suffering as the boy achieved the top step. Pointing at the box, Ian Damu spoke a few words to the Englishman, who did not respond. Then Craft turned away abruptly, and Ian Damu dragged the crate across the porch to the doorway, where he sat down on it to watch the Englishman for the rest of the day.

"You must understand, Collins, that it's simply the right thing to do," Craft said later that afternoon. He had come across to the American's office for tea. "That boy will not leave me alone. And those floorboards are damned dirty, after all. His father won't do anything to help me, out of spite, I think. I'm not a ghoul. The box means nothing to me."

Collins spooned tea into his cracked porcelain pot.

"Weathering a lost cause, eh?" he said.

Early the next morning Ian Damu and Muttah appeared in Collins's doorway. The boy's thumb was in his mouth. The ball lay at the child's feet and he carried a packet of rice in his free hand. His cheeks were splotched with dirt. He wore a T-shirt, as always, but this time he also wore a pair of brand-new red shorts. He was barefoot. Muttah remained behind the boy, peeking around him, surveying the floor and grimacing.

"Hello, Ian," Collins said. He stood up from his desk and walked out onto the porch. At first Ian Damu had been very shy in Collins's presence, finding succor in his thumb, unable to speak. After a few months, though, he had become used to the large American and had found it easier to speak with him. The combined languages the boy spoke — Iban and English with a pronounced Edinburgh accent — made conversations with him quite comic. Ian Damu mixed words and constructions freely in a singsong, childish speech, incomprehensible to any Tuan who did not speak both languages.

"Hullo," he said. With the completion of each reply, his lips secured themselves once more around his thumb.

"You've been playing?" Collins asked.

"Aye."

"Where?"

"Mr. Craft's steps."

"With your ball?"

"Aye. And the dog."

Collins leaned on the wooden porch railing. He noticed Craft watching him from his office. Muttah retired to the shade at the end of the porch.

"How's your mother?"

"Good."

The Englishman hunched over the papers on his desk. Collins began speaking Iban with Ian Damu, to avoid being understood by Craft.

"Is the Tuan a nice man?"

"Aye."

"He's not mean to you?"

Ian Damu shrugged his shoulders. He sat down on the porch and rolled his ball down the length of it. The ball meandered toward the wall, rolled along it beneath the railing, and fell to the ground.

"He's funny," Ian Damu said.

"How?"

"He looks like a bird. He looks like the Lang."

A mythic bird, important in the origin of the tribe, Lang had great salutary powers. The sound of his full name, Sengalang Burong, carried more of his true weight. He was a grand kite-bird, a predatory, celestial hawk who gave the Ibans the very sense of their own being. Fearful though he was, children loved Sengalang Burong. He was the great war chief. He had been present at the creation of the universe.

Craft reached down to swat a mosquito on the back of his leg.

"Reminds me of my father," Ian Damu said.

"But how is that?" Collins asked. Ian Damu knew nothing of the empire and its snooty suppositions. Just the same, Collins thought, the boy must see how his father was different from the Englishman.

Ian Damu shrugged again. He removed his thumb and examined it a moment.

"Dunno," he said in English. "Just think so."

He put his thumb back in his mouth.

"You do too," he mumbled.

"Has your father talked to you about Mr. Craft?"

The boy moved toward the stairway.

"Aye. Told me not to play there," Ian Damu said in Iban. "Good-bye."

He walked down the steps. Muttah got up and followed him. When Ian Damu reached the ground, he ran beneath Collins's building to retrieve his ball, then walked the thirty feet to the stairs to Craft's office.

As the boy climbed the stairs, Craft suddenly busied himself at his desk. He took a few sips from a cup of tea, and when Ian Damu arrived, he lowered his head over his papers. Ian Damu stood in the doorway. Craft looked up, saw him, and motioned to him to get off the porch. Collins read the Englishman's lips: "Go away, boy." Ian Damu and the dog remained where they were.

Craft came to the doorway, took Ian Damu by the shoulder and turned him toward the stairs. Ian Damu resisted him. Finally he held the packet of rice out before him. Exasperated, Craft knocked the packet from the boy's hand, and Muttah leapt on it.

"No!" Ian Damu shouted. He grabbed for the packet himself. Muttah snarled, suddenly vindictive. She bit the boy's hand. His voice rose to a clear, high-pitched scream. Craft kicked the dog in the side, and Muttah turned on Ian Damu. The boy fell to his knees, screaming. The dog bit him in the head and shoulders, knocking him to his stomach. She mauled the boy's back, bringing up narrow ridges of blood where her paws broke his skin. Craft kicked her again and backed her down the steps. She fell back snarling and ran away into the trees above the river.

Collins hurried to Craft's office and reached the porch as Craft was turning the boy over on his back. There were puncture wounds on the side of Ian Damu's head and a laceration across his right shoulder. He screamed and tried pushing Craft away.

"Get McGregor, Dan," Craft yelled.

Collins ran down the steps toward McGregor's house. As he ran, he heard Ian Damu's small voice rise into painful screaming.

Collins found Sati getting ready to go to the school. He told her what had happened, and she went immediately to Craft's office. Collins continued on to the rubber groves, where he found McGregor in one of the processing huts. Alarmed,

McGregor returned with Collins to the offices. Ian Damu lay in Sati's lap on the porch, breathing fitfully. He had paled and the blood had begun to congeal on his head and shoulder. Craft had brought the children's shirts from his office and had torn them into rags to daub the boy's wounds. McGregor called some of the Ibans over from the longhouses. He instructed them to find the dog and kill it. Then he asked Collins to drive into Simanggang, a hundred miles away, where there was a Chinese doctor who had been educated in New Zealand.

Craft stood in the doorway to his office. Ian Damu's blood had splotched his shorts and shirt sleeves. He appeared confused, unable to move. When McGregor lifted Ian Damu into his arms, the Scotsman looked at Craft, then turned away.

"Mr. McGregor," Craft said.

"Get out of here, Craft," the Scotsman said. "You don't belong here at all, and you've nearly killed my son. Get out of here."

He walked down the stairs, Sati following behind. Collins went to his Land Rover, which was parked behind the offices. He cursed himself for not having done something about the dog weeks before. He looked back once at Craft, who remained, colorless and stricken, in the doorway.

The Ibans brought Muttah back from the longhouses, where they had found her lying in the shade later that afternoon. They had shot her. It was determined she was not rabid. Two days later a dozen Ibans arrived from Sati's longhouse in upriver Skrang. Collins went to visit them at McGregor's house. Sati's father, Gru, was an aged man with gray-white hair, lacking most of his teeth. He sat with his back to the porch railing, smoking a cigarette. His wife was inside the house with McGregor, Sati, and Ian Damu. The others on the porch, relatives from Gru's longhouse and other friends of McGregor, talked about the rains, about how the spirits affected the emotions of animals, and about the arbitrary ways in which the spirits acted. Rags and baskets littered the porch. Large green leaves were opened up on the mats to reveal strands of cooked chicken and vegetables.

Collins sat on the top step. His hands were folded between his knees. His shoulders were hunched over, shaded by the straw hat he wore. There had been no word from Craft, and Collins planned to complain about him to the Agriculture Ministry. He did not feel Craft had willfully caused the attack. He did think, though, that there was real callousness in Craft's attitude, especially in his absence since the accident.

Collins looked out across the yard into the rubber groves. He saw movement in the trees, someone walking far away. After a moment he made out a white shirt and white legs. Collins's hands hung loosely above the steps. His mouth opened and it remained open as the figure from the grove broke into the open sunlight.

Craft carried a small packet in his right hand. From his other hand dangled the shoeskates Tracy's children had left behind. He approached the gate, fumbled with the wood and rope latch, and entered the yard. An immediate flurry of interest arose among the Ibans. It was natural, they thought, for such a prestigious man to visit one of his countrymen in this terrible time. The Ibans themselves had only seen Craft from a distance. They gathered themselves together for the visit. This was something historic.

The Englishman appeared to have gotten little sleep. His face was gray, almost obscured by his brightly reflecting shirt. Solitary in the center of the yard, with no shrubbery or backdrop to soften the heat, he walked with his head down. When he raised up his head toward the house, the sun shone straight into his eyes. He held a hand before his face and looked at Collins. For an instant, there was an expression of relief. Evidently he had not known what to expect at McGregor's. Collins's presence seemed to give him confidence. One of the boys on the porch went into the house. Presently McGregor stepped out onto the porch. He leaned on the rail as Craft paused at the bottom of the steps.

"Pardon me, Mr. McGregor," Craft said. "I've come to ask about your son, whether he's all right?"

"As well as can be expected," McGregor said. "His wounds are bad. But the doctor told us he'll recover. He won't be disfigured, luckily."

Craft looked down the length of the porch. The Ibans peered at him through the diagonal railing supports. The porch was filled with faces, silent, waiting.

"I have something here for him," he said. "May I give it to you?"

"Well," McGregor said, "yes, I suppose so," and Craft mounted the stairs.

Collins had stood up and moved halfway down the porch, where he leaned against the railing. Craft's isolation, which had so etched him against the yellow earth of the yard, grew extreme as he stood on the porch, surrounded by the Ibans in their loincloths, with their tattoos and parang knives.

"I've been . . . afraid, frankly, to come visit you," Craft said to McGregor.

"For God's sake, why?"

Craft averted his eyes.

"I don't blame you for thinking the worst of me."

"What is it you want, Craft?" McGregor asked.

The Englishman surveyed the Ibans at his feet, and finally replied. "Would you give him this? For me?"

Craft handed the packet to McGregor. It was a serving of sweet rice wrapped in a green leaf and secured with a string. The gift brought whispers of approval from everyone on the porch. McGregor held it in his open hand, staring at it.

"And these?" Craft handed over the skates. "They're something Ian Damu might like," he said.

A look of humorous distrust appeared on McGregor's face. He did not want to accept the gifts. But for the moment he did nothing. He simply looked at the Englishman as though he were waiting for something more. Finally the strange kindliness of Craft's request appeared to move McGregor. His fingers closed on the rice.

"I will," he said. "Thank you."

Craft shrugged. "Of course, it's a bit muddy here for skating, isn't it?" he said.

A grateful murmur came from the Ibans. A few of them reached out to touch Craft's hands, and he pulled them away. The

Ibans persisted, offering their gratitude with guileless caresses and, in Gru's case, a hand-rolled cigarette. Gru stood up before Craft and handed it to him.

"Tuan McGregor told me you were responsible for my grandson's injury," he said.

Craft looked to Collins for a translation. The American held up his hand, waiting for Gru to finish.

"I resented it," Gru continued. "But I believe, now, that you're a good man. Maybe even a kind man."

He offered his hand.

"What's he say, Collins?" Craft asked.

"He's grateful for your kindness," Collins said. "Shake his hand, dammit!"

Craft acquiesced. Pumping Gru's hand, he looked down at the others. He remained isolated and uncomfortable. He turned to McGregor.

"It's just that Ian Damu's been . . . well, company to me in the last few months," Craft said. "I didn't realize it."

He looked to the side, as though the admission embarrassed him. Collins became irritated by the Englishman's reticence. But he suspected Craft actually loved Ian Damu, that love for the boy had flushed him out. Craft moved from the crowd of Ibans toward the top of the stairs.

"Sad part is, I've made a habit of that kind of thing," Craft said. "For some years."

"What's that?" McGregor said.

"Misleading myself."

He said this in a mutter, barely discernible.

"I'll never have a family myself, and I've seen what it can mean to someone like you, a boy like that," Craft continued.

He paused at the first step and looked back.

"The fact is, I envy you, McGregor," he said. "Will you let me know if there's any change in Ian Damu's condition?"

McGregor folded his arms. The rice packet was nestled in one hand. The skates rested against his stomach.

"I'd hate to see anything happen to him," Craft said.

"I'll do that," McGregor said.

The Englishman walked down the steps and across the yard. A patch of dark sweat glued his shirt to his back. When he reached the gate, he made sure to secure it, and before turning away toward the groves, he waved. The Ibans, nodding with gravity, waved back.

McGregor held the packet in his hand. After a moment he turned toward Collins. He appeared angry. But his grimace was more of confusion than rancor.

"Well, he did come here, didn't he?" McGregor said. He held the skates before him. "He did bring these."

He gestured toward the others on the porch.

"And he did stand among us, the bastard."

Clutching the packet of rice, McGregor turned back toward the door.

"Damned difficult to understand, these English."

Within three weeks Ian Damu recovered. His upper body was badly scratched. He had lost considerable weight, and his legs looked like stalks. His shoulder was still bandaged. One morning Collins saw him climbing the steps toward Craft's office. He was wearing the skates.

On the porch Ian Damu ricocheted back and forth from the railing to the wall. His good arm flew out to his side. He had no skill with the skates, and he walked on them as much as he rolled on them. When he arrived at the doorway, he stood in it a moment, looking for Craft. The Englishman was in the back of his office, out of Collins's line of sight. Ian Damu placed his hand on the doorjamb and peered into the office. He caught himself as the skates flew out from beneath him. He regained his balance, and Craft soon appeared at his desk. He laid a few papers on the desktop and came to the doorway. Craft examined Ian Damu's face. He commiserated with him and caressed his scabbed cheek. He took Ian Damu's hand.

"Go away, boy," he smiled.

Ian Damu turned and skated along the ruts of the wooden porch. Hidden in the shadow of his own office, Collins saw Craft's face open up and his eyes soften to an expression of regret and happiness. Then he returned to his desk. Ian Damu skated back to the doorway. He skated once more to the end of the porch. Craft listened as Ian Damu careened along the wall and appeared, flailing, in the doorway again. Craft placed his forehead in his hand. He appeared dizzied by Ian Damu's laughter. He laid his head down on his folded arms, while Ian Damu turned and skated away. The boy continued skating, noisily, the rest of the morning.

4 / The Champion

Collins put the Land Rover into first and let out the clutch. The wheels spun, taking him deeper into the mud. He pushed it into reverse, let out the clutch, and sank a few inches more. He got out of the Land Rover to check his progress.

The road, if it could be called that, had been this bad most of the way from the turnoff. More a track than a road, in some places a mysterious, wandering trail, its gashes and potholes had caused Collins's luggage to be strewn all over the back of the Land Rover. Collins now understood why the government wanted him to supervise building a new road out here. Besides, this was to be the showpiece, the first of an entire system of access roads from the gravel highway between Kuching and Sibu. He looked toward Saratok. He was only a mile from the town, but at this rate it would take him an hour or two to get there.

He shielded his eyes against the sun. A monolith emerged from the coconut trees far ahead. Faded and green, with a corrugated tin roof that shone white in the sunlight, it looked to be about a hundred feet tall. Collins guessed it was the summit of some religious structure, a grand pyramid, perhaps, from a previous Muslim dynasty. Strange, a thing like that, he thought. He had not been aware such archaeological sites existed in Borneo. He got a shovel and started digging himself out.

The building *was* a hundred feet tall. It was made of wood planks, painted green, and situated across the playing field from the Saratok Chinese school. Collins parked the Land Rover in some shade and walked toward the open door at one corner of the building. He could hear shouting and laughter inside. When he reached the doorway, a white shuttlecock bounced to his feet. Collins picked it up. A Chinese man thrust his head out the door into the open air, then recoiled, shocked by the sight of Collins. The American offered him the shuttlecock.

"Hello, I'm here to build the new road," Collins said in Malay.

The man's mouth hung open a moment. Then he reached out and grabbed the birdie from Collins.

The American followed him into the building. Several Chinese sat around the perimeter of a single badminton court. To his amazement, Collins discovered the building's only purpose was to house the court.

"This is the fellow who has come to build the road," said the man who had taken the birdie. There was a rumble of disapproval, followed by laughter. "Welcome, Mr. . . . Mr. . . ."

"Dan Collins."

"Ah, yes." The man approached the rear of the court and prepared to serve.

"What's your name?" Collins said.

"Lew Ling," the man replied. "I am . . . "

He gestured toward the roof far above, then about the entire room.

"I am the champion here."

Saratok was such a small town that there was nothing notable about it, except the badminton building. The Malay kampong contained about a hundred houses randomly nestled among the coconut palms upriver. Downriver was the Chinese bazaar.

The kampong was quite peaceful, a place where laughter counted for more than hard work. There was music and the smell of warm tea. The light at dawn was soft enough to be enjoyed, gray-blue and watery. The bazaar was quite different. There, in the two blocks of plank buildings next to the river, the shops withstood the blazing sun through the day and, if anything, grew furiously busy toward the middle of the afternoon. The siesta, which occurred every day at three, seemed unnatural to the bazaar, as though the Chinese were simply bowing to slothful custom.

Even before he found a house to rent, Collins learned the real importance of the badminton building. Lew Ling had lobbied the Interior Ministry in Kuching for the building years before, then raised construction funds from the local Chinese business organization. It had been a very political maneuver, involving subministers, the British District Officer, the American Peace Corps, everyone.

Collins had been number three seed on the University of California tennis team in 1948 and 1949; when he had thought of badminton at all in those days, it was as a poor cousin to his own game. Watching Lew Ling, though, Collins realized that in Saratok badminton was more than just a sport. The hearts of the Chinese truly rested in their champion. Collins saw that becoming as good a player as Lew Ling would be a way to gain their cooperation. More important, it would be a way he could get their respect.

Right away, though, Collins was intimidated by the ferocity of Lew Ling's game. He played noisily, without grace. His feet slammed against the court. He simply could not be beaten unless, for some private, self-humoring reason, he intentionally lost a single game, almost as a gesture. Collins saw an opportunity in this. At his previous post at the Skrang rubber plantation, Collins had already become a well-known figure, the "Yankee Tuan." Now, assigned to Saratok for the access road, Collins knew his success would depend on the Chinese. They owned almost everything in the town itself and much of the land surrounding it.

Strangely, from the start none of the Chinese would play with him. They laughed when he asked for a game. Collins resented this rudeness, suspecting they simply wanted to keep the court to themselves.

D. K. Singh, the Sikh headmaster of the secondary school, offered another explanation.

"They do not know how to be a gentleman," he said. Singh was a round, tan man who wore thick, horn-rimmed glasses that overwhelmed his gray beard and enormous, pointed moustaches. He spoke excellent English. "If you make a perfectly presentable joke," he said, "like 'Why did the chicken cross the road?' they do not understand, they laugh loudly in your face. It takes a properly brought-up man to get on with these people, Mr. Collins. And, of course, since they will not play with you . . ."

Singh pointed to his chest and bowed.

"I will be honored."

Singh was a terrible player, who moved about the court without finesse and with little resolve. After two months Collins had had enough of the Sikh's good intentions. He decided to declare himself directly to Lew Ling.

There were twenty shops in each of the long, wooden buildings on stilts that made up the bazaar. A wide, dirt track ran between them. The wood sidewalks were cluttered with open barrels and bins filled with green beans, sago palm worms, nails, and rambutan fruit. The planks seemed packed with dirt, worn like neglected leather.

Collins walked down the sidewalk toward Lew Ling's shop, where the champion sold school supplies. The shopkeepers lounged about, propped up on sacks of rice or on short wooden stools. Collins waved once at Wo Sam, who was seated at his cash drawer reading a Chinese newspaper. Wo Sam's café, its peeling, white walls pocked with water stains and moss, was empty of customers. Collins turned into Lew Ling's, which was next door.

The champion stood between two racks of pens and pencils in front of a table piled with mounds of cheap plastic school bags and notebooks, which had wilted in the wet heat, their covers curled and stained. Collins greeted him in Malay. Although Lew Ling spoke English, it was not of a kind Collins could understand.

"You've taken up the game, eh, Tuan?" Lew Ling said.

Normally, the use of the term *Tuan* embarrassed Collins when it came from a Chinese. The word bobbed on an undercurrent of satire. Tuans were always white and generally well liked by the Ibans and the Malays. On those two counts alone, as far as the Chinese were concerned, they were suspect. But white people also indulged in false friendliness all the time. British, Australian, American . . . it didn't matter. They were all the same. The Chinese found such ingratiating patter misleading, phony.

"Yes, I have," Collins replied. "It's a good game, isn't it?"

Lew Ling shrugged his shoulders. He was a solid man, even tight. His eyes were remarkably black and clear. There was little humor in his face.

"And you're improving so quickly," he said.

"Thanks."

"You need some pencils, Tuan?"

Lew Ling's false teeth shone in the light. He gestured across the counter.

"No, actually I came to . . . "

"Erasers?"

"No, I need some shuttlecocks."

"Yes, I have them."

Lew Ling reached up among the sandals hanging from the wall. He wore a T-shirt and dark blue shorts, cinched at the waist with a string.

"Your game is getting much better, Tuan."

"Thanks. Someday," Collins smiled, "I hope to win a game or two from you."

"Yes, I will wait. You've won against Mr. Singh. Very good. Mr. Singh beats everyone."

"Oh, he does not," Collins chuckled.

Lew handed a packet of two shuttlecocks to Collins.

"Try these. They are very good," he said.

"Thanks. They're just the kind . . . "

"You must run faster, Tuan."

Lew Ling bowed his head with deference.

"Excuse me?" Collins replied.

"You too slow," Lew Ling said in English. He laughed. "Nevah win."

He smiled, paused a moment, then held out his hand.

"Two dollah," he said. The thoroughness with which he demanded his money showed the conversation was finished. Collins was being thrown out. Insulted, he searched for a reply. Lew Ling waited silently, his hand held out before him. Collins brought money from his shoulder bag, paid, and left.

He went next door to Wo Sam's for a glass of lychee juice. Wo Sam was the only player in town who thought Collins stood a chance.

Wo wore thick glasses that slid down his nose. He dressed in khaki pants and flip-flops, with no shirt, and his hair flew from the back of his head in a spray of unmannerly black. There were several gray hairs in his sparse beard, which grew from the end of his chin. A wasted, ghostly man, he moved quickly on the court and displayed such subtlety in his net play that his opponents did everything they could to keep him in the backcourt. Collins liked him because he was serious and very pleasant.

"There was a teacher ten years ago at the secondary school," Wo Sam said, as Collins sipped from his juice, "Tamil, here on contract from India. I don't remember his name. He beat Lew Ling. But only two or three times. He flew across the court like a sail. And dark. Black. The Chinese . . . at first we were afraid of him, I remember. But he was a kind man. White teeth."

Wo Sam shook his head.

"These Tamils are so tall, so thin," he continued.

"How did he beat Lew Ling?" Collins asked.

"He wasn't afraid. And he lost, too. Many times. But he never was afraid. That seemed to be the only real difference between him and the others."

Wo Sam's mouth hung open a moment, revealing several brown, gapped teeth.

"Lew Ling can be beaten by a superior player," he continued. "You must be certain you can do it. Certain. Then it can be done."

"But you've never beaten him."

"No," Wo replied. "No."

They looked out at the mud track. Beyond the bazaar the badminton building soared against the blue sky. Above the meander of the palm fronds, in the few breezes, the building was graceful, serene.

"Yes," Wo Sam said, following Collins's gaze, "it's the most beautiful building in town." He uncrossed his legs and leaned on one hand. "As well as the most important. Lew Ling is the best player and the most prestigious shopkeeper here."

Collins turned back toward Wo Sam. The note of bitterness that had entered his voice, a sudden chagrin, an impatience, surprised Collins. It disturbed his impression that Wo Sam was a tranquil man. It carried an edge of jealousy.

"It's been that way for years," Wo Sam continued.

He placed his hands on the table.

"It would be very different to have a new champion here. It would be, it would be . . . "

He crossed his legs again and stared a moment at the badminton building.

"Well, no one has ever imagined what it would be like. Lew Ling has always been in charge. His family, you see, they've always been so. His father. His father before him, old Lew Ching, and Mai Soo, the old man's wife."

"You've never liked that," Collins said.

Wo Sam shrugged his shoulders. He retreated into silence.

"You would like to be in charge."

Wo Sam remained leaning on his palm. He did not reply. Collins, circling his glassful of lychee juice about the tabletop, looked at the few gecko lizards immobile on the back wall of the café. He knew he had guessed it right.

Collins practiced several months more. There were about twenty men in the bazaar who played regularly, and he held his own against almost all of them. Even Lew Ling deigned to play with him after a while. Collins became known for his ability to retrieve impossible birdies. He had lost little of his tennis agility, and he developed a masterful half-dropshot that he executed best on the run, popping the shuttlecock in such a way that it expired just as it gasped over the net. No one could get it. Finally only two players could stay with Collins well enough even to give him a game, Wo Sam and Lew Ling himself.

Then one day Collins lost a game to Lew Ling by just three points. Lew won finally after an exhausting exchange of volleys at the net. It was a contest that the other players watched as though the championship itself were at stake. The game included so many long volleys and speedy backcourt rallies that neither man had time to stop and catch his breath. After Lew Ling won, there was a longer than usual period before the next game. Lew normally insisted on no more than two minutes. He took the court, finally, after ten, complaining cheerfully that the Tuan had been too much for him.

Something had happened. As he recovered on the bench with his towel over his head, Collins realized all the other players were watching him. In the pregame rally with his next opponent, Wo Sam, Lew Ling appeared distracted. He glanced at Collins frequently, and Collins recognized the unique appearance of uncertainty in Lew Ling's eyes.

The next game began, and Collins watched silently as Lew Ling ran up an immediate, commanding lead. Singh approached and sat down next to the American.

"Good show, Tuan," he smiled. The man's affectionate humor relieved Collins's exhaustion. "It is really, now, just a matter of time."

Singh sat back and folded his arms.

"Who would think that you and I, both born so far away, would have such common goals?"

The grave formality of Singh's question actually made it comic. Collins waited for more.

"After all," Singh continued, "a bloke from Amritsar and a Yank from, from . . . "

Singh's teeth sparkled.

"San Francisco," Collins said.

"Ah, yes. Frisco, isn't it?"

"Yes."

"You've lived there a long time?"

"All my life."

Singh pulled at his beard.

"I expect there are very few Sikhs in Frisco," he said.

Collins thought of his neighborhood in North Beach, the various apartments he had lived in since college. In the twenties, Joe DiMaggio had been raised a block from Collins's apartment on Mason Street, and the ballplayer's father had repaired fish nets in the playground across Columbus. Collins imagined the Yankee Clipper, angular and suave, approaching home plate in a turban.

"Very few," Collins smiled.

"And you were an engineer there?"

"Yes. I worked for a large firm," Collins replied. He enjoyed Singh's questions because they recalled the fondness he felt for San Francisco. For Collins, a comparison of that city with his current surroundings was almost impossible to make: on the one hand, a European-like metropolis filled with Italians and Irish, French bread, and the Forty-Niners; on the other a collection of rickety wood buildings patched with tin, which clung to the edge of a watery forest. He had left San Francisco happy with his life there. The cold air on a clear day brightened the light. Here, there was no cold air, ever, and he missed it.

"We built freeways," Collins continued.

"Freeways," Singh said. "What are those?"

"In England, I believe they're called dual carriageways." The British usage made more sense to Singh, and again he broke into a large smile.

"Ah yes, I see," he said. "Quite right. We have few of those in Amritsar. None, actually. The Punjab is rather behind Frisco in that respect."

Singh leaned close.

"But here in Saratok we have much in common, Mr. Collins, you and I. We play badminton."

Lew Ling, lunging for a shuttlecock that had barely cleared the net, shouted with laughter as his return sailed past Wo Sam's outstretched racket.

"And we have a common opponent," Singh whispered.

"Who?"

"Lew Ling! Mr. Collins. Who else?"

Collins wiped his hands with his towel and let it drop to the floor.

"You see, Mr. Collins, your pursuit of him, your mastery of him, has meaning for the rest of us."

"The other players?"

"Well, yes. For all of us who are not, well, not so wise in business."

"But that has nothing to do with it, Singh."

"For you, perhaps not. But Lew Ling is not liked by us. He is, how shall I say, rude. He is a money-grubber. Yes, he is a cheat."

Collins watched as Lew Ling won the game with a long drifting shot to the backcourt.

"It is very important to us that you win, Mr. Collins."

Collins leaned forward and retrieved his towel from the floor.

"But who are *you?*" he asked. "Who wants me to win?"

Singh glared at him with surprise.

"Everyone who is not Chinese," he replied.

Collins groaned.

"Look, I don't feel that way."

"Oh, but Mr. Collins, the Chinese will defeat you if they can."

"Come on!"

"They will. They feel sorry for you if you are not one of them. But then they use that against you. Even against you Yanks."

Singh placed his racket in its case and stood up. Lew Ling approached the bench.

"Even you Yanks, Mr. Collins."

"Well played, Lew Ling," Collins said in Malay.

"Thank you," Lew replied. He bowed to Singh.

"The bloody champion," Singh muttered in English.

The following day Collins received a letter from Kuching, from his boss, Evan Buchan.

Dear Dan:

We've received word from the D.O. in Saratok that the Chinese there don't want the road. It seems to be this chap Lew Ling, principally. He believes it will spoil the signifi-cant riverboat cargo business he's set up over the years. In my opinion he doesn't understand the finer points here; the road will increase, not decrease, his business. Have a look at it, will you? Get his support. It's very, very important to our efforts, and I see it as your task to make sure the Chinaman goes along. We'll be rather disappointed in you if that does not happen. Rather.

Best,
Evan

Disgruntled, Collins wondered where the D.O. had gotten his information. There's nothing wrong with the road, he thought. Coming along, just as it always has. Have a look at it, eh? Collins thought. So far, with a crew of thirty Chinese, Collins had dug, tractored, and pushed his way through two miles of jungle. There had been no objection from anyone. If anything, the locals had shown a great deal of patience with Collins, the aggressive white man with his abrupt, certain plans.

But as he walked through the bazaar, Collins realized that such a letter was no idle thing. There had to be a reason for it. He wondered how Lew Ling could possibly object to a road that would shorten the trip to Kuching from two days to six or seven hours. It made no sense. And Lew Ling had never mentioned it to Collins.

At the badminton court his few questions met with laughter. Lew Ling wondered how the kind people in Kuching could think such foolishness. It was a wonderful thing, Lew said, such attention.

That evening Collins sat reading in his house in the kampong. Outside the cicadas maintained a kind of liquid hum at several pitches. Fireflies crowded the wet shrubbery. Collins's gas lamp cast harsh light in a circle around his chair.

He heard footsteps on the dirt path outside, and Martin Lew Quan, Lew Ling's son, appeared in the doorway. Shaped like his father, with a thinner, more open face, he excused himself as Collins invited him into the house.

"I hope you don't mind this late visit, Mr. Collins," he said in Malay. He wore black-rimmed glasses that in the hard light from the lantern threw shadows across his eyes. "My father would like to see you. He needs your help."

"Right now? What kind of help?"

Martin lowered his head with embarrassment.

"If you can be patient, Mr. Collins. I know it's late. I would appreciate your kindness."

Alarmed by Martin's obvious discomfort, Collins agreed, and the two descended the stairs and walked up the path toward a waiting trishaw. The driver, a young Muslim, lounged in the passenger seat as the two men approached. He got up quickly and moved onto the bicycle. They wheeled slowly through the village toward the bazaar.

The buildings in the bazaar formed a crumpled, black silhouette against huge, silvery clouds. Collins was reminded of old graves, the stones akimbo and fallen. The bazaar gave way to groves of rubber trees, then to a solitary shack. As the trishaw approached, the light through the doorway took on the blue glare of a Coleman lantern. Lew Ling sat beneath the lamp at a table with raised sides lined with green felt. A cloud of moths speckled the light.

"Tuan. Come in, please. Sit down."

Lew Ling was sweating freely. His confident manner put Collins off.

"I hope this is not an inconvenience," Lew said.

"Well, it is, somewhat."

"I wanted to show you something, Tuan. Something I enjoy."

Lew Ling waved Martin from the room. Then he reached beneath the table for a small cloth bag.

"These."

He opened the bag and sprayed the green felt with several dozen rubies. Their color, a purple-red of extraordinary depth, lightened as the mantles in the lantern suddenly dimmed. Lew Ling stood up to pump the lantern. Collins stared at the rubies without speaking. After a moment Lew Ling brought out a second bag and poured them onto the felt as well.

"Where do they come from?" Collins asked.

"Burma. Through Thailand, on their way to Australia."

"How did you get them?"

Lew smiled.

"I have an interest in these things," he said.

"But how did you get them?"

"In sacks of rice."

Collins leaned closer to the jewels.

"But I wish to speak with you about something else, Mr. Collins."

Lew Ling's use of his name, the first time ever, took Collins by surprise.

"I want to talk to you about badminton."

Lew Ling sat back in his chair. His face shone with sweat.

"We will have a challenge match soon, you and I," he said.

"Yes."

"And I . . . well, I have never lost such a challenge."

Collins rolled his fingers about the rubies. They seemed to him like beads of water.

"Until now, I hope," Collins muttered.

"I have always been the champion in Saratok, and if I were not, well, my position would be diminished. So I am serious when I say I don't want to lose."

"Oh, Lew, you have every chance of winning."

Lew Ling's face turned from the light.

"My family's position, you see . . . " His hands sagged above the table. "The rubies, Mr. Collins. Do you like them?"

"Pardon me?"

"Would you like some for yourself?"

Collins retreated a moment. At first he was insulted. He wanted only to play badminton, fair and square, just like everybody else. His sense of honesty flared up in him. Americans don't do this! he thought. But he worried he was just being naive. Lew Ling doesn't care that there are other ways of going about this, he thought.

But then Collins realized the depth of Lew Ling's desperation. Lew's face sagged into a frown. He obviously disapproved of Collins's reluctance. A bribe was nothing new to him, and he wanted the championship badly. He was just offering a commission, that's all. But I have an obligation to myself, Collins thought, to my own morality, to the way I'm supposed to be doing things out here.

He picked up a ruby and examined it.

"I like them very much," Collins smiled.

"Good," Lew Ling replied. "Excellent."

"But I can't accept them."

"You can't?"

"No. My government would not allow it."

Lew Ling shook his head.

"How would they know?" he asked. "I've often made such arrangements before."

Collins paused, swallowed, then pressed on.

"Well, there is something else I want," he said.

"What is it, Tuan? Women?"

"To finish the road."

Lew Ling's eyes seemed to thicken. He shook his head.

"Give me the road," Collins said.

Lew Ling grimaced. "We don't need the road," he said. "It serves no purpose."

"It's for your own good. It will improve your business."

"No!"

"It will, Lew. Believe me, it will."

"No. A road will mean that certain methods of delivery of certain goods must change."

"So it may be."

"Tuan. Please." Lew Ling sighed, looking for the correct words. "It is so difficult to transport quietly on a road. On a boat, yes. Or on a man's back . . . . But with a road, I *must* transport by truck, and the government patrols the roads. They search trucks."

"But the only thing I want is the road."

Lew Ling ground his teeth.

"This is not fair," he said.

Collins stood up. He knew the offer of the championship was a bribe as well, and he worried about what would happen to him if the State Department learned what he was doing. He could be censured, maybe fired. Collins had wanted his work to be straightforward. He had wanted to build the road, nothing more. The idea of bribing Lew Ling made him queasy. He saw that it might even put him in Lew Ling's control were Lew to accept it. But on the other hand, Collins thought in a moment of crystalline pleasure, it may give you the completed road, stretching off into the forest gravelly and beautiful. So to hell with the State Department. His heart seemed to open up suddenly and to glow.

"If we can't arrange it here, Lew Ling, it will be arranged on the badminton court," Collins said.

He turned to leave. Lew Ling held up his hand.

"I want the championship, Mr. Collins."

Collins stopped in the doorway.

"And you will get the road," Lew Ling said. Angrily, he looked down at the floor and spat. "*If* I get the championship."

The American turned back and shook Lew Ling's hand.

All the badminton players in Saratok and most of the Chinese merchants, some two hundred people in all, turned out for the challenge match. The crowd shouted for Lew Ling throughout the first game, which went very much against the American. Collins felt stiff, ungainly. The touch on which his game depended was nonexistent. He tried to play aggressively, to look as if he wanted to win, and he simply botched it.

Between games Collins ignored Lew Ling's few words of encouragement. No matter what, Collins resolved, he wouldn't lose the second game. He would play as well as he could, at least for the second game.

He won the first three points, lost one, then won two more. His nervousness disappeared. His stride became smoother, and he found he could extend his reach, easily retrieving one of Lew Ling's seeming winners and forcing Lew off the court with an excellent backhand return. For the first time there was applause for Collins, and Lew Ling returned to the baseline muttering to himself.

At 15–15, Collins ran off six straight points to win. He made shots so decisively that he found he had won over some of the crowd simply by the way he played. Collins even angered Lew

Ling by making soft shots where smashes would have been more appropriate. And once he rifled the shuttlecock past him when Lew obviously expected something more delicate. Finally Lew Ling watched in despair from the backcourt as Collins won the last point, lifting the birdie lightly over the net, clearing it just in front of his opponent. Collins made the shot in the same spirit he would have thumbed his nose.

"Good game, Tuan," Lew Ling said as they sat down on the bench. His breath came quickly in gulps.

"Thanks."

"Final game coming up."

"That's right."

"You keep playing like that, you're going to win."

Lew Ling stood and walked onto the court, not waiting for Collins's reply.

Collins raced ahead 12–0. Lew Ling had given up, it seemed. Running listlessly about, he had fumbled easy returns, even double-faulting twice. But as Collins turned to serve once again, he saw Lew Ling watching him. There was a grin on his face.

Suddenly Collins remembered the bargain. The ferocity of the competition had taken him over, and now he cursed himself for getting carried away. To lose now, his own game would have to fall apart completely. He'd have to scramble about looking for ways to be defeated. It would be crushing. He leaned over and grimaced at the floor. He realized Lew was making a fool of him.

All right, Collins decided, I'll get the damned road some other way. Being humiliated isn't part of it. He retreated beyond the baseline to serve again.

The shuttlecock left his racket and sailed slowly toward the far court. Lew Ling put the return down the line, out of reach, and took the next five points. He had come back to life. He played once more furiously, noisily. He charged about the court, his game electric with revenge. The crowd screamed with each point of his resurgence, and Collins struggled to hold him off.

Finally, at 19–19, Lew Ling called time. He joined Collins at the net. Lew Ling spoke between gasps.

"You know the rules, Tuan."

"Yes," Collins said.

"Tied like this, we add on three points, right? First one to 22 wins."

Collins pulled his shirt from beneath his belt and wiped his brow.

"That's right," he wheezed.

Lew Ling took the lead.

Collins took it back.

At 21–21, the champion gained the serve. He stepped up to the line and held the birdie before him. There was loud shouting from the crowd, yet Lew waited quietly a moment, composed, glistening.

So now, Collins thought, it's time to blow the match.

Lew Ling served low and to the right. Collins's return was deliberately poor. There was an untroubled serenity in the passage of the birdie across the net. It fell through the noisy air like a petal. But it came back like a rocket, skittering to the floor a foot beyond Collins's desperate lunge.

Lew Ling raised his arms into the air. The crowd exploded.

"Lew Ling! Lew Ling!"

Gathered up on the shoulders of the spectators, Lew Ling shouted his victory. He waved his racket in the air, as Collins stood silently at the back corner of the court.

"Lew Ling," the crowd chanted. They paraded around the court. Their shouts echoed through the building like a recurrent storm, then swept out into the night.

"Lew Ling! Lew Ling!"

Only Singh and Collins remained behind. Alone, a towel in his hand, Collins waited. After a moment the Sikh shrugged his shoulders and stepped across the court.

"A few problems," he said. "But on the whole, Tuan, you played quite well."

The American wiped his face.

"Thank you. He surprised me, coming back as strongly as he did. Beating me when I thought I had him."

"It doesn't matter," Singh smiled. Dejection darkened his large eyes. "At least you lost . . . what is it you Yanks say? Fairly and square?"

Collins grunted.

"Yes," he said. "Fairly and square."

5 / The Truth

Before dawn Collins was awakened by the voice of Hajji Mahmet
bin Saleh, the crier at the mosque next door to his house. At first
Mahmet's morning recitations had annoyed him, coming as they
did so early every day. But Collins had grown used to them and,
after living in Saratok for a year, he actually enjoyed them. In
Arabic, sung in a high nasal drone, the calls to prayer were made
even more meaningful by Mahmet's having made the pilgrimage
to Mecca. But Collins could not understand a word. They
represented only sound and verve to him. Yet what sound! They
seemed to come from the forest beyond the village, as the drone
of the cicadas did, like the monsoon rains. Mahmet's voice was
warm and delirious. It floated through the liquid forest. The end
of each phrase was a clipped, upward bleat, an abrupt exhalation
that gave way immediately to another lush passage decorated
with the sounds of laughter and argument coming from the
village, with the putter of boat engines starting the trip downriver, with the lyrical Malay music — light voices, gongs, and
violins — coming from the radios everywhere in the kampong.

And he brings light to the village, Collins mused as he
watched the sun rise over the river. Initially he saw the black-gray
silhouettes of the palms, which appeared frozen in the morning
darkness. Then gloomy sprays of green against the brightening
sky. The gray gave way to the sunlight finally, then to the glare.
Mahmet was able to bring it about, Collins liked to think, with
the simple urging of his voice.

Collins's house was a wooden frame building on stilts, which protected it from the river's daily high tide. He rented it from the mosque, so that Mahmet was also his landlord. The Malays were honored to have Collins living in their kampong. Dignitaries such as he were normally put up in the government guest house or at the District Officer's large home overlooking the river from the hill at the end of the bazaar. But it was the political importance of the Malays that had made Collins decide to stay in their village. They did not own nearly as much land as the Chinese or even the Ibans, the local tribesmen. But the Malays — a passive, pleasant people — had ingratiated themselves to their British rulers over the years with their trustworthy, efficient lassitude. Now, the governing of the country was theirs, a gift to them from the recently departed colonialists.

Collins liked the Malays a great deal. Mahmet often dropped by Collins's house with gifts of sweet cake or flowers, and he never asked for the rent. Noting Mahmet's shyness as a businessman, Collins always made a point of paying on time.

Collins got up and dressed, then prepared a cup of coffee and two slices of toast and jam. He walked the path through the Malay village toward the Chinese bazaar. He approached his office, which was on the second floor of a cement-block government building. A single palm tree twenty yards from the building cast its shadow on the blistered ground. Otherwise there was no respite from the sun anywhere near the building. When Collins arrived in his office, he turned on the ceiling fan immediately. It would continue turning all day at full force. He had placed his desk directly beneath it, and the small piles of paper, neatly arranged, were each held down with a large stone.

At nine-thirty, Collins heard Jim Eustace's footsteps on the stairs, and after a moment the missionary stepped into Collins's office.

"Not too warm for you, I hope," he said as he sat down across Collins's desk. His forehead gleamed like a wet plate. His shirt appeared to have been dipped in water, especially around his neck where sweat ran down in small streams. Collins, with whom he had tea every morning, placed a tray before Eustace, a pot, two cups and saucers, a tin of sugar cubes, and a can of evaporated milk. Eustace himself brought the leaf tea, a tin of the Earl Grey he received in the mail from England every few months.

"Makes you perspire, you know," he said. "Good for you, that."

Collins, who always reacted to the tea with an unstaunched flow of sweat himself, could not understand the virtue of so much secretion. Eustace removed the tin from his shoulder bag and spooned out enough for a full pot. Pouring the water into the pot, he sat back to watch the slip of steam rising from the white spout.

"It's God's will," he said.

"What is?" Collins asked. He sat down to his own cup and pushed a packet of salt-crackers toward Eustace.

"Sweat. It makes the body sing. Music of the spheres, you see. You hear it all the time out here."

"If you say so, Jim."

Collins glanced out the window at the hills across the river. They were low and green, one after another. Far from graceful, the jungle had a throwaway quality, something slovenly and dull.

"You do! Listen for it, Dan," Eustace laughed. "The forest here is in a state of grace. Everything can be explained by it."

Eustace was a round man with white hair that shot from the sides of his head like wires. Bald on top and sweating, his head reminded Collins of fine porcelain. He was sixty-seven years old and had lived in Sarawak half his life, with the exception of the years during the war when he had been an Anglican chaplain with the British army in Malaya and North Africa. Eustace spoke all the local languages, as well as Cantonese and Mandarin, fluently. He was quite short and ragged looking. His body had the shape of a lumpy bowling pin, ill-carved, hand-hewn.

"Well, Dan," he said as he settled back in his chair with the cup and saucer resting on his lap. "I've decided to pack it in."

He lifted the cup to his nose, smelled it, then lay it back on the saucer.

"I've written the letter to the Mission, and I'm going to post it this afternoon."

Eustace took a handkerchief from his pants pocket and wiped his forehead.

"You mean, retire?" Collins asked.

"That's it. I hope that doesn't come as a surprise."

"No, not really," Collins replied. "After all, you've been out here for years. You're getting . . . "

"Older, yes."

"I was going to say you're getting so well known that everyone takes you for a Muslim."

Eustace chuckled.

"Then you don't deny I'm getting older," he said.

"No, but it doesn't matter."

"And I can still chop down an ironwood tree as well as anybody?"

"Of course, yes, that's true."

"Right you are."

Indeed Eustace's hands *were* like a laborer's — cut and chipped — because he enjoyed working in the woods with the local tribesmen and the Malays. He was not the sort of man Collins associated with sanctity.

"I'll be leaving in a month or two, I think," he said.

"Where to?"

"London. My sister is there. She was married to a clergyman as well, poor man."

"What, that he was a clergyman?"

"No, that he's dead."

"I see."

"Like so many others."

Collins sipped his tea.

"It's difficult to imagine so complete a change, though, Jim. The jungle to London. It's like heaven to hell. Or hell to heaven." Collins grinned. "Or something," he continued. "It makes no sense."

"Yes, it's cold there," Eustace replied.

"Will you miss things here?"

At first the question got no response. The airiness of the conversation had not prepared Collins for Eustace's sudden regretfulness. The missionary set the cup and saucer on the desk and laced his fingers behind his head. He looked out the door into the sunlight.

"Missionary work carries a lot of drudgery with it, Dan," he said. "You don't see much that's miraculous out here, I'm afraid."

He paused, staring out the door. His eyes were red with the morning heat.

"Except for the occasional cup of tea with the occasional American, one's enjoyment of the work sometimes flags."

Eustace appeared to lose his breath for a moment. He looked into his cup.

"Besides, I'm afraid, you see . . . I'm afraid God will take me," he said.

"I'm sure He will." Collins sat back and grinned.

"Yes, but I'm afraid He'll take me too soon, you see. Now."

A small loop of steam caressed his face.

"Before I've done what I want to do."

In the silence that followed, Collins became embarrassed by his own gleefulness. He had been expecting the sort of patter their conversations usually contained, fueled by Eustace's intense enjoyment of his Earl Grey. Both men had come to depend on these morning meetings: Eustace to complain breathlessly about the foolishness of being a missionary, Collins to laugh at the Englishman's comic dismay. He did not believe that Eustace could be disappointed with himself. Eustace was a success out here, and Collins envied him. He was known up and down the river. He was loved.

"But you see, half the people here are Muslims," Eustace said. "And there's little I can do about them. Some of the Chinese are interested, but I worry it's only for business reasons or some-thing. And that leaves the tribes out in the hills. Wonderful people, hard working and all that. But they don't care much for Christ's teachings. They're worried more about their rice, about their rubber. And I for one — well, I can hardly blame them.

There's just too damned little of it—the rice and the rubber, that is."

He placed his chin on the palm of one hand and exhaled. For a moment neither man spoke. Outside a burst of hurried talk came from across the yard.

"So sometimes I worry," Eustace said, looking toward the door, "that the only success I've had as a man of God is with myself."

Collins stood and walked to the door. Beneath the palm tree, Mahmet and several other Malays shouted back and forth at one another. They clung to the minute oval of shade and appeared intimidated by Collins's office. They looked at it often. They debated. Collins stepped out onto the porch and Mahmet, clearly relieved, hurried toward him. He was a very small man, wearing long black pants and a white shirt. His arms were crooked at the elbows, a habit of carrying himself that made him look older than he really was. His legs and arms were very thin, and he resembled a rickety statue.

"There is a white man up in the forest, Tuan, a crazy man," he said.

Collins leaned on the metal railing. In the morning sun it felt like crusted, hot rust, and he pulled away from it.

"In the caves," Mahmet continued as he pointed upriver. "And he won't come out."

Mahmet shielded his eyes. The other Malays had followed him across the yard and now stood in a group behind him. Collins recognized several of his neighbors. Eustace walked from the office, his cup of tea in his hand.

"What is it?" he asked.

"Will you help us?" Mahmet asked. He nodded toward the Englishman. Like most of the Malays in Saratok, Mahmet recognized Eustace's religious kindness. Though a Christian, he was an affectionate man, and he could be trusted. In that, he and Collins were alike. Mahmet walked toward the stairway and Collins gestured to the others to come up as well.

The Malays ascended the stairs and turned into Collins's office. The American put a fresh pot of water on his butane burner, and the men sat down on the rattan mat just inside the doorway. Collins took a new packet of Rothman's cigarettes from his desk, opened it, and placed it with a box of matches before the men. Several took cigarettes from the packet, gave polite thanks, and waited for their tea as Mahmet explained the situation.

"He's very strange, Tuan. A tall man but quite thin."

Mahmet made an enormous circle with his hands about his face. Smoke from the newly lit cigarette fluttered into the air.

"And he has a beard, like this, very thick. Like a bird's nest."

"But what's he doing up there?" Eustace asked.

Mahmet waited a moment in silence. He seemed at first not to understand the question, and his dark, lined face remained stolid.

"He talks," Mahmet replied. "But he makes no sense."

"What do you mean?"

"Well, he doesn't speak Malay."

Collins finished preparing the tea and arranged several cups on a tin tray. He placed the tea on the mat before the semicircle of men and poured a cupful for each.

"But that is not the problem, Tuan," Mahmet continued as he took his cup from the tray. "The problem is that he talks continuously. In English, of course. But I'll wager . . . "

Mahmet placed his right hand on his chest and nodded toward the two white men.

"I'll wager even you will not understand him."

He pressed his lips together and shrugged.

"He barely waits for us to ask him a question," he continued. "He just talks. Points across the valley and talks. Addresses us as though we were studying Allah's words, as though he were the master and we . . . "

Mahmet leaned forward and nudged the ash from his cigarette onto the floor.

"And we were the pilgrims. He doesn't understand that we don't understand him."

"The man is up there raving!" Eustace said in English. Collins sipped from his own tea and went to the coat rack to get his shoulder bag. He placed inside his sunglasses, a second packet of cigarettes, and a notepad.

"Well, we ought to go see," he replied.

"He won't let us approach the caves," Mahmet said. The others sitting with him grumbled agreement, and Collins sat down with them.

"What do you mean?" he asked.

"He has a rifle." Mahmet lowered his head. "I mean, we think he has a rifle."

"You're not sure?"

"No. But we've approached the cave, and he stands before it and gestures us away. He pretends he is shooting at us."

Collins lowered his cup to the floor.

"You see," Mahmet explained. "He aims at us as though he has a rifle in his hands. And he makes a sound with his mouth, like a shot. But really it is not a rifle."

"What is it?"

"Air," Mahmet said. "Nothing."

"Where is he?" Eustace asked.

Mahmet pointed at the hills upriver.

"Fifteen minutes' walk. In my cave up near Kampong Ulu."

"Well, come on then," Eustace said in English. "Let's have a look."

Mahmet led the way as they walked into the forest. After several minutes they saw yellow-white cliffs pushing up from the tree line far ahead. The cliffs appeared to have collapsed inwardly, into the caves, as though the very weight of the rock had crumpled them. Only one cave was large enough to be entered on foot, and it was normally used by Mahmet and the others to store their rice. Collins strained to see the mysterious white man. A voice was the first indication of his presence. It was high, complaining, like a preacher's on the street.

"Don't come up here," the voice said. "Get away."

Collins and the others stopped to listen. The voice was nasal and clear, though it was barely loud enough to be heard.

"I know you're coming to get me."

Mahmet crouched behind a tree and waved to the others to gather around him.

"That's him, Tuan," he whispered. "Listen. He'll say more."

The man muttered and stormed. Sometimes he shouted as though the forest were empty. He said he was Joe. He said he loved mankind.

"No question about it, though," he said. "Sons of bitches don't deserve it. Never have."

"What does he say, Tuan?" Mahmet asked.

"I'm not sure yet," Collins replied.

They continued slowly up the trail. Their efforts at quiet were ruined by the cracking of twigs and ferns. Collins cursed to himself as he stumbled over a root. They heard more noise from Joe, disconnected mutterings and raves. Finally, when they cleared a rise and had an unimpeded view of the caves themselves, they saw him.

He rose up from the cave entrance with disheveled dignity, in rags in the open sun. His feet were bare and filthy, and his shorts, green fatigues that hung loosely about his thighs, had not been washed in months. His Hawaiian shirt was much too large; its garish flowers were crusted with filth. The left sleeve had disappeared altogether while the right clung to the rest of his shirt like a rag hanging from a line. His beard was as Mahmet had described but far larger. On the ground in front of the cave were the remains of a campfire from which a thin line of smoke rose into the air. Joe's gesturing hand passed through the smoke as he talked.

"Beautiful place. Yeah," he continued. "Me too. Beautiful."

"Australian," Eustace whispered to Collins. "I would have thought so," he chuckled.

They moved closer. Collins had seen people like Joe before but never in as remote a place as this. They approached him in cities like Kuala Lumpur or Bangkok, hitting him up for a cigarette or a place to stay. Usually wasted and dirty, they made jokes about drugs. They were world travelers, but they had no money. Collins avoided them whenever he saw them, which in Asian cities was frequently.

Standing in the sun, Joe continued talking. He wandered through private conversations that were truculent and serene at the same time. He railed against the world but seemed to want to explain it. His explanations made no sense. He preached, and his words disappeared into the woods. In his madness, he conversed with the air.

"I'd better try to talk with him," Collins said in Malay.

"Be careful, Tuan," Mahmet whispered. "Remember the gun."

"But you said there was no gun."

Mahmet nodded. His lips turned down.

"Yes, but you should be careful with a man like this."

"Well, at least I'll be able to speak English with him," Collins nodded. He turned to Eustace. "Same language, you know. That'll help."

He stood and walked toward the cave entrance. When Collins was thirty yards away, Joe spotted him. Stepping to a boulder, he reached into a pack leaning against it, pulled a pistol from the side pocket, aimed at Collins, and fired.

Collins jumped into the underbrush off the trail.

"Did you see that?" he shouted.

The Malays scrambled about in the underbrush, shouting confusedly. They ran down the path and disappeared into the forest. Mahmet remained behind with Eustace, while Collins crawled toward them, using the ferns for cover as Joe shot at them again.

"My God, Dan, what's going on?" Eustace said.

Collins's heart pounded. He brushed his hair back and dirty sweat came away in his hand. His knees shook, and as he lay to the side of the path, he rested his forehead on his palms. The thought raced through him that he could be killed. He looked for Eustace, who hid with Mahmet behind a granite boulder covered with ferns. Eustace brushed at his own mouth, then touched his tongue with the fingers of one hand. There appeared to be no saliva, and he wiped his fingers on his shirt. Collins crawled down the path and joined them.

The three men waited a half hour. Joe's vigilance gave way after a while to more conversation. Collins listened, trying to pick threads of sense from it, some idea of who Joe was.

"Come around here trying to toss me out," Joe said.

He whispered a few moments. The beard below his chin jabbed the air.

"Won't have it, dammit. Never listen to me."

His voice raised to a shout.

"Listen! I'll show you the way!"

The man rambled with semiphrases and small bits of information, mostly argument and reverie. His shoutings were filled with despairing wonder. He'd been mistreated all his life. He begrudged the world.

"What are we going to do?" Eustace whispered.

Collins turned around and sat up with his back to the boulder.

"We've got to get him out of there," he replied. "But I don't know how."

Collins looked down at himself. Sweat dripped from his face to the ground. He realized he had cut his knee when he dove for cover and he examined the wound with a muddy hand.

"We'd have to go down to Simanggang to get the police," Collins continued. "It'd take us a couple of days!"

"I might be able to speak with him," Eustace said. He looked up at the caves. Joe could not be seen, but his voice sputtered into the trees.

"I'd forgive 'em if I could, dammit," he said. "I would and that's the truth."

"He's so lost," Eustace continued. The sympathy in his voice, sincere as it was, worried Collins.

"But it's far too dangerous, Jim," he said.

"Maybe."

Eustace swallowed and glanced once more at the caves.

"No. Of course you're right, Dan. I can't go up there."

Mahmet, who had been watching the caves as well, exhaled with surprise as Joe stepped again into the sunlight.

Now he wore no clothes, and sweat gleamed from his body. Nonetheless the whiteness of his skin shone through the streaked dust. His shoulders and stomach particularly glistened, and a dark V-shaped line of tan down his chest showed how long he had been traveling. He carried his shirt in his hand, and looking out into the forest toward Collins and the others, he threw it in their direction. The shirt fluttered a few feet into the air, then caught on a bush and hung there as Joe shook his fist.

"Come up and get me, you bastards."

Behind them came the sounds of loud crashing and men running through the forest. Collins and the others crouched down with alarm as the Malays returned carrying shotguns and rifles.

Mahmet threw his hands up to stop them. But immediately they fired at the cave entrance. The puffs of smoke from their shotguns rose into the ferns and trees. A scream of fear came from above, and Joe, sprawled in the mud, hurriedly crawled back into the cave. His voice rose to a wail as the gunfire continued.

Eustace had dropped down onto his stomach. He shouted at the Malays to stop, but they would not listen to him.

"Mahmet! Mahmet!" he yelled.

Eustace crawled quickly to the Malay's side and shook him by the sleeve of his shirt.

"Stop them!" Eustace said.

Mahmet turned and shouted at the others, but the men continued firing. Joe's voice rose through the gunfire in despair.

"Goddamn it!" Eustace cried. He stood and moved through the underbrush toward the path. "Goddamn it!"

The Malays stopped shooting. They ordered Eustace out of the way. But he continued walking slowly up the path, his hands in the air.

"Jim!" Collins wanted to knock Eustace down, to get him out of the way. Eustace staggered and kept walking. He appeared to be entranced. His white legs, protruding from his walking shorts like sticks, wobbled as he slipped again in some mud. Smoke from the gunfire floated through the trees and obscured Eustace's body.

"Jim, stop!" Collins said.

"Wait, Tuan," Mahmet said as he laid a hand on Collins's arm. "He's trying to save the man. Leave him alone."

Mahmet watched Eustace intently. His mouth hung open, his lips not moving.

"Ridiculous," Collins said, and he stood and walked up the path toward the Englishman. He had almost caught Eustace when Joe stepped out from behind one of the boulders. He pointed the pistol at Eustace, who abruptly stopped.

"Joe, wait," he yelled. "I'm a priest. I can help you."

Joe pulled the trigger. The pistol did not fire, and Joe pulled the trigger once more before gunfire erupted from the Malays. Grabbing Eustace, Collins pulled him into the underbrush.

"Let go of me," Eustace screamed. Collins lost his grip. He slid through a patch of mud against a tree trunk and struggled to his hands and knees.

Eustace stood up again in the line of fire. Mahmet exhorted the Malays to put down their guns, and the echo of the gunfire rumbled through the forest, diminishing farther and farther away. Collins pursued the missionary. So much smoke swirled about that it was difficult for Collins to see ahead. He arrived at the cave a moment behind Eustace.

Joe lay crumpled against a boulder. He had been hit in the chest and had died immediately. His mouth was open, as were his eyes. Collins's breath came in gasps. He could not put the chaotic noise of the gunfire from his mind. The danger had been so extreme and so quick that only now did he comprehend it, and he tried slowing his breathing to ease the shaking in his chest.

In the sudden quiet Eustace's voice sounded drained by disappointment. "I don't know who he is." He leaned over and took up Joe's soiled hand. "Could have saved the bloke, and I don't even know him."

Collins glanced at the backpack, which had ripped on one side and been sewn haphazardly back together with a leather strand. He knelt down and flipped open the cover. He pulled out a shirt, quite dirty, and a pair of rubber flip-flops, one of which had no heel. Collins pushed aside the other rags and clothing in the backpack, trying to avoid the sodden odor that came out of it. There were small hashish scales, some tobacco, a few tinfoil-wrapped packets, wet rolling papers, and a half-eaten rice-ball. At the bottom Collins found a passport.

He stood up again and moved to Eustace's side. The photo showed a clean-shaven man with glasses. Joseph Maurice. Thirty-three.

"Tells you everything you need to know, doesn't it?" Eustace whispered.

Eustace took the passport. Collins looked back at the Malays below. Mahmet stood apart from them in disgruntled silence. He came up the path, followed by the others.

"But he wasn't listening to you, Jim," Collins said. "He could have killed you."

"Poor man's reason deserted him."

Eustace turned away from the body.

"Life, happiness . . . " He looked down at the passport photo once more. "Dan, I don't know. Everything deserted him."

He knelt once more and placed his hand on Joe's lips.

"We deserted him."

"Oh, Jim, come on!"

"We did!" Eustace whispered a profanity. His lips turned down with disappointment. His eyes widened like dark blemishes. "I've worked with these people for years," he said, gesturing into the shaded forest.

When Mahmet arrived, he looked down at Joe's body, then placed his hands in his pockets and murmured an apology.

"And they've meant a lot to me," Eustace continued.

"This is a terrible thing," Mahmet whispered.

"But poor Joe. You think he wanted to kill me, Dan. But the gun . . . the gun was just a gesture."

"Jim," Collins muttered. "That's nuts."

"And he was one of ours."

"Are you kidding?"

"Shooting at me didn't matter. I could have brought the poor fool back."

Eustace lowered his head.

"I could have saved him, Mahmet," he said in Malay.

Eustace touched Joe's bleeding chest. His fingers rested a moment on the wound, and Eustace suddenly grimaced.

"The truth is, though, I probably couldn't have."

He glanced at Collins, who was struck by the loss that appeared in Eustace's eyes.

"I mean I didn't, did I?"

Eustace sat down next to Joe and fell into silent mournfulness. No one spoke for several minutes.

Finally Mahmet motioned to the others to take up the body. He laid a hand on Eustace's arm. The Malays slung their weapons onto their shoulders, placed Joe's arms over his chest, and picked him up. Collins took Joe's pack, and they began descending the path. Eustace's sadness was profound, and it was obvious to Collins he could do little about it. They followed the path down through the forest, farther down toward the river and the village. Eustace's shoulders slumped, and he seemed to pale into old age.

6 / The Lost D.O.

"What are you Americans doing out here?" Hartland asked. "In Borneo, of all places?"

Collins looked down at the river. A late breeze had come up, oddly making the afternoon warmer.

"Helping with the transition, I guess," Collins replied. "You British are leaving. Malaysia's a new country. A lot of problems here, and we think we can bring something to them."

"Well," Hartland said as he turned toward the window to watch the river himself. "You're bloody welcome to try."

The Englishman's hair was gray and straight. His eyes were sheltered by large, graying brows, which formed a straight line above his aquiline nose. He was a tall man, though quite stoop-shouldered when he walked. His fair complexion, after thirty years in tropical Africa and Malaya and three months as the District Officer in Saratok, had fallen into disrepair. Hartland's cheeks were crisscrossed by wavering red lines between which the skin was the color of fresh salmon. His arms were also red, though his legs were fishy pale with few marks. Hartland wore the standard colonial outfit—a carefully pressed khaki shirt, khaki British walking shorts, light tan knee socks, and a pair of brown leather shoes. He had asked Collins to his office to talk about the access road. But so far there had been no talk of the road at all.

"Hard working, these Ibans," Hartland said.

"Yes."

"Need direction, though. I suppose you know that. You speak the language, I understand."

"Yes."

"And you've seen those human heads they've taken, in the longhouses?

"Many times," Collins replied. "Remarkable practice, I think."

"Barbarous."

"Oh, I suppose. It was very effective against the, the . . . "

"The Japs," Hartland interjected.

"That's right."

"Rather. Though I think it's a good policy we have here of not allowing them to hang the heads in their houses. Perhaps it's all right to do that in upriver Skrang, in their own pale so to speak, but not down here."

Collins laughed and waved a hand. "This is still their own pale, you know," he said. "Here in Saratok."

"It is not. It's the government's pale."

"But there was ceremonial importance to the practice," Collins insisted. "Rite of passage, et cetera. It wasn't just blood-thirstiness."

"Oh, quite, quite, Mr. Collins. No need for the lecture."

"I'm sorry. I don't mean to."

"Of course. It's just that . . . well, you know, I've seen self-mutilations and scarrings in Africa. India, too. All sorts of repellant practices among the blacks. But I must say, this one — well, this one rather takes the cake, doesn't it?"

Hartland hooked his thumbs in his belt and assumed an upright, planted look with which he surveyed the horizon. Several Chinese students stood beneath a tree in the road below. Their dark blue shorts and white shirts appeared crisp and pressed despite the heat. They practiced the Malay kick-ball game, keeping a small rattan ball in the air by kicking it back and forth with the side of the foot. As always, the Chinese appeared more exacting in their practice, far more intent than the Malays, who usually played with graceful languor, and who usually won. The road led into the Saratok bazaar, two rows of decrepit buildings shaded by palm trees. The river paralleled the bazaar, then turned into a meander and disappeared into the forest.

"You know, Collins, it strikes me that with every place we've been . . . " Hartland continued. He turned his head toward Collins and nodded. "That is, the English." He chuckled. "And the Americans as well, of course." He turned to look at the view once more. "And others of our ilk. With every place, it's the little enclave of civilization like this that saves us all."

"You're kidding," Collins grinned. "Like Saratok?"

"Yes." Hartland stood silently a moment, his hands joined and resting on his stomach. A breeze blew through the palm trees outside. The fronds, at the same level as Hartland's second-story office, rattled pleasantly, confusedly, a blur of sound that surrounded the stolid Englishman. He pointed into the forest. "Out there there's no order. There are headhunters and chaos. We must do what we can to avoid that."

"I'm not so sure you can avoid an entire culture . . ."

Hartland scratched the back of his head and remained silent.

" . . . Especially when you're surrounded by it," Collins continued.

"What are you talking about?"

"It's just that what you see as chaos is simply different, that's all."

"Of course it's different."

"But it's a practice that can be explained. It isn't chaos you're looking at out there. It . . . "

"Heads hanging in a basket can be explained?"

"Yes, they can."

"Mr. Collins, I suggest you give up this practice of trying to understand these people. You won't get anywhere with that."

Hartland moved toward his desk. So tall a man, he appeared confined by the small wooden room.

"Sounds harsh, I suppose. But I've found that you must maintain yourself out here. Keep your privacy, that sort of thing. Otherwise . . . " He pointed toward the window. "Otherwise they'll take you over."

Leaving the office, Collins walked upriver into the forest. The air was cooler here, and Collins enjoyed the clouds—high, sculpted bunches of white that appeared motionless in the marine sky. They cast dark shadows on the hills, which looked softer, more negotiable than in fact they were. These jungles were not the impenetrable slash more prevalent upriver. There were trails and settlements here. The district was well inhabited. But the forest was difficult anyway because it was so dreary. The hills went on and on, covered with forest and occasionally broken up by rivers and streams. If moments of actual intrigue did arise, they were brought on by the light as it changed throughout the day, especially in late afternoon when the air beneath the tree cover darkened quickly. For the moments of transition from day to night the forest took on a menace that excited Collins. Only then did it exhibit the misanthropic extremes he had found in other parts of Borneo—the noise of the night animals, the gloom into which the trees so rapidly disappeared, the promise of total darkness. The forest would thicken, the air grow heavy. In the gloom Collins feared the orangutan and wild boar, perhaps even the predator headhunters themselves. A moment later, though, the wild boar would turn out to be a domestic pig running to shelter. Small lights would appear in the darkness, the lamps the Ibans used to light their houses. From the silence, voices, a turn of laughter, muffled argument, the noise of meals in the long-houses. No, the forest here was quite safe, Collins thought. He smiled as he thought that, despite Hartland's fears, it was even friendly.

He walked to a trailhead above the river. Descending the path, he continued a quarter mile more to a pool into which a cascade fell from a cliff. Collins enjoyed swimming under these falls. This far up, the streams were clear and cold, though the air was fetid with the smell of fallen papaya. Collins removed his clothes. The trees formed a pavilion of dappled light. Below the falls a spray of sunlight fell on the water. Collins jumped in and swam toward it, thinking about Hartland.

The Englishman gave off an antique stateliness that Collins found amusing and, to a degree, intimidating. He embodied the cliché of the well-bred colonialist overseeing the British raj. But now, in 1966, the empire had rapidly deteriorated, bringing a sadness to Hartland's character that actually appealed to Collins. His career had come to this — an aging D.O. in an unimportant part of an ex-colony.

Collins floated back toward the shore. The water from the falls was much colder than that in the larger stream, and it seemed not to mix completely. Rather it swirled about his arms and legs in small patches of cold. He dried himself with his shirt.

Indeed there was a lot of sadness in Hartland, Collins thought, shielding his eyes. When Hartland walked through the groves of rubber trees, he proceeded like a slow bird. At a distance his voice could be heard in patches of inquisitive talk. He spoke with all the polite disapproval Englishmen seemed to have in the performance of their duty. It seemed to Collins that Hartland now was an anomaly in this country. His appearance outshone his purpose, so that he was grand with little to do to fill the day.

As he put on his shorts, Collins looked back across the pool. He was blinded by the sun as it lowered toward the cliff across the way. The falls splintered in the light.

For a moment Collins wondered when he too would become isolated out here. Like Hartland, he worked alone. But Collins's duties still sustained him. It was interesting work, and there was prestige to it. Just learning the languages forced him to surround himself with the sweat and effort of the people. But he knew he already *was* isolated. As he wandered about these places, a foot taller than any of the locals, a kind of precise, pale giant, Collins was simply an oddity. And nothing will salve your dismay when you see that you're no longer needed, he thought, or that you no longer need this place. He imagined himself like Hartland, mock self-assured and useless. Then, Collins thought shivering, your duties won't help you. They'll be, like you and like the Englishman, empty.

When Collins returned to his office, the sun had gone down, and he spent a moment straightening his desk. A note had been left on his chair.

Dear Mr. Collins —

I wonder if you would join me for a drink this evening at my home. I've received a bit of bad news and I'd like to speak with you about it. If you'd be so kind as to call, I'd be very grateful.

Nigel Hartland

Collins walked from his office toward the D.O.'s residence. It stood on a hill at the far end of the bazaar, overlooking the Malay village that bordered the bazaar itself. In the semidarkness the house blocked the sky. The house contained so much authority, even in this crummy place, that it appeared ominously monumental. It was the center of everything. Collins ascended the hill worried about what Hartland wanted to tell him. A bit of bad news? Collins grimaced. Hartland was a far older man than he, with far greater experience in the East. Collins was flattered to be asked, but he worried he could be of no help to the Englishman.

He was met at the door by a dark Malay man dressed in a white shirt and black pants, with bare feet, who wore the songkok, the traditional Malay black cap. His head was exceedingly round, like a fine, featureless ball. When he spoke, he broke into a sad frown that startled Collins.

"Tuan Collins, I am Yussuf," he said in Malay. "Tuan Hartland's servant."

"How do you do?"

"Very well," Yussuf said. The frown deepened. "And you?"

There was uncertainty in each motion Yussuf made, in the way his breath grumbled as he waited for Collins's reply, in the manner he held the Coleman lantern behind him in his right hand to hide its brightness. His eyes were watery and large. He was very shy. His handshake, delivered with a deep bow, slithered from Collins's grasp. But he seemed relieved that Collins had arrived, and he gestured to the American to follow him down a dark hallway.

"Ah, Collins." Hartland stood up from his desk. "Thank you for coming, old man. I didn't intend your making the climb up here in the middle of the night like this."

"I don't mind, Mr. Hartland . . . "

"Please. Nigel. I'd prefer we used that. The other is too formal."

"All right. My name's Dan Collins, of course."

"Quite. It doesn't do to become too friendly too soon. I suppose you agree."

Hartland's desk was surrounded by a collection of artifacts from his previous posts. Behind his chair, two crossed elephant tusks from Kenya rose into a slim white arch. There were headdresses and pieces of beaded jewelry hanging from the walls. His ten years in Malaya were represented by large, laughing shadow-puppet figures mounted on one wall, and by photos of the D.O. residences he had had in the cities of Kuala Kangsar and Penang. Far more resplendent than his house in Saratok, they really were mansions, with grillwork and grounds and servants lined up on the covered porches.

Hartland's living room was very gloomy. The breeze that passed through his open windows did little to disperse the damp odor in the room. He pulled from a cabinet a bottle of Haig and Haig Pinch, which he brought to his desk. Pouring two glasses, he passed one to Collins and motioned him toward a chair.

"Really, I am sorry to have asked you up on such short notice."

"I'm happy to come."

"I can't imagine why," Hartland sighed as he sat down on one corner of his desk.

"I haven't been here long," Collins said. "In Saratok, I mean. And I worry you think we're trying to horn in."

"Who?"

"The Americans. The State Department. People like me."

Hartland laughed and moved to the chair behind his desk. He sat down and took his glass of whiskey between both hands.

"You needn't be. The empire has a history on which I can fall back when necessary. Glories for the most part, I should think."

"I suppose."

Hartland raised his glass and drank down the entire whiskey.

"You suppose."

His voice grew tight.

"You Americans — your efficiency . . . " He set the glass on his desk. "You'll never understand."

"I beg your pardon?" Collins said.

"You won't know what to do with these places."

"But we aren't going to take them over."

"Oh, come now. You can't expect me to believe that. We see what you're doing in Vietnam."

Hartland waved a hand in the air and looked toward the window. The discomfort of the exchange, its hostility, caused both men to fall silent.

"But my day is over," Hartland said finally. He nudged the glass away from him with the ends of his fingers. "I've been — well, we English would say I've been sacked."

He opened the top drawer of his desk and took out a letter. It was from the Interior Ministry and told Hartland his retirement would be required sooner than had been expected, that he would be replaced as D.O. by Inche Bol Fahd. Collins looked up from the letter.

"Yes," Hartland muttered. "A goddamned Malay. Almost half my life in the service and I end up in this awful place. And now they don't even have use for me here."

He poured more whiskey, then sat down in his chair and put his feet up on the desk. He folded his arms and stared at the photos on the wall, shaking his head.

"Excuse that remark about the Malays, Dan."

Collins shrugged.

"Sometimes it's just that I fear I haven't done much with my life," Hartland continued. "I was married once. Didn't work out. Never did much at all, really, except live out here with my servants and my miniscule powers. People like Yussuf and so on."

He removed his feet from the desk and leaned forward so that his elbows rested on the large blotter that covered it.

"Incidentally, Yussuf tends to be frightened. Never figured it out, really, except that it has caused him to take good care of me over the years. I suppose he's afraid of me."

"He might just respect you. You're his employer."

"Well, whatever. Devoted servant, in any case."

Hartland sighed and looked about him.

"But really it didn't mean much, all this. It was just a job."

His eyes turned down. In the moment he remained silent, his head seemed to lower, his shoulders to lose strength. His dismay overtook him, and Collins felt he saw a moment in which anguish, like a blanket, covered Hartland over.

"This is awful, Dan."

Hartland looked up once more but was unable to meet Collins's sympathetic, embarrassed look.

"Awfully kind of you to come here."

"Are you going to be all right?"

Hartland's head shook and a long exhalation of sadness came out of him.

"Of course," he replied. "It's just that I hadn't expected it — this moment — to be so bad. But here it is, and it's quite bad. I'm amazed to be unhappy leaving a shithole like this."

"But it's not the place, is it?"

"No, it's my life, of course. It wouldn't matter where I had served, or for how long." Hartland cradled his head in his hands. "I've enjoyed it, all these years. Enjoyed these places." He lowered his hands to the desk. "Good Christ, Dan, whatever am I going to do in England?"

Hartland looked down at his hands, too distressed to speak. They looked like they would fly apart were he to let them go. Collins became frightened by Hartland's sadness, so much so that he could not answer the Englishman's question. He thought of the mementoes in his own house: the ironwood sculpture of an Iban hunter, the blowgun hanging from his wall, his own shadow puppets like gregarious skeletons, and the photo of himself standing on the porch of his shack at Skrang Scheme with his bright smile and sunburn, a chicken on the railing. A few years from now Collins would take them all down in silence, and he would hate doing it.

For the American the D.O.'s dark house and the dumpy town only sharpened the finality of the conversation. The place *was* a shithole for a man like Hartland. Where there had been black tie and glory, authority and celebration, now there was only the damp evening gloom. As he left, Collins told Hartland he would call on him in the morning. Gratefully, the Englishman walked him to the front door.

"The trouble is there aren't many people here I can speak with about this. It's an imposition asking you to listen, since you probably can't imagine what I'm talking about. But at least we speak the same language. And I can see . . . "

Hartland touched Collins's arm. His fingers were thin and cold.

"I can see you're a good man."

Two hours later Yussuf came to the door of Collins's house. He pushed his way in, very agitated. He removed his cap and took the chair Collins offered him.

"Tuan, Mr. Hartland has disappeared."

Collins gave him a glass of orange squash and sat down across from him.

"He walked out into the jungle," Yussuf said.

"What do you mean?"

"After you left, he had more to drink. Much more. Whiskey . . . "

He shook his head slowly.

"A terrible thing, this drinking of alcohol." Yussuf caught himself up and looked at Collins apologetically. "Pardon me," he continued, "but it is a Christian habit. A Muslim would not, would not . . . "

Collins nodded agreement. "But where is he, Yussuf?"

"I don't know. He walked out."

"Which way?"

"Into the jungle."

"But the jungle is in every direction."

Yussuf nodded. He looked up at Collins and his eyes widened as he spoke.

"I'm afraid he'll be killed out there," he said. "The Ibans, if they find him, they'll attack him."

"Yussuf, they wouldn't kill the D.O."

"But in Malaya we always hear about them, how fierce they are."

Barely listening, Collins put on his shoes.

"I've never seen him like he was after you left, Tuan."

"You have a lantern?" Collins asked.

"Yes. Out on your porch. Why?"

"We've got to go look for him."

"But where?"

"In the jungle, Yussuf, in the jungle."

They walked out into the Malay kampong. Already the villagers had learned of the D.O.'s disappearance. Collins met Mahmet bin Saleh, who had brought the village dignitaries together. Fifty people gathered around them, and they walked into the Chinese bazaar, where they encountered Lew Ling.

"He's gone off into the forest?" Lew Ling asked.

"I'm afraid so," Collins replied. The two men spoke in Malay. "Yussuf says Mr. Hartland had been drinking."

"Ah!" Lew Ling replied. "Misfortune."

Collins nodded. He did not wish to go into the details, and Lew Ling did not enquire of them, for which Collins was grateful.

"Well, we've got to find him," Lew Ling said. Other Chinese came out of the shops carrying flashlights and lanterns. They assembled in the street behind Lew Ling, opposite the Malays who stood about behind Mahmet. Everyone deferred to Collins. Despite his own anxiety, he was amused by the rigid separation between the two groups.

"Lew Ling, will you go downriver? And Mahmet upriver?"

"Yes, yes," Lew Ling said. "And if we find him, we should bring him to . . . "

"The D.O.'s house," Collins said. "If he's dead, we'll have to contact Kuching, of course."

"A terrible thing, Tuan," Mahmet said. "The D.O. is too important. We mustn't lose a man like him."

"I'll come with you, Mahmet. Lew Ling, if you get over to Rumah Bukit and the Ibans, be sure to tell them what's happened. They can help you."

"If they haven't chopped off his head," Lew Ling chuckled. The other Chinese broke into laughter, and Yussuf groaned out loud. His voice wobbled.

"Lew Ling. Please!"

"Excuse me, Mr. Collins. A joke."

They split up and headed toward either end of the bazaar. Collins looked back once before turning up the path into the forest. At the far end of the street the bobbing light from the Chinese lanterns revealed sticklike legs, swatches of skin, half-faces, and feet. The palm trees jutted like rags into the cloudy sky.

Lanterns shone up the trail. Where light fell on the undergrowth, it broke into specks of jittery green and yellow. Fireflies scattered through the trees. Collins could see nothing, and the darkness reared up high, black, without relief. It does exist, Collins thought—the chaos in the forest, the danger. He looked around, his breath cut off abruptly in the dark. But it was a danger that came to real intensity only with human failure. Drunk and wandering, begrudging his loss, hating himself, Hartland was ripe for victimization out here. A low branch or a misstep, nothing much, some minor detail could do him in.

As Collins and the Malays split up into smaller groups, their lights became so dispersed that from a distance they were indistinguishable from the fireflies that glutted the woods. Collins found comfort in Yussuf's large Coleman lantern, and he forced the Malay to lead the way.

"But Tuan, I would prefer your taking the lead," Yussuf said. They faced one another on the trail.

"I take the lead, I get the lantern," Collins replied.

"Why?"

"Because I'd be the one facing the danger, Yussuf. I could step off into a chasm, and you would be safe, standing on the edge, holding the lantern up high to see me fall."

Yussuf remained silent a moment. Grumbling, he pushed past the American and continued up the trail.

"You should have your own lamp, Mr. Collins."

The glaring light gave them a few feet of safe vision on every side, though its brightness also made the surrounding darkness even more profound. By two in the morning the clouds had passed and the sky had become filled with stars — so many of them, they seemed to cluster in the minute breaks in the tree cover, so that even the darkest forest was encrusted with touches of silver.

The hum of insects filled the forest. Orangutans chattered violently in the distance. Collins could not get rid of the disastrous images that beset him. Hartland, lost and falling down a gully to some hidden death. Or wandering, nuts, upriver into the hills. Outside Saratok and its Malay village, he would be lost completely. Got to find him, Collins thought, though at the same moment he cursed Hartland's foolishness. He surely doesn't realize the danger into which he's put himself.

"Yussuf," Collins said. The Malay turned about and faced Collins. He sheltered the light with his free hand, the fingers of which were outlined in burning red.

"Would Hartland kill himself?"

Yussuf's face was just visible in the darkness.

"I don't know. Do the English do that?"

Scared, Collins did not answer, and Yussuf held the lantern up before him, the better to see Collins's reaction.

"Do they?"

There were others in the forest. Initially Collins could not see them. But Yussuf, preceding him on the trail, stopped and listened a moment. There was nothing ahead except the black woods, the black distance.

"I don't like this," Yussuf whispered. "Outside the village, it's not a good place at night."

"Oh, it's all right, Yussuf."

"Perhaps. But a Muslim should not be out here at night. The Ibans don't like the Muslims."

A light shone ahead, then another. Yussuf lowered his lantern and stepped back behind Collins. There were lights behind them on the path as well.

"Mr. Collins?"

"Yes?"

The lights came closer.

"You will protect me?"

"Yes," Collins replied, though his own fears swirled about wildly.

The lanterns were solitary and small in the darkness. Collins heard laughter, an epithet in Iban, anger at the forest and how it swallowed men up. He recognized the voice of Lundu, headman of Rumah Santah. The Ibans lived in the upriver regions and farmed dry hill-rice and vegetables. They kept separate from the Malays and the Chinese and resisted any friendship with them, fearful that to lose their own customs would bring the tribe to ruin. They were the headhunters, though they had not pursued the practice for some time now. The departing Japanese had been their last victims. Even now, though, the Ibans felt the practice had been a good one, that it had improved life and had been unjustly squelched by the too-reserved British. A very old man, Lundu carried a small lantern with a single mantle. Collins saw only his feet as he approached. But when Lundu brought the lantern up next to his face, his expression came out in harsh angles of glare and black. Yussuf began shaking. He stood close behind Collins, peeking around the American's shoulder.

"Did you know the D.O. is lost, Tuan?" Lundu asked.

"Yes."

Lundu paused a moment. His silence seemed impatient and overlong. Finally he spoke once more.

"So have you seen him?"

"No, we haven't."

Collins had to translate for Yussuf, who was too rattled to listen much anyway.

"We heard he was wandering out here," Lundu said. "And we came out to help find him."

He gestured into the forest with his lantern.

"A man shouldn't be out here alone at night. Easy to get lost," he said. "And even if you don't get lost, there are the kraits."

"What is that?" Yussuf whispered.

"It's a kind of snake," Collins replied. "He's right, you should watch for them. They're dangerous. Poisonous."

"But how can we see them in the darkness like this?"

Collins translated the question for Lundu.

"I don't know," the Iban said. He held the lantern up once more, and his face glowed in the darkness. His grin was nearly toothless. "They're difficult to see even during the day."

They turned up the path and were joined by other Ibans who came, singly or in couples, quietly out of the forest itself. Indeed the jungle seemed suddenly crowded with men slipping through the ferns and underbrush. They walked for miles, up and down paths, cross-country through the jungle, past many other long-houses. The search continued several hours more until gray light finally appeared in the sky.

They cleared the top of a hill and headed down a switchback through dense underbrush and trees, stumbling over wet shale as they went. Collins heard the sound of the falls through the trees and realized he and the others had made a large circle during the night. Now they were close to Saratok again. They headed for the pool where he had been swimming the day before. Stopping on a rise above the falls, Collins saw many people below in scattered movement, barely discernible in the gray-blue light of the morning.

A hundred tribesmen milled about, clustered in the small clearing. The men wore dark loincloths and were heavily tattooed. They were spattered with mud. The surrounding trees darkened the clearing, so that their tattoos and brown skin were even further muted. There was so little contrast between the men and the surrounding forest that everything appeared to be the same few colors — brown, dark-green, and gray.

Collins shivered. The men had gathered around something that held their interest. They looked down at it, talked with each other about it. Collins swore beneath his breath. He knew what had happened. They had found the body.

Collins ran down the path. The falls grew louder as he descended past them to the pool. In this light the water cascaded dirty brown and white. He pushed his way through the crowd of Ibans. Yussuf hurried behind him, muttering with fear. Collins couldn't imagine what he was about to see. Hartland, his head half blown away, akimbo in the mire. Or Hartland, face down in the mud, his life rendered meaningless in the end by his wandering, dark collapse.

At the pool's edge a wounded tribesman tended to a gash on his foot. The others, gathered about and solicitous of the man's pain, made fun of him nonetheless. He had slipped and fallen on a muddy log. Hartland was nowhere to be seen.

Lundu joined them at the edge of the pool. His frail chest and arms made him look like an elderly child. When he spoke, Collins could barely hear his voice for the roar of the falls across the pool.

"You should go back to Saratok," Lundu said. "Notify the head white man in Kuching."

He looked up at Collins. Lundu's eyes were red-rimmed with lack of sleep. But there was a look of such sympathy in them that Collins, so tired himself, nodded and took the Iban's hand in his.

"Thank you," he said. "I'll do that. It's very kind of you to help us."

"It is nothing, Tuan. Everyone here is happy to help. The D.O. is an important man. The D.O. is always kind. The D.O. is our leader."

Collins recalled Hartland's caution to avoid the chaos in the forest.

"Yes, I agree," he said.

He walked up the hill toward the D.O.'s house with Yussuf. The Malay wept as they approached the building. The empty hallway seemed to convince him finally of the fact of Hartland's disappearance, and tears blotched his face.

Collins escorted Yussuf up the hallway toward Hartland's office. They heard a cough, the sound of papers being shuffled about. As they entered the living room, Hartland looked up from his desk and broke into a broad smile.

"Collins!"

"Tuan!" Yussuf cried. He hurried to the desk and dropped his lantern to the floor. Holding his right hand to his chest, he tried to speak but could not. Tears ran down his cheeks.

"Good Lord!" Hartland said in English. He looked over Yussuf's shoulder at Collins, whose own surprise battled against the fury that suddenly, instantly, gathered up in him. "What in hell is going on?"

"Goddamn you!" Collins said.

"Tuan, you're alive," Yussuf interjected.

"Of course I'm alive," Hartland replied. He stood and placed a hand on Yussuf's shoulder. "Stop crying, Yussuf. Stop!"

The Malay lowered his head and wept with joy.

"What's happened here, Dan?" Hartland asked in English. "Where have you two been?"

"We've been out in the jungle, for Christ's sake."

"Well," Hartland muttered. He was clearly surprised by the strength of Collins's epithet. He raised his eyebrows, and his voice settled into a gentle, preemptive tone of self-defense. "No need to be so upset."

"But we've been looking for you!" Collins said.

"Me!"

"We thought you'd disappeared."

Hartland sat down again at his desk, and Yussuf, begging the D.O. to let him prepare a pot of tea, turned to leave. He raised his eyes toward the ceiling.

"Thank Allah you are alive," he said as he hurried from the room.

"Do you realize what you've put him through?" Collins asked. "Or me? Or anyone?"

"I can't imagine, old boy."

Collins sat down across from the Englishman. He leaned forward and joined his hands on the desk. They were splotched with mud. His arms were badly scratched. Looking down at himself, Collins saw he was covered with wet, yellow grit. He tried brushing some of it away.

"You haven't been out there at night!" Hartland said. He laughed out loud. "I'd never go out in the jungle at night."

"We know that," Collins shouted. "Now we know that."

He sat back, slouching in the chair.

"I merely went out for a stroll," Hartland said.

"But where?" Collins asked.

"In the village. I've lived here three months, and I've never really toured the place. I thought I ought to, you see, after what happened to me yesterday."

Hartland held his hands out before him and shrugged.

"Last hurrah, that sort of thing," he said.

Collins stood and walked toward a window. Outside a group of Chinese students walked up the bazaar, pointing at the D.O.'s residence on the hill. They still thought the D.O. was missing.

"You've inconvenienced these people terribly," Collins muttered. "You've frightened them."

"But, Dan, that isn't fair."

Collins turned and faced the Englishman. "It's the truth, Hartland."

"Dan, Dan," Hartland said. He stood and walked across the room toward Collins. He laid a hand on the American's shoulder and gazed at him steadily, without anger, but rather with kindly amusement. "Forgive me, old boy. I meant no harm."

"That doesn't give you the right to use them as you did last night."

"I did not use them," Hartland replied. "An American like you, you'd never understand something like this. You must realize that these people will always do that, don't you see? They always have."

At that moment Hartland's face hung before Collins's. He seemed to fill everything, and for Collins his enormity became frozen and indistinct, like a gigantic white moon.

"Of course they were afraid for me," Hartland said. "After all, I'm the D.O."

7 / A Rite of Passion

Collins reached out to wipe the condensation from the wind-shield. Water ran from his fingers down the Land Rover's green metal dashboard. The monsoon season had begun, and it rained now every afternoon and evening, so heavily that the river was the color of red mud. Gertie leaned against the window of the Land Rover watching the rain. Her thick red hair, braided beneath a white kerchief, swung against her neck with the ragged lurches of the truck as it bounced down the dirt road. Her skin was freckled, ravaged by the constant sun in Sarawak. Her cheek-bones were quite thin and gave an elegance to her profile that seemed out of place in the muddy heat.

Collins liked her. For one thing. Gertie was interested in life in the outback, which surprised Collins since much of his work seemed so obscure to the other Americans in Borneo. An AID engineer in the jungle. An itinerant American doing what his British and Australian counterparts, more gentlemanly sorts, would seldom dream of doing. A month earlier, at a reception in Kuching, Collins had been introduced to Gertie, who was a teacher with the Peace Corps in Sarawak. Stuck in the relative sophistication of the capital, she really wanted to get into the jungle to see the Ibans and their longhouses far upriver. It was this adventurousness that appealed to Collins. Few people he had met were so genuinely interested in the forests and the ramshackle villages.

Now as they drove into the Saratok bazaar it began raining very hard. Collins wheeled the Land Rover to the side of the road in the center of the bazaar before Wo Sam's café.

"Hello, Dan."

Tom McGregor sat at a table to the rear. His red hair and white legs appeared lit up against the surrounding gloom of the café.

"So this is your American friend," he said.

"Yes," Collins replied. "Gertie Gringold meet Tom McGregor."

Gertie sat down and Collins ordered two bottles of Tiger Beer.

"And Rumah Bintulu is having a festival for you?" McGregor asked.

"Yes," Gertie said. "That's why I'm here."

"Well, you'll enjoy yourself." McGregor leaned far back in his chair and placed his fingers on the edge of the table. "As much as Collins here will, I'm certain. He's being pursued, you know."

"Pursued? By whom?"

Collins let out a sigh. He lowered his eyes to the table and slumped in the chair. McGregor's face, which was usually a mixture of stern angles and reticence, broadened into a grin. Collins shook his head. He implored him to stop.

"By him," McGregor replied. He pointed into the road. Collins followed his gesture and cringed as he saw the object of McGregor's interest.

Bulan, headman of the Rumah Bintulu village, walked up the road, followed by three other Iban tribesmen and a young woman, Bulan's daughter Binta. Bulan wore a loincloth and a soiled T-shirt. His customary tobacco and rolling papers were stored in the plastic sack hanging from his right hand. Bulan's feet pushed up small dikes of mud with each step. The sack appeared to float above the ground like a soiled rag.

"What do you mean?" Gertie asked.

"Well," McGregor replied, "it's just that, that . . . "

"Bulan wants me to marry his daughter," Collins grumbled.

"Oh!" Gertie said. "That's nice for you!"

She looked out at Binta.

"And she's so pretty."

Binta carried a basket of green beans on her head. She walked
carefully, working to keep her balance. For her visit to town she
wore a Malay blouse of black lace and a red and brown batik
sarong. Her face was very small and far thinner than that of her
father. Her skin had a clarity that was brightened by the many
brass earrings she wore. The Chinese in the bazaar paused to
watch her. Her soft, black eyes remained fixed on the back of the
man before her. Binta's careful gait beneath the basket caused her
to appear aloof, but Collins realized this was also due to her
shyness. Embarrassed by her own beauty, she knew she was
being shown off by her father.

McGregor sipped from his beer.

"Bulan's got it right," he said. "He sees Collins here as Binta's
savior."

The American slouched in his seat and tapped his thumb
against the beer bottle.

"Financially, that is," McGregor said.

Bulan's passage up the street, magisterial in the sun despite his
obvious poverty, saddened Collins. Bulan was a tribal eccentric
who displayed such self-importance that even his fellow villagers
laughed at him. The truth was that after fifteen years as headman
he was noted most for his daughter's looks. Bulan came to town
on Saturdays to play snooker on the rutted, barely level table in
Wo Sam's pool parlor. In the dark room, lit on one end by
the glare from the street, the Iban challenged the few Chinese
hanging around, to whom inevitably he lost.

"So if you marry her, he benefits from your wealth?" Gertie
asked.

"That's the idea," Collins replied.

Gertie leaned on the table. Her fingers lay across her cheek.

"*Are* you wealthy?"

"By their standards, I should say he is!" McGregor said.

"Oh, stop it, Tom," Collins muttered. "You're making a joke
out of a serious matter."

"I know it, Dan. Just can't help myself." McGregor turned
toward Gertie. "We like to have a spot of fun with the Yanks, you
see, Miss. But this is a wonderful thing you'll be attending

tomorrow, a festival like this. These people extend themselves a great deal to see that you enjoy yourself. They're remarkable for that, really. And Bulan . . . well, he is odd, I suppose."

McGregor looked out into the road. Bulan and his entourage had disappeared into the pool parlor.

"But they have good methods up there. Good farmers. He's had something to do with that."

He took up his beer once more and sipped from it.

"And beautiful women." His voice wandered into silence as he gazed back out to the road.

Collins stood and walked with Gertie from the café onto the wooden sidewalk. He did not mind so much being kidded by McGregor. What bothered him was that he had come up with no effective answer to Bulan's intense pursuit of him. Binta, paraded about as she was, had few rights in the matter at all. There was little recourse for Collins either. His employers in Kuching would not hear of his abandoning his project in Saratok simply because of an amorous-minded father. The road Collins was building was far too important.

They descended a set of stairs to the Land Rover. Collins held the door open for Gertie. As he made his way to the other side of the vehicle, he saw Bulan walking up the dirt track toward him. The chieftain hurried like a man chasing a bus. Collins stepped into the Land Rover and started up the road toward the Malay village where he lived. A wave of mud flew over the hood, and Gertie ducked as it slapped against the windshield.

"Why the hurry?" she asked.

Collins did not answer.

At Collins's house Gertie packed the few things she needed for the next day's trip and sat down in a chair to read. Collins watched her from his bedroom. She picked up a newspaper from a pile in a corner of the room. A month-old copy of the *Straits Times,* it rattled noisily as she opened it, and the sun, coming in through the door, glared against the yellow, aging newsprint. Gertie's hair floated about in the light.

A section of the newspaper fell away, and she leaned over to pick it up. Collins heard bare feet on the stairs to his front porch. Bulan appeared in the door.

The Iban stood silently looking at Gertie. His dark feet were splayed outward, and his legs were bowed. He appeared confused as he spoke to her. Collins realized Gertie understood nothing Bulan said.

"Where is the Tuan?" Bulan said. "I want to see the white man."

Gertie turned toward the bedroom, where Collins was still hidden from Bulan's view. The Iban removed the long parang he wore from a rope slung around his waist. He gathered up the rope, then pulled a length of it sharply as though to test its strength. Collins recognized the gesture as Bulan's effort to give himself some authority, though in fact he didn't know what to do in Gertie's presence. But the knife and the rope clearly frightened her.

"Pardon me, lady, but is the Tuan here?"

"Dan," Gertie said. "Help me please, will you?"

Collins walked into the living room.

"Ah, Tuan," Bulan said. "I am here to speak with you about my daughter."

"What does he want?" Gertie asked.

"He's here to make me another proposal," Collins sighed. He turned to the chieftain. "Bulan, this woman is from my own country."

"I assumed so," Bulan said. "She is very pretty, Tuan."

"Is he angry with me?" Gertie interjected.

"But I wish to speak with you about my daughter," Bulan said.

"Angry?" Collins said to Gertie. "Oh no. He's just—well, I'll tell you later. You might look outside on the porch. I'm sure Binta's out there. She's afraid to come in."

Gertie stepped out the front door. After a moment the two women came back into the house. Next to Binta, Gertie's legs and arms were like slim, straight branches, isolated and long. She was so tall by comparison to Binta that she seemed to soar. Binta's face, which was darker and fuller than Gertie's, was made up, as Gertie's was not. But Binta's expertise with the makeup was minimal, so her lipstick was smudged and the rouge far too heavy. She grasped Gertie's hand, frightened at having to enter Collins's house.

"You should marry her," Bulan said, pointing to Binta. "I will give you land as her dowry, Tuan. I have some animals. Some silver coins as well."

"We've talked about this before, Bulan," Collins said. "Binta would be happier with one of your own bachelors. We white men, we're not dependable. I'd have to take her to my own country, and she wouldn't like it. Big place. No Ibans."

Binta giggled and Gertie patted her hand.

"So you still won't do it?" Bulan asked. "Not interested?"

The Iban turned his eyes up toward Collins. Like his daughter, he was slightly built but squat. His long, black hair shone with strings of gray.

"She'll make a good wife to someone here," Collins said. "You shouldn't press her on me."

He stepped toward the front door of the house.

"And now I hope you'll excuse me, Bulan," Collins continued. "But my friend and I have to get ready for the festival tomorrow. We'll meet you at the boat in the morning."

"We will wait."

"You can't!"

Bulan pointed with his parang toward the door.

"We will wait on your porch," he said.

"But, Bulan!"

The chieftain grunted at Binta. He turned her about and pushed her toward the door. He ignored Gertie's effort to hold on to Binta's hand.

Bulan followed his daughter onto the porch. They sat down abruptly on the wooden planks, and, in silence, Bulan faced the doorway. He dropped his hands to his lap. He appeared affronted. But Collins had seen this reaction before, and he resented it. Wants to sell her, that's all, he thought. Wants me for my money. Binta's wishes were of no worth. Collins did not even know what they were.

He walked back into his bedroom.

"I'm not going to do it," he muttered. "He thinks I'll give in because I have to have a woman."

He faced Gertie through the doorway. Holding his arms out from his sides, his palms up, he shrugged in an exaggerated imitation of the chieftain.

"'A man cannot live without a wife, Tuan,' he tells me. 'Who will cook? Who will clean?'"

"You've never courted her?" Gertie asked.

"Never, for Christ's sake."

Gertie leaned against the jamb and folded her arms.

"Pardon me, Dan. I didn't mean to offend you."

Collins leaned over his bed.

"It was an innocent question," Gertie said.

Her hands fell to her sides. She remained leaning against the doorjamb.

"I'm sorry," Collins replied. He turned away, scratching his head. "It's just that Bulan's spent many nights on my porch. It'll rain tonight, and he and Binta will move inside to stay dry. He knows this, you see. He thinks I'll be driven crazy, sexually mad, I guess, by her proximity."

Gertie looked over her shoulder at the front door. Her fingers tapped against her thighs. Collins looked down at her legs, then quickly at her eyes as she turned about to address him again.

"Does that happen to you around women?" she asked. "I mean, are you driven crazy by them?"

"Well, by some women."

"Not by Binta."

"Gertie, she's fourteen."

"Oh, I see."

A few hours later Collins took Gertie out for a walk around the kampong. He had made a dinner for her of fish with soy and sugar, a mixture of fried vegetables, steamed rice, and a selection of Wo Sam's pastries that reminded her, she said to Collins's amusement, of erasers.

"Out for a stroll, eh, Tuan?" Bulan said as they made their way past him and Binta. The porch was narrow, so that Collins and Gertie had to pass by them in single file.

"Yes."

"A beautiful woman," Bulan said, pointing with his lips at Gertie as she descended the stairs. She wore a madras-print blouse, a jeans skirt, and flip-flops. She slipped on the damp bottom stair, holding herself up by grabbing on to the railing. Her legs splayed like two thin boards.

"But clumsy," Bulan concluded.

Collins hurried down the stairs.

"Not a good worker," the Iban said.

"What'd he say, Dan?" Gertie asked. Collins helped her to her feet.

"Nothing. Just commiserating, that's all."

"Oh." She turned toward Bulan and smiled. "Thank you!"

Collins led Gertie to the path. The kampong was so settled in darkness that the lantern lights shining in the houses and along the dirt track appeared antique and soft, as though the mantles themselves were covered with moss. It was very warm.

He heard laughter from the houses as the Malays watched them pass. For them it was appropriate that Collins have, as they put it, a new wife. They guarded their daughters strictly when it came to the American, not because they felt he was brutish or dangerous, but simply because he was not a Muslim. So Gertie, one of the big, wan, Christian women they saw so infrequently, gave them reason to be happy for him. She was, after all, one of his own kind. They thought the ease with which Iban women married almost anyone — Chinese, Tamils, whites — was disgraceful, though understandable when you considered they were just savages.

"These people defer to you, don't they, Dan?" Gertie asked as they approached the river at the end of the path.

"Yes, they do," he replied. "And sometimes, like with Bulan, it can be embarrassing." Collins shrugged. "And I've had occasions when I felt it could get me into real trouble."

"But why do they do that? It's not just that they see you as rich."

"No. I think it's the Brookes. The history of the place." Collins sighed and shook his head. "Something as unworkable as that."

The Brookes were the white rajahs, a British family of adventurers who, as reward for quelling Iban uprisings during the nineteenth century, obtained Sarawak from the Sultan of Brunei. They had ruled the country for a hundred years until the Japanese arrived.

"They brought civil servants here from Britain and encouraged them to marry with the locals. The Brookes were quite kind, you know. They didn't get into repression and cruelty like other English did in other countries. So as a result the Malays and the Ibans love the English."

"But you're an American," Gertie said. She slipped her hand through his arm.

"Oh, I know. And in Kuching, where people have been to school, they understand the difference. But up here, they don't make such distinctions. I'm a Tuan. I'm like the Brookes, it's simple. So when it comes to a dispute or a request for money or the need for salvation, if I happen to be around, I get chosen."

"But have you ever explained to them that that doesn't matter anymore?"

A single fisherman returned in the darkness, a lantern hung from a stick on the prow of his longboat. He passed before them on the black river. He could just be seen, standing in the stern, his body a dark shadow against the water.

"I've tried. They're amiable, interested. But in the end it doesn't matter, as far as they're concerned."

"How do *you* feel about that?"

"Well, I'm amiable too," Collins chuckled. "I think I'm considerate. But I'm careful as well. I care about myself and my own integrity. I mean, I have a lot of self-respect, see? And that's one of the biggest problems I've got, because what kind of self-respect can I have when it comes to someone like Bulan? He must think I'm cruel, awful, the way I treat him."

"Don't be so harsh with yourself," Gertie said. "You do have the right to your own privacy."

"It's just that, upriver, I'm the only Tuan they ever see. Solitary," Collins said. His lips tightened.

"I know."

"And I've got to protect myself."

Collins looked up above the hills across the river. Even in the darkness he could make out the bulky clouds of approaching rain. He took Gertie's hand and walked up the path. The first drops began to fall. The wind blew through the low palms outside the houses. Rattling fronds flickered before the lanterns. The two Americans turned up the pathway toward Collins's house.

"It's interesting to me why so many people come out here, though," Gertie continued. "Americans. English. In my case, it's a lark. The Peace Corps, a few years. . . fun! But others, like you, you seem so much more involved."

"Some come out because they're failures, I guess," Collins replied.

"You've met some like that?"

"A few."

Collins grinned and turned toward Gertie.

"Although I've only dealt with British, really," he said. "So it's hard to say."

Gertie paused at the bottom of the stairs and leaned against the bannister. The wind was so heavy now that her hair blew about. She held it down with a hand.

"Are you one of those?" she asked.

Strands of her hair buffeted her fingers and covered them over.

"No, not at all," Collins replied. "My reasons for being out here are far happier than that. Less complex."

"How?"

"It's simply a matter of exchanging something I knew about, was familiar with, nine to five, office, chair . . . " He sat down on a stair and rested his hands on his knees. "For something I just couldn't imagine."

From time to time a kind of elation, like a wash of fine color, swept through Collins's heart. It happened at moments when he felt convinced he had made a successful choice somewhere, that his senses had led him to a unique change. He could not explain it, except that it surged through him without qualification. Possibly it was love, he thought. Some grand feeling reserved for very few, and very seldom reserved at all. It gathered in him now, so that as he glanced at the trees beyond the path, bowing in the wind and the fresh rain, his breathing paused. He wanted to hold the moment and savor it.

"That's why I came out here," he said.

It rained heavily all night. The combination of the downpour and a high tide brought water up over the riverbanks beneath the houses. Collins got up to close the window shutters. On their pilings the houses in the village huddled beneath the black palm trees as they roared in the wind. The noise of the fronds, like a storm of loose sticks, was overtaken by that of the rain itself as the storm rolled up the river.

Collins looked into the living room. Gertie lay on the extra mattress beneath her mosquito net. On the far side of the room he saw a collection of arms, rags, baskets, and tins — Bulan and Binta with the gear they had bought in the bazaar.

Collins's mosquito net wavered slowly in a breeze that had gotten through one of his shutters. The storm turned violently about his house. He returned to his bed but was unable to sleep. He worried Bulan was awake, waiting, hoping.

The rain abated and, at first light, stopped altogether. There was still a heavy cloud cover, and on the river, a gray fog grasped the ironwood trees on either shore. Large drops fell from the palms, so that there remained a remnant of erratic rain. When Collins awoke, he looked into the living room. Bulan and his daughter had left for the river.

He awakened Gertie, and they went out to Wo Sam's. The café owner had prepared a breakfast for them of cooked vegetables, white rice with a raw egg, and black tea. Afterwards Collins and Gertie descended to the river, where the Ibans waited.

As their boat moved upriver in the fog, Collins leaned against the gunnel to watch the forest. The river meandered every quarter mile, and very little of it was actually visible at any one time. Each turn gave a view of a stretch of new shore, but each shore was similar to the last, and to the one before that. During the cool morning the fog did not lift. As the boat passed in and out of the mist, large walls of forest were revealed clearly, then broken up in the insubstantial light, and swallowed again in the gloom. The trees were heavy and blue, as though they were themselves underwater.

"I only wish I could see more," Gertie said finally.

She looked across at Bulan's boat. The chieftain lay sleeping in the front near Binta. Wrapped in an old blanket, he had cradled himself against the baggage in the boat.

"Have you courted any Iban women?" Gertie asked.

"No."

"Why not?"

Collins laid his head against the gunnel. The fog obscured the trees above.

"Well, there's a procedure."

"I know that," Gertie grinned. "But what's that got to do with it?"

"No, I mean a social procedure. Their way of going about these things is different from ours."

"What is it?"

The boat passed along the edge of a bank of fog, and the air heated as they passed from it into the open light.

"The young men come out in the night," Collins explained.

Gertie laughed. "So what's different about that?"

"They enter the girl's room in the longhouse where her family lives. You know, these villages are all in one building, rooms end to end?"

"Yes."

"And each subgroup in the family—the little kids, mom and dad, the grandparents, you see—each group has its own mosquito net."

Collins dropped a hand over the side and let it slide along the river's surface.

"And so does each eligible daughter," he continued.

He looked at Bulan's boat.

"Like Binta, for instance. An interested suitor will visit her in her family's room late at night. Someone from another longhouse. He'll sit down outside her mosquito net and wake her up."

"Is it by chance?"

"No. They've made the arrangement previously, you see. But she'll sit up, surprised to see him. Shocked at the intrusion."

"Really?"

"It's just a play-act. There'll be a conversation in which he's supposed to convince her of the worth of, of. . ."

"Of his becoming her lover."

"Yes, that's right. They use special language. Rhyming. Erotic words. And when she's convinced that this man is the one she loves, she lies down again. It's an invitation."

"You've done this?" Gertie asked.

"No."

"Why not?"

"It's not that I haven't wanted to."

"I can imagine," Gertie said. "It sounds wonderful."

"Perhaps it would be wonderful if we were Ibans, or if this were the way it's normally done in San Francisco or someplace. But I couldn't take one of these women back with me to the United States."

"You could stay here."

"No, I won't do that, Gertie. I'm not like Tom McGregor."

Collins leaned on one hand against the baggage.

"And I won't do it just for fun, either. Because it would ruin Binta."

"Binta! So you have thought about it."

Collins grinned.

"Of course. But look, if I were to court her and then not follow through with an offer of marriage, she'd be treated like a whore. Tuan's girlfriend, see? It would be very cruel. Very."

When the boats arrived at Rumah Bintulu, the sun had dropped behind the surrounding hills, and the air, darkened by the forest, was a clear blue. A party of Ibans awaited the boats' arrival. When they saw Gertie, the women broke from the group to help her, and two boys took her bag up to the longhouse. Bulan stepped from his boat and escorted Collins and Gertie toward a waiting group of dignitaries. One of the Ibans, whom Collins recognized as Sahap, Bulan's brother, wore a loincloth and a ragtag, double-breasted coat. He had quite long earlobes, which had been ceremonially stretched in his childhood with brass rings. His skin was very dark by comparison with Bulan's, and his two front teeth were framed in gold when he smiled. The coat hid his tattoos, except where they extended down his wrists.

They walked up to the longhouse, which was a thatched, wooden building on stilts overlooking the river. It contained rooms for fifty-two families. The building was so long that it seemed an imposition on the forest, which did little to obscure its size. Inside, Gertie was shown to the rear of Sahap's room, where she would be sleeping. Sahap and his wife had given up their own bedstead and mosquito net to Gertie. When she protested, Sahap told Collins to explain what an honor it was to have her as a guest.

"Do as he says," Collins said. "It's an important matter for him, it really is."

Gertie acquiesced and placed her bag under the bed. "But where will you sleep?" she asked.

"I'm not sure yet," Collins said. "Bulan wants me to sleep in his room, of course."

They changed into fresh clothes and were given dinner.

"What's going to happen?" Gertie asked as she swirled strands of pork about in a bowl of sauce.

"There'll be singing and dancing. A lot of rice wine—you know, the tuak. Drunkenness."

"For everyone?"

"Almost. But that's not a bad thing. For the Ibans, drink is an occasional matter. It doesn't change them for the worse."

At the far end of the porch, musicians practiced on the gamelan. Gertie watched their methodical, disinterested rehearsal until, suddenly, they began to play, and the porch filled with people. Sahap approached Collins. He explained there would be a ceremonial poem, recited by him and several other men.

"For our friends from England," he said, holding his hands tightly before him and staring at the floor. For the sake of accuracy Collins translated England to the United States. "We thank the Spirits who have sent you," Sahap continued. "And also the government, of course."

Sahap walked to the far end of the porch, where he joined several other men. They began a slow thumping of the floor with long, carved walking-sticks. Sahap sung in a monotone chant, the words frequently rhyming, and the others followed him in chorus the length of the house to the far end of the porch. They turned and continued back, still chanting.

"What are they saying?" Gertie asked.

"It's difficult to say," Collins replied. "The language of these things is very different from what I speak with them. Far more elevated. They tell about great warriors. Battles. I really don't understand it. And it's early yet. Some of these recitals go on for days."

The poorly thatched walls, patched by weathered boards or pieces of galvanized tin, allowed light from the outside as the evening grew darker. But it was light in small flecks, thrown off by the lanterns of visitors coming through the forest from other longhouses, by fireflies, and by candles held in the hands of revelers on the outside porch.

"They're like wraiths," Gertie said as the line of singers passed up the porch yet one more time.

"Do they scare you?"

"No. No, they're wonderful."

At midnight the festival grew noisier. Gertie, unaccustomed to the strength of the rice wine, laughed at the drunken dancing of the Iban men. The house was filled with a confusion of bodies dancing the length of the porch, of cooked pork and rice, of tuak and laughter. Gertie was sweating in the smoke and dim light. It began raining, and the noise of the storm through the forest overwhelmed the gamelan music. Yet the musicians continued playing, the poets made their way up and down the porch, and young men, bachelors from other houses, disappeared into various rooms.

"You see," Collins said as he pointed at one teenage boy who waited outside a room. "It's a remarkable way of going about it."

Distracted for the moment, Collins did not notice as his knee touched Gertie's.

"It's a real rite of passage. Very elaborate," he said.

"A rite of what?" Gertie laughed out loud. She leaned closer.

"Of passage," Collins yelled.

"Oh. I thought you said 'of passion.'"

"That too."

The bass gong formed a resonant stream through the entire house and flowed beneath the higher-pitched, nervous tone of the gamelan. Collins caressed Gertie's hand as he sipped from his glass of tuak.

"This is so beautiful, Dan," Gertie said. She leaned her head on his shoulder. Collins, himself dizzied by the wine, moved to put his arm around Gertie when Bulan suddenly appeared before them.

He startled Collins because he looked so angry. Bulan swayed with drunkenness. His lips hung open, and his eyes were ringed with red. A glass of tuak hung from his fingers. His free hand rested on his parang. He glared at Gertie, and for a moment Collins feared the Iban was going to attack her. But Bulan pointed toward his room.

"Tuan, you see how Binta is waiting for you?"

Binta stood before the door with several older women. Though the others giggled and watched Collins's reaction, Binta was clearly embarrassed. One of the women pushed her forward, as though to display her. Binta turned away and angrily pushed her way through them into the room.

"What's going on?" Gertie asked.

Bulan cleared a place for himself among the Ibans surrounding the two Americans. He put his hand on Collins's arm.

"She is your wife," he said, and he pointed toward the door. "Take her."

The women followed Binta into the room and closed the door. Their derisive laughter sounded condemning, as though Binta were being a fool.

"Please, Tuan." Bulan laid both his hands on the rattan mat.

He leaned close to Collins. The clear anguish in his remark surprised both Americans.

"Dan, what's happened?" Gertie asked.

"My daughter is your wife," Bulan shouted. "Your wife!"

"This is bad," Collins said in English.

"What's happened?" Gertie asked.

"He's making a scene. About Binta. He's insisting I sleep with her."

"But she doesn't want to," Gertie said. "It's obvious. You saw her."

"I know, Gertie. But what am I going to do? I mean, all these people think Bulan's being an idiot, but what can I do about it?"

Gertie surveyed the Ibans, who muttered among themselves about Bulan's brash misbehavior. She glanced at Collins, then at her own hands.

"Maybe I can help," she said.

It was obvious the rough-sounding language of the Ibans, their dance, and their tattoos excited Gertie. She looked down the porch at two boys walking slowly along the line of doors. They talked with each other joyfully. Their hands fluttered in the dark, and after a moment each of them entered separate rooms.

Gertie leaned toward Collins and kissed him. The odor of tuak in her breath mingled with that of the sweet cigarette smoke. She took Collins's shoulder and kissed him again. The Ibans seated around them laughed with approval. Hurriedly, Bulan poured fresh wine and thrust a glass of it into Collins's hand. But Gertie stood up and excused herself.

"I'm going to bed, Dan. Tell them, won't you? Tell them I've had a wonderful time."

Collins translated for her, and Gertie walked unsteadily across the porch. She stopped briefly at the door to Sahap's room and looked back. Her face gleamed a moment in the dim candlelight. As she turned into the room, her lips formed a kiss. It was intended for Collins, and it was met with glee by the Ibans.

Bulan's eyes flickered. They were very dark, like black stones. His mouth was turned downward so that when he sipped from his glass he appeared to be moping. He stared at the door as it closed behind Gertie. His large hands hung over his knees. His bare feet, which were quite thick and cracked, lay on their sides sole to sole.

"Forgive me, Mr. Collins. But I often think white men don't understand the reality of things."

"Pardon me?"

"You are happy here. You would love Binta, the beautiful forest, your children growing up with their own people, here."

Bulan lowered his eyes. He spoke without the tone of opportunism that had so troubled Collins before. He fumbled with a packet of tobacco.

"She would give you happiness, Tuan."

He pushed the tobacco aside.

"Children," Bulan whispered. Disappointment accompanied his sigh. Bulan's self-assurance, which for Collins had been so disreputable, had disappeared entirely. In his unexpected sadness, Collins sensed that the opportunity the Iban had looked for with him really was in his daughter's best interest.

"Children," Bulan repeated.

He loves her, Collins thought.

The music from the gamelan swirled about the porch. Collins stood and excused himself. He walked quickly toward Sahap's room, accompanied by a chorus of well-meaning, lewd laughter. He entered the room and searched out the mosquito nets in the semidarkness. All except one were gathered up in large loops above the floor. In the light from a single candle they resembled Victorian summer bonnets of lace. On two of them the protruding puffs of netting turned about slowly with a gracefulness that softened the din outside. At the back of the room Sahap's mosquito net had been undone and now hung down over the bed. Within, Collins saw a dark, rumpled line, the silhouette of Gertie's reclining body. He crossed the room and sat on the edge of the bed, outside the netting. Gertie sat up, as though startled. Collins leaned forward and placed his elbows on his knees.

"I hope you don't mind that I came in here," he said.

She touched his arm. Through the mosquito net her fingers glowed in the light from the candle.

"I've so loved this," she whispered.

The line of her bare shoulder disappeared against the pattern of the rattan wall behind her. Collins could barely see her face.

The door opened behind him. Collins looked over his shoulder and swore to himself when he saw Bulan's profile in silhouette.

"Dan?" Gertie said.

Her hand pushed aside the netting, and she reached out to take his arm. She lay back, pulling him toward her. Abruptly the door closed, and Collins and Gertie were again alone. He took Gertie's hand and kissed it, then lay down beside her. His legs became tangled in the netting, and as Gertie clasped the back of his head with one hand and kissed him, Collins reached back carefully to set himself free.

8 / The Well

When Moot arrived from the river with Collins's freshly dried clothing, he put a round, steel plate over the two burners of the American's butane stove to heat the iron.

"The ironing will take me a half hour, Mr. Collins," he said. "Then I'll take a look at the rain barrel on the roof."

Moot Zawawi was the only Malay in Saratok who had any money. For this, he was suspected of moral degeneracy by the other Malays in the kampong, and the fact was Moot was not a friendly man. He was too direct. He did not bother with the flowery wandering so pervasive in the speech of the other Malays. He appeared to dismiss his neighbors in the village impatiently. Collins had long ago noticed he spoke mainly about money.

Moot owned thirty acres of rubber trees upriver from Saratok, and he had the most modern processing equipment of anyone. He also owned several houses in the kampong, and the Chinese merchants came to Moot the Malay instead of other Chinese for building materials, an arrangement unheard of in other towns. Despite all this — despite even the fact that Moot owned a Land Rover of his own, very old and decrepit but nonetheless the only private one in Saratok — Moot was still referred to around the kampong as the night-soil collector. As it happened, he still *was* the night-soil collector. He had begun his fortune years before by provident parlays of that one activity into many others.

Moot drove the American's Land Rover, did his wash, and bought his food. In recent months Moot had begun providing workers for the access road. On all the other projects Collins had supervised, the workers had not been dependable, and he had to spend hours every day looking for them, complaining to them, and making them redo work. Few ever showed up on time, and all worked slowly. Collins was patient, perhaps even lax when it came to project discipline. He had learned that orders only caused laziness and that disgruntlement from him was a source of offended humor for most of the workers. But still it bothered him that work that could be done in the United States in one month usually took five months to do here.

With Moot's workers, it took one month and no more.

But Moot's efficiency was another matter that brought him under suspicion in the kampong. His neighbors felt that a man who suffered so little self-doubt was not to be trusted.

"Shall I iron these, Mr. Collins?"

Moot held up a pair of Collins's khaki walking shorts.

"No, just fold them."

The Malay put them aside and rummaged through the pile of garments at his feet. His skin was dark brown and mottled with light splotches left over from childhood chicken pox. His face was like his manner, and a lack of good humor showed in the taut muscles that kept his mouth closed and that directed his eyes almost always straight ahead. His few teeth were dark brown and rested at angles from each other. The gray stubble on his chin, along with a graying at his temples, gave him a look of disapproving grizzle. As he ironed, his elbow jutted out and back, so that he reminded Collins of a water pump ceaselessly working on its own.

Collins leaned over the plans on his desk. He had gotten some money from the U.S. consulate in Kuching for a village well he wanted to build for the Malays in Saratok. It was intended as a gift, offered in thanks for the kindnesses his neighbors had shown him during the year he had been living in their village. Despite his presumed Christianity and his flat, nasal accent in their language, the Malays treated Collins with considerable hospitality. Usually a Tuan would be put up in the government guesthouse outside town. That Collins had expressed a preference for the Malay kampong had greatly flattered the Malays, so much so that the day he moved in Collins had been feted by the village leaders with flowers and glasses of orange squash.

The town of Saratok was located on the Krian, a tidal river that overflowed its banks several days a month. The Malays washed their clothing in the river and got their drinking water from rain barrels on the roofs of their houses. The river tide was not dangerous to the houses in the kampong, which were up on stilts. But Collins worried about the smell that was left when the tide went out. The water simply was not healthy. Also the rain barrels remained full only during the rainy seasons. During the dry periods the water eventually became acrid and in some years dried up altogether. No one had ever thought to dig a well in the kampong. To his astonishment a few months earlier, Collins had discovered none of the Malays knew how to do it.

Sitting at his desk — a broad plank held up by two upended metal trunks — Collins leaned his head on one hand. His fingers were cracked and soiled with the residue of mud from his work on the road. He pulled at his unkempt hair, then scratched the top of one foot where a fly had been landing over and over again for the last few minutes. Collins wore the cheap, plastic sandals he had decided were best suited to work in the jungle. For one thing, they didn't rot. He found he could wash his feet conveniently without removing the sandals. A drop of sweat rolled down his forehead, dribbled onto his hand, then fell onto a sheet of paper. He daubed his forehead with a Kleenex. Looking about, he saw Moot had stopped ironing.

"When will we start on the well, Mr. Collins?"

"The day after tomorrow."

Moot studied the ironing board a moment. He stepped out from behind it and rested his hand on its end.

"I have a problem, Tuan."

The use of the word Tuan was new for Moot, who usually would have nothing to do with it. He stood before Collins in an attitude of shy quiescence. With his hands folded together, he appeared to be mulling a confession. Collins laid his pencil on the table and waited.

"What problem?" he asked.

"I can't get any workers, Mr. Collins. For the well."

Moot spoke in a clipped mutter. He gave the information as though it were being forced from him.

"Why not?"

"You're not paying them enough."

"Not enough? Moot, you're the contractor. It's up to you to arrange these things."

"Yes, Mr. Collins. But ten ringgit a day is not enough."

Collins knew the Malays usually worked for eight ringgit a day, sometimes even seven. But for a project like this he had felt he could be more generous, and he had told Moot to offer ten.

"This doesn't sound right, Moot. Is there some other problem?"

"No. The workers are asking for fifteen. I've tried to protect your interests, of course."

Moot smiled brightly. The appearance of such cheerfulness so quickly, with so little preparation, worried Collins. It was uncharacteristic of Moot. But Collins was too involved with finishing his plans to worry about this. Besides, the well would require only three or four days to dig. He turned back to the papers on his desk.

"OK. Offer them thirteen," he grumbled.

Two days later Collins was up early to begin work. He stepped out onto his porch into the morning mist. One wide path ran the length of the kampong. On either side many of the wooden houses were hidden in the fog. Others could be made out like drawings not yet completed, their windows and roofs giving way to indistinct outlines, then to nothing. Collins descended the steps of his house to the dirt track that led past the mosque, which was itself a simple wooden building like his own. Its water-stained plank siding was warped above the stilts that held it up over the mud. The thatch roof was quite old and almost black with the ravages of monsoon rains. Coconut palms rose up in slim bunches. There were hundreds of them throughout the village. In the mist the fronds canopied the houses like silken umbrellas.

Collins had planned the well for a site at the far end of the kampong on a rise away from the river. It was an open place, where many people could gather while waiting their turn at the water. Now a group of fifty villagers awaited the American. To keep the hole that would be dug from filling with rainwater, Moot had arranged for a thatch cover. It lay at the foot of a palm several feet from the well site. Collins wore a fresh pair of shorts, one of his newly ironed white shirts, and his San Francisco Giants baseball cap. As he passed through the crowd of villagers, he spoke with several, thanking them for coming.

Collins enjoyed his work for the Interior Ministry. The roads he built meant a great deal to these people, and he felt he was doing something of real value for them. But the well was another matter. Water — fresh, clean water rippling up from the mud — was something of which the Malays simply had too little, despite the months of heavy rain each year.

No one replied to Collins's ambling greetings. Moot awaited him also, standing apart from the others with five Chinese men. One of the Chinese leaned on a new shovel Collins had obtained for the project. Moot smoked a cigarette and awaited the American's orders. Collins looked back at the villagers, from whom disapproval — downturned mouths, slumped shoulders, and steady, downcast eyes — shone like darkness.

"Moot," Collins whispered. "I thought you had Malay workers."

"No Malays here," Moot said proudly. "We want to use good people."

"But that's not what *I* want," Collins replied. "This is a well for the Malays. It's an insult to them to use these Chinese."

Collins turned to look at the workers. The Chinese, realizing something was wrong, talked among themselves.

"I want you to hire Malays, Moot. Apologize to these men, but I want Malays."

"Mr. Collins, they aren't as good."

"Moot. Hire Malays."

When Collins arrived at the well site the next day, Moot awaited him with five Malay workers and a smattering of others from the kampong. Moot stood next to the thatched cover among the tools, smoking another cigarette. Collins greeted him, then took up a shovel and turned toward the workers.

"I want to thank you for coming here this morning," he said. He spoke slowly in Malay. "With this well, your families will have fresh water to drink all year long. Your clothing will be fresh. There will be no need to boil your water to make it clean. It's an honor for me to be a part of it."

He grinned and extended his arms. Then, leaning over a patch of muddy grass, he pushed the shovel into the earth with a thrust of his foot and turned the dirt over.

"And now," he grunted, "let's go to work."

No one moved. After a moment Moot took up another shovel and held it out before one of the workers.

"You, Ismael, take this one," he said. "Dig."

Ismael paid no attention to him. Instead he stared shyly at Collins. Moot pushed Ismael by the shoulder.

"Get to work," he said.

Ismael turned again toward Collins.

"Tuan, we're happy to work, but we have to talk first."

"No talk. No talk," Moot said.

Collins put out a hand to restrain him.

"What is it, Ismael? What's wrong?"

Ismael was a tall man, almost as tall as Collins himself. He was also very thin, and a sprig of hair jumped from the back of his head like a small geyser. He was the assistant at the mosque and one of the most devout men in the village. When Ismael prayed to Mecca, he wailed.

"Excuse me, Tuan," he said now. "But we are not being paid enough."

Moot turned his back and retreated toward the thatch cover. He looked into the woods.

"I think I'm giving you more than a fair amount," Collins replied.

Ismael sought out the others. They were too shy to speak and remained at a distance.

"We appreciate your gift of the well," Ismael said. "But six ringgit a day is not enough."

"Six!"

Ismael pointed at the spot where Collins had turned the earth with the shovel.

"We don't know how deep we'll have to go. There may be rocks . . . "

Collins turned and walked toward Moot, who moved away from the well site down the path toward the village. Collins caught up with him.

"Moot, we agreed on thirteen," he said.

The Malay continued walking.

"Not eight," Collins continued. "Not seven. And *not* six, Moot."

"I'm the contractor, Mr. Collins," Moot sputtered. "I have to be paid, too."

"You are being paid. This, this is robbery. Of them, and of me."

Moot shook his head. By now he was almost running, and Collins let him go. Moot's arms pushed out to the sides as he retreated, like an elderly sprinter's. When Collins walked back toward the other Malays, he saw they were all laughing.

"Ismael, you're the new boss," he said. "Dig the hole about a meter and a half deep. A meter across."

He turned to leave, then stopped himself. His hands were shaking with nervous anger.

"Don't forget to put the cover there over the hole. Very important. I'd like to see you here tomorrow at nine o'clock."

He waited a moment. The Malays did nothing except to take on the attitude of embarrassed lingering Collins had seen moments before.

"And you'll be paid a proper amount," he said.

With an eruption of talk the Malays began digging.

A half hour later Moot knocked on the door to Collins's house. Collins stepped out onto his porch and saw that Moot was very agitated. Collins invited the Malay in, and as soon as the door was closed behind him, Moot began speaking.

"Don't make a fool of me in front of my neighbors, Mr. Collins."

"If you treat them fairly, that won't happen."

Moot paced toward the kitchen, then turned to the front door. He was sweating, and small rivulets of perspiration ran down his cheeks as though his skin were made of bark.

"They're fair people," Collins continued.

"Those bastards? Their mothers wouldn't know an honest face, Mr. Collins. They think I'm shit, like the shit I take from their outhouses."

Moot blustered silently a moment. His hands flew about.

"All my life I've been treated like a servant. All my life."

Collins walked to his desk and leaned back against it. Moot removed his black songkok from his head. He slapped it against one leg, raising a cloud of dust.

"But they don't ask for much, Moot," Collins said. "Just fair pay. All you have to do is treat them fairly."

"Fair pay," Moot grumbled. "You think that's all they want from me?"

The Malay stepped toward the door.

"You arrange the work, Tuan."

"Moot."

"See how they dig your well without me, the idiots."

"Moot, please."

"Or dig it yourself."

Moot walked out onto the porch and hurried down the steps. His hands hung straight down at his sides. The back of his dark head glimmered beneath his cap. He reached the main path and turned toward his own house, fifty yards away, which was the largest in the kampong. A spindly man, Moot listed to his left, his shoulders at a wavering angle to the ground.

That night it rained heavily. The sun the next morning was hidden by mist and clouds. But it came out within an hour—a hot white ball in the blue sky. Collins stood on his porch and listened to the radios in the kampong. They all played the same program—Radio Sarawak's early morning Malay music show. Through the glistening trees drifted sweet-hearted love songs, mostly duets in which a man and a woman raised their voices over violins and gongs—our love is forever in the lovely rain, God will smile upon it.

Collins stretched, placed his hands in the pockets of his shorts, and descended the steps. He walked up the path to the well site. When he arrived, he discovered Ismael had forgotten about the thatched cover. A canvas tarp the Malay had used to cover the hole had sunk deep into it beneath the weight of the rainwater. Collins saw only one corner of it curled up and spattered with mud. He pulled the tarp from the hole. A two-foot-high ridge of shiny mud surrounded the well site. The hole itself was filled with water.

Collins stared into the hole for several minutes. He took up a bucket. He attempted a resigned sigh, keeping Ismael's kindliness in mind. But finally he gave in to the rage he truly felt.

"That idiot son of a bitch," Collins growled.

He dropped to his knees and lowered the bucket into the hole. The water divided and swallowed it up, leaving swirls of light and dark brown on the surface. Collins's knees sank into the ridge of mud, and he could not pull the bucket from the water. He fell forward, just saving himself from tumbling in, and the bucket sank deep to the bottom of the hole.

Mud twirled about like smoke on the surface. Finally Collins eased his legs, then his entire body, into the water, which came up to the middle of his stomach. He found the bucket with his foot.

He bailed for half an hour. With each bucket of water removed, the hole remained just as full. Collins pulled himself from the hole and stood with his hands on his waist, staring malevolently at the water. He removed his shirt and threw it over by the thatched cover. None of the workers had arrived yet, and as Collins stepped back into the hole and continued bailing, he grumbled that this was Moot's fault, all this, that if Moot had been more honest none of this would have happened.

Mahmet bin Saleh and Ismael walked up the path toward the hole. Mahmet, the crier at the mosque, was an important man in the kampong. The top of his head reached the middle of Ismael's chest, but he moved with such calm authority that Ismael with all his height seemed only to be tagging along. Mahmet's black pants flickered in the sunlight. He paused to pick up Collins's shirt. He held it out and examined it, then placed it flat on the thatched cover.

"The sun is strong, Tuan," he said. "You'll have a dry shirt soon."

Standing in the water, his shoulders stooped with fatigue, Collins thanked him.

"I'm sorry for this problem," Mahmet said. Collins climbed from the hole and sat down at its edge. The two Malays hunkered to either side of him, and all three men stared into the water. They resembled a small gallery of birds.

"Given an opportunity," Mahmet said finally, "a hole in the ground will fill up with water."

Mahmet took up a dollop of mud and rolled it in his fingers a moment. "It's the nature of things," he continued. He tossed the mud into the hole.

"Yes," Collins replied. "But if the cover had been placed over the hole as I instructed, this wouldn't have happened."

Mahmet's face tightened, and he looked away.

"Do you know where the other workers are, Ismael?" Collins asked.

"No. I suppose they didn't come because of the rain last night."

"But that shouldn't have stopped them. We have work to do."

"You can't dig a hole when it's full of water, Tuan."

"Go get them for me," Collins said. The tone of his voice, so suddenly gruff, surprised both Malays. Collins knew he was insulting them. But he could not help himself. For once they would have to give in to his needs, rather than otherwise, the way it had always been. This time Collins would not obsequiously negotiate, as he so often did, for the sake of everyone else's good feelings. "Get them, dammit," he continued in English. This was even more of an insult, since neither man understood the phrase, which was given nonetheless with obvious disgruntlement.

"Ismael," Mahmet said. He nodded toward Collins and smiled. He held his hands out, palms up in a gesture of conciliation. "Do you have any cigarettes?"

Ismael shook his head.

"Tuan, do you?" Mahmet asked.

"In my shirt." Collins gestured toward the garment. His packet of cigarettes showed through the wet cloth. It resembled a clod of dirt.

"Well," Mahmet said, "Ismael, would you go to the mosque and bring us all a packet of cigarettes and some dry matches? We need to talk, and we can't really do so without a good smoke."

Ismael nodded and stood up. He walked down the path and headed into the village.

"Tuan, it's important we speak in private," Mahmet said after a moment. "I know you didn't plan all this to come out in such a way."

He gestured toward the hole, and Collins nodded.

"There are a few things you don't know about our village. I wish you had known them. You could have avoided these problems."

The sunlight that filtered through the palm fronds played across Mahmet's face in thin shadows. His eyes were imbued with mournful discomfort.

"But Moot is not a kind man," he continued. "He doesn't care much for us. He doesn't seem to understand us."

The hole lay open before them, a maw filled with indistinctly colored mud and water.

"The people are jealous," Mahmet said. "They think you value Moot's friendship more than you value theirs."

"But Mahmet, I only want to give the kampong a gift."

"Yes, Tuan."

"Some water."

"Yes. I understand. You understand."

Mahmet looked over his shoulder and pointed toward the village.

"But they do not."

The Malay looked down at Collins's legs. The mud, in splotches and long, dribbling lines, had already begun drying. Collins's shorts were clotted with light terra-cotta.

"They fear you are in league with him. To enrich him at their expense."

"In cahoots," Collins muttered in English.

"What is that, Tuan?"

"An American phrase. It means the same thing."

"Yes," Mahmet nodded. "As you say. And they don't wish to believe it, because you have been so kind to us otherwise."

"Has anyone tried to be kind to him?"

"Yes, Tuan," Mahmet sighed. "But Moot resists."

Collins stood and walked toward the thatched cover.

"We are a friendly people," Mahmet said. "We take care of our own. But there has always been an anger in Moot. I don't know where it comes from. We've always treated him with the greatest kindness, of course."

"Of course," Collins grunted as he attempted moving the thatched cover toward the hole.

"I knew you'd understand," Mahmet replied. He stood up to help Collins. The two men brought the structure to the hole and covered it over. Collins brushed his hands and put on his muddy shirt.

"I have a suggestion, Mahmet," he said.

The Malay nodded and waited.

"We have the belief in my country that all problems can be solved through talk, through negotiation."

"Very civilized, Tuan."

"Surely that can be done here with this problem."

Mahmet remained silent.

"Will you call a meeting of the village leaders? Tomorrow?" Collins asked.

"Certainly. But why?"

"A meeting Moot can come to?"

Mahmet placed a hand on his chest, as though he were clutching for a breath.

"Moot?" he said.

"A lot of this has been my fault," Collins continued.

Mahmet shook his head in protest.

"Yes, it has," Collins said. "But it can be solved, easily, by talk."

"Tuan, please, may I suggest . . . "

"I really must insist, Mahmet. I want to do what's best for the kampong."

"But, Mr. Collins . . ."

"And if you would help me with this, I'm sure the dispute could be solved quickly."

"Please . . . "

"I insist."

Mahmet, suddenly at a loss, nodded his head.

The following morning Mahmet welcomed the village leaders into his house. Bom bin Mustapha, whose gut filled his yellowed T-shirt as though it were a great basket, entered the living room and headed directly for Collins. Barely on his feet, Collins felt his hand being secured within Bom's as though the Malay were cadging it for later use.

"Tuan, we are honored."

"Thank you." Since Bom would not let go of him, Collins shook the Malay's hand with equal enthusiasm. Bom moved on to Mahmet and shook his hand in the same way. He ignored Moot in order to shake Ahmad Trengganu's hand.

"How is your rice this season?" he asked.

"The same, the same," Ahmad smiled. He drew on a cigarette. "The rice never changes."

Until his recent retirement, Ahmad had been the headmaster of the Saratok Malay school for thirty years. He was a happy, argumentative man of about seventy. He was not a native of Sarawak. Having grown up in Kuala Trengganu in Malaya, famous for its batik, he wore sarongs of bright reds and greens decorated with ceremonial birds and borders. The other men in the village dressed in more customary machine-printed sarongs with large patterned checks. Ahmad's dress was not the only thing that set him apart from the other villagers. He was also well traveled, having been sent twenty-nine years before by the British colonial government to New Zealand for a course for English teachers. He had been in Wellington for two weeks, and always treasured the experience. Collins had never exchanged a word in English with Ahmad. As far as he knew, the Malay didn't speak it.

Zahir hobbled up the steps on his wooden crutches. His left leg had been withered by a childhood disease, and it hung from his body like a rag. He lived at the far end of the village in a small house with two rooms. He owned no land and was very poor. He was a village elder, however, because he had the power of prognostication. He had foretold bad marriages and untidy deaths. People feared Zahir's smile, which was constant. He had been very helpful to Collins upon the American's arrival in Saratok, when Collins had been offered houses by Mahmet and by Moot. Mahmet's was a wood-frame building next to the mosque, drafty and comfortable enough, but of a drab design that was of little interest. Moot's was a more palatial edifice, faced with a large porch and situated on a hill overlooking the kampong. Zahir's silence had swayed Collins from renting Moot's house. At the time he had not known who Moot was, but he had gotten the clear impression from Zahir that Mahmet's was — really — the better choice.

Zahir greeted everyone in the room, then went to the doorway between the living room and the kitchen. Above the door hung a black and white photo of President Sukarno of Indonesia. Though at the time Malaysia was at war with Indonesia, and Sukarno was therefore the enemy, his picture hung in almost all the Malay homes. He was a great hero in the Malay struggle for independence. The present war would fade eventually, everyone thought, and Sukarno would remain a hero. Zahir pushed aside the cloth partition and greeted Mahmet's wife.

"Do you have orange squash for us?" he asked.

There was high laughter, like breaking glass, from the kitchen.

"Yes, and sweet cake. Especially for you, Inche Zahir."

The cloth was pushed aside and Mina appeared. During meetings of this kind she usually sat in the doorway, just behind the cloth partition, listening to the talk. Other women, and children as well, sat in the kitchen listening. But unlike these others, Mina spoke. When she wished to add something to the talk, her hand reached for the cloth and pushed it aside. Her voice bolted into the room, and then the hand retreated behind the cloth again. Collins had witnessed this on a number of occasions. Mahmet, always patient, waited silently, his head buried in one hand while he and the other men listened.

She walked now across the room toward Collins and offered him a piece of yellow, sugary cake and a glass of orange squash. Collins accepted the cake and tasted it while Mina awaited his approval. Though quite full, her face was covered with lines. Powdery makeup filled the wrinkles. Her smile revealed teeth that were black with years of chewing betel nut, and her red lips got their color from her saliva.

"Delicious," Collins said. The cake, like a dry sponge taking on water, slowly filled his mouth. He took a glass of orange squash, and Mina continued about the room. After all the others, she served Moot, who took a piece of cake without reply. Mina held the tray before him. It was laden with crumbs. Her lip was turned up, and as he stared at her, she turned back toward the kitchen.

"Tuan Collins asked me to have this meeting," Mahmet said, "so that we can talk about the well he has so kindly offered the kampong."

Grumbling whispers moved through the room. All the men sat on rattan mats that were spread out on the polished hardwood floor of Mahmet's living room. Collins watched the palm trees outside, bright and motionless in the morning sun.

"He asked me to invite our neighbor Moot to join us, since there is a question about his involvement in the project."

Moot's head hung low between his shoulders. He studied his feet.

"Yes, I . . . " Collins held himself back. He glanced at Mahmet, whose rather lost look caused him to hurry on. "I feel we can work out our problems here. With the well, I mean. Moot has always helped me on my projects, and I . . ."

The cloth in the kitchen doorway fluttered to one side.

"Eh, night-soil man."

Mina's voice, like pieces of flint, clattered into the room.

"Helping the Tuan, eh?" she said.

The cloth fell once again, and Mahmet held his hands up before him in an effort to interrupt.

"Yes, I help the Tuan," Moot said. "More than you do. More than any of you do."

Immediately the room filled with voices. Disapproval, like the rush of heavy rain, coursed through the house. Zahir's high voice rose above everyone else's as he pushed himself up on his hands and protested. Ahmad wrung a corner of his sarong in his fingers and shook his head. Finally Mahmet, holding out his hands with the palms facing the floor, quieted everyone.

"Let Tuan Collins speak, please," he said. Collins, sweating, leaned forward and sipped from his orange squash. His large face hung above the half-empty glass.

"I'm to blame for the problem here," he said.

Again there was an upsurge of talk, though now it had a sympathetic tone. Collins lowered the glass to the floor and continued speaking.

"I asked Moot to hire workers for the well, but I didn't specify Malay workers."

Collins looked at each man in the room. For the moment he had their attention.

"We use Chinese on the road project, and . . . "

"Yes, we've wanted to ask about that, Tuan," Bom said. Collins, still immersed in his own thought, paused a moment.

"That is, why haven't Malays been used on the road?"

"Well, it's because . . . "

"It's because I've been given the job by Mr. Collins of finding the best workers," Moot interrupted. "And do you know why I don't hire Malays?"

He split the remains of his piece of cake into two and popped one of the pieces into his mouth.

"Because they are lazy," he said, chewing rapidly. "Because they can't follow orders. Because they are stupid."

"We hired your father!" Ahmad interjected. He leaned forward and pointed an index finger at Moot. His Trengganu batik seemed to flame, and spittle gathered on his lips as he spoke. "To carry our shit away years ago. What about that, Moot? Was he lazy?"

"You treated my father like an animal," Moot said.

"At least he knew his place," Ahmad cried. His brow furrowed into a scowl. "He did not have airs, as you have."

Collins tried interrupting but was cut off by Ahmad.

"Moot was this way in school, Tuan. Always arguing. When he was there, which was not often."

"Who would come to your school, Teacher?" Moot asked. He looked about the room. "What could Ahmad possibly know?"

"Bom," Collins said. "You're right, of course. I was foolish. I know there should be Malays on the road project, and tomorrow I'll see to it."

He cursed himself. He realized that by letting Moot handle all the arrangements he had made a terrible mistake.

"Your father was lazy," Bom said. He had not heard Collins.

"Although we can't say that about your mother!" Mina shouted from behind the curtain. "She wasn't lazy!"

Laughter rose through the room.

"A whore!" Zahir said.

"She was not," Moot replied.

"She came from Simanggang, didn't she?" Zahir grinned. "Disgraced, thrown out of her father's house."

"That's not true, you bastard," Moot said.

"I remember," Ahmad nodded. "Your father loved the whores in Simanggang. Went there all the time."

Collins hurried to intrude. "There was another problem," he said. "The pay. The pay. Moot and I misunderstood each other. He offered six ringgit because he didn't understand what I wanted."

"And everyone knows the whores down there don't care who they fuck," Ahmad chuckled. Mahmet, who had kept silent for the moment, began laughing. He hid his mouth behind the fingers of his right hand.

"Well, ask your daughter about that, Ahmad," Moot replied.

The laughter in the room halted, and Moot, caught for a

moment in the silence, inhaled. He had gained momentum, and he hurried to press it forward.

"Though my father wouldn't even have noticed your daughter."

Now he laughed himself, his throat constricting so tightly that the sound came out in brief coughs.

"In fact, ask all your daughters," he continued. His laughter, isolated in the now otherwise silent room, sounded like wheezing. "Or ask your wife."

"Moot!" Mahmet cried. His mouth fell open, and his eyes, downcast and fluttering, seemed about to fill with tears. "Respect the memory of the dead."

In the heat outside, the coconut trees did not move. Collins wished he were in the shade of one of them right now. All around him were shaking fists and vitriol. He could do nothing. He pleaded. His own voice tightened. He wrung his baseball cap in his hands, then tossed it to the floor as he began shouting himself. But he could not be heard in the babble of voices.

"Cruel man," Mahmet said.

Moot thrust his chin out, ignoring the tumult of protests.

"Louse-ridden dog," Ahmad grimaced. Sweat glistened on his neck.

Collins retrieved his cap, stood, and placed it on his head. He stepped out onto the flight of stairs leading from the house. Behind him, voices rose in gusts of argument. He put on his sandals at the bottom of the stairs and hurried up the path. As he retreated, yelps, shouts, and accusations poured from the house. Collins headed for the well site. His hands were stuffed into his pockets. He walked very quickly, as though being propelled toward the hole by a stiff wind.

Collins struggled a moment with the thatched cover and finally was able to pull it aside. He looked back toward Mahmet's house. At the bottom of the stairs, Moot put on his leather shoes. His left hand shook in a fist above his head as he walked toward the main path. Mahmet—understanding, malleable Mahmet— inveighed in the doorway against the retreating night-soil man. The others hung out the windows while many villagers gathered around the house to watch and laugh. The river — very dark brown and apparently motionless — reflected the thick, cotton-white clouds overhead.

After a moment Collins took up a shovel and plunged it into one of the mounds of mud at the hole's edge. He dropped the spadeful of dirt into the hole, and the resultant plash muddied his sandals. He took up a second shovelful, then a third. The water now spilled over the banks of the hole. Collins removed his shirt and continued shoveling. Sweat dribbled down his face. He bent and dug.

He tried calming his nerves, but could not. Kindness, an altogether worthwhile thing in itself, had brought him to this — Collins the witness, no, the catalyst to the reopening of the village wound. He paused, a shovelful of mud in the air dripping to the ground. But it wasn't kindness at all, he thought. The well really was just one more chance to do things your way. The right way. He let the shovel drop to the ground, and mud oozed from it like an amoeba. Efficiency, he thought. American productivity. Those are what you've been trying for with all this, instead of seeking something far less superficial. Such as simple surrender, maybe, to the way things are.

He took up the shovel once more, thinking he was being too severe with himself. The well *was* going to bring them water. It was supposed to be a good idea, a kindly one even. He dropped the dirt into the hole. Perhaps it was not *just* affection for the Malays that was pushing him along, Collins decided, but with all the other reasons, his simple wish to help out was at least a part of it. He looked around once more at Mahmet's house. The Malay remained on the top step. From the distance he appeared to be watching Collins. Mahmet raised his hand to wave.

A Malay woman came up the path from the river. She carried two buckets of water suspended from opposite ends of a long stick she balanced across her shoulders. With each heavy step, the stick bowed. Water spilled from the buckets onto the path. She stopped a moment.

"Filling up the hole, Tuan?" she asked. She spit a large glob of betel-induced saliva onto the ground.

"Yes," Collins grunted as another shovelful of dirt disappeared into the well. He did not look up.

"No water down there?" the woman asked.

She peered into the hole.

"No," Collins sighed. "None."

9 / The Wo Family

The Australian soldier rose up at the front of the bus like a forest animal, some sort of rare, muscled primate. His fatigues were crusted with sweat. He blotted out the window behind him.

"Where is he?" the soldier asked. His voice gargled, as though the sweat that poured from his skin ran down his throat as well. He looked out the door of the bus into the sun.

"In the back, Captain Brownly." Another Australian stood outside. He pointed the length of the bus. "On the left. The skinny Chink with the straw basket, next to the white man."

Collins noticed that Wo Sam was tapping the rim of his basket with his fingers and straining to see what was going on outside, but the bus windows were so caked with dust that the figures surrounding the bus appeared as yellow shadows.

"Come with me, Perkins," Brownly said, and he moved up the aisle. Most of the passengers were Ibans transporting their goods into Kuching for the weekend market. They were in awe of the man's sweaty might. The noises of their animals — small pigs trussed up in rope baskets, fighting cocks clucking from their bamboo cages — only emphasized the silence of the passengers. No one spoke. Indeed it seemed as if no one breathed. Private Perkins slung his automatic rifle over his shoulder, and the butt clattered against the seats. Collins became alarmed by Wo Sam's obvious nervousness. The rimless glasses propped on the end of Wo Sam's nose and the very thin beard that grew from the center of his chin made him appear wise and reserved. But his hands were visibly shaking as he held tight to the rope sling of his basket.

Collins stood to intercept the Australian. He and Wo had ridden on this same bus through this same checkpoint many times, and there had never been trouble.

"Maybe I can help here, Captain," Collins said. He pulled a diplomatic passport from his shoulder bag.

"But you're not Chinese, are you, Yank?" Brownly asked.

"Of course not. This man's traveling with me, and I can assure you . . . "

"Sit down then."

Collins extended the passport toward the Australian. The two men stared at one another.

"I'm sure there's been a mistake," Collins said. His fingers left grimy prints on the passport. His arms were clotted with sweat and road dust.

"I didn't ask to see your passport," Brownly said.

"Look, I'm with the U.S. State Department and . . . "

The Australian looked beyond Collins at Wo Sam.

"Papers," he said. Wo Sam did not move. "Come on, then, let's see them," Brownly continued.

"He doesn't speak English, Captain," Collins interjected.

"Documents," Brownly said, this time in Malay. Wo Sam brought his Malaysian identity card from his basket. Brownly took it from him and perused it a moment.

"You see, Captain," Perkins said. "Same description. Chinese. Not the same name, but I thought it'd be worth a few questions."

Brownly's eyes moved back and forth between Wo and the identity card. His cheeks were purple, and his perspiration dripped onto the document.

"Right," he said after a moment. "Take him off."

"Wait a minute," Collins said. "You can't do this."

The Australians hauled Wo into the aisle.

"Mr. Collins, Mr. Collins," Wo said. He looked over his shoulder at the American. His eyes jumped with fear, and as Perkins pulled him up the aisle, Wo's hand flew up before his face. "Where are they taking me?"

Collins followed the men from the bus. The camp in which the bus had stopped was made up of several palm-leaf buildings with tin roofs. The forest had been cleared to accommodate the camp, leaving no trees to shade the yellow earth. In the open sunlight the buildings resembled bright graves.

Guerrillas, most of them indigenous Chinese, were fighting against the new Malaysian government in many parts of Sarawak. They hoped to take advantage of the war Malaysia was fighting against Indonesia in order to take the state of Sarawak by force. But they needed food, and the government had retaliated by fencing off hundreds of square miles of rice paddy in suspect areas. Farmers going to work in the morning had to pass through gates in the cyclone fence to get to their fields. They were checked carefully every evening for clandestine stores of rice. Without the rice the guerrillas could not survive.

One of the most suspect areas was this one, along the main road south of Simanggang. The government had placed this checkpoint in the center of a valley populated by farmers sympathetic to the guerrillas. Soldiers of the Australian army, specialists in counter insurgency and much admired by the Malaysian government, had reduced guerrilla activity almost to a standstill.

Collins followed the two Australians across the compound to the largest of the buildings. They pulled Wo Sam up the stairway, then turned to the left along the wooden porch to a doorway. Wo had dropped his basket, and Collins swept it up as he mounted the stairs. He turned through the doorway into an office. Wo Sam was being led to a chair next to an old wooden desk.

"What's he being charged with, Captain?"

Brownly turned from the desk and placed his hands on his hips.

"What do you want?"

"What's the charge?" Collins said.

Private Perkins sat down across the room. He was a tall man, very young, with a florid, whiskerless face.

"You have to charge him with something," Collins continued.

"I do not," Brownly replied. "I have the right to question him. I have the right to question you, for God's sake."

He laughed, and his teeth shone in his watery mouth. Collins's clothing was covered with yellow dust. As he removed his straw hat, a light cloud of it billowed around his head. Dust had clotted the sweat on his neck. Thin lines of it wound in rings down into his shirt. He took off his sunglasses and folded them, putting them into his shirt pocket.

"But I doubt you're giving help to the guerrillas, Yank," Brownly said.

"Neither is he."

"Well, we're not so sure of that."

"I am," Collins said. "Wo Sam's never done anything like that." Wo Sam, the owner of the only café in Saratok, was a kind, very reserved man and a good friend. He had lived in Saratok fifteen years. When Collins was not traveling, he had his meals in Wo's café. During the day Wo sat at his cash table reading the Chinese newspaper and watching the activity in the bazaar. He seldom moved from his chair, and he perused his newspaper from a distance, without humor, as a scholar would an original manuscript, with his glasses far down his nose. Wo also happened to be an exceptional badminton player.

Brownly pointed at him.

"I'm questioning this friend of yours because we think he's been helping the guerrillas out here. That's reason enough."

Wo Sam sensed the anger between the two men. He looked at the floor.

"I don't know what the hell you're defending him for, anyway," Brownly continued. "If he is a bloody guerrilla, you'd be one of his first targets."

"Mr. Collins!" Wo said. His voice jumped into the conversation, so that he startled both men.

"Help me. Please," Wo said. "Don't leave me out here."

"Captain, you can't hold this man," Collins said. "He hasn't done anything."

"We'll let you know about that."

"I insist you let him go."

Brownly looked across the room at Perkins, who stood and approached the two men.

"Mr. Collins," Brownly continued. "That's the name, isn't it?"
"Yes."

"Right. I think the best thing I can tell you is that there is one of you and many of us. We say you're wrong."

"Captain . . ."

"So, back on the bus."

Collins's insistence, more bluster than he wished to admit, fell away as he realized there was nothing he could do. He clutched Wo's basket. He turned toward the Chinese, who saw Collins had failed.

"I have to go, Wo Sam. They won't let me stay."

"Then see my brother in Kuching. His name is Wo Ting, on Merdeka Road. He'll help."

"But how can he . . ."

"Please. It's important you see him."

Wo slumped once more, and a glaze of anguish came over his eyes.

Late that afternoon Collins walked up Merdeka Road from the Kuching wharf. The two-story buildings were made of construction brick and cement, distinguished only by the green mold and discoloration caused by the heavy rains. Each building contained a single shop on the ground floor and living quarters above. The fronts of the shops were open to the street.

This part of Merdeka Road was occupied by gold merchants, and the signs above each establishment told the name of the shop's owner. The heavy Chinese characters, carved into wooden slabs and painted as well, gave the street a cluttered, jumpy look that belied the drabness of the buildings. Long sticks hung with laundry jutted from the windows of the upper floors, so that the sunlight was obscured by socks, underwear, shirts, and rags.

One sign was painted with gold characters against a red lacquered background. Beneath the characters, in English, "Wo Ting — Proprietor" was written like an afterthought. The shop was full of customers. A fat Chinese man — a laborer, Collins thought — about fifty years old, sat on a stool to one side of the entrance. He wore a dirty white undershirt, dark blue shorts, and rubber flip-flops. He had an enormous stomach.

"Excuse me," Collins said in Malay.

The man looked up and smiled quite broadly. All his teeth were lined with gold.

"Yes, John," he said.

"Is Wo Ting here?"

The man stood and assumed with importance his full height of about five and a half feet. He placed a hand on each side of his stomach and cleared his throat.

"Yes, John. I am Wo Ting."

"You!"

"Yes."

Collins glanced inside the shop. Clerks scurried about behind the counters. Collins had expected a more presentable man — a white dress shirt, long pants, moneyed aplomb.

"My name is Dan Collins," he said.

"I'm honored." Wo Ting extended his hand.

"I work up in Saratok, in the Second Division, and I'm a friend of Wo Sam."

The hand closed, and Wo Ting drew it back.

"Wo Sam," the Chinese said.

"Yes. Your brother."

"What do you want with him?"

Collins laid his shoulder bag on the sidewalk with Wo Sam's basket.

"Nothing. I'm his friend," he said.

"Has he done something?"

"No," Collins replied. "I mean I don't know. But he needs help, and he told me you were the person to speak with."

Wo Ting exhaled and sat down again.

"Yes, we are brothers, Mr. Collins."

He gestured to the bench next to him, and Collins sat down.

"But we do not get along," Wo continued. "You are British?"

"No. American."

"American! From San Francisco?"

Collins leaned back against the wall and crossed his legs. Although he was much larger than Wo Ting, his sandaled feet appeared more delicate than those of the Chinese. Wo's thick toes spilled from the sides of his flip-flops like sausages.

"Yes, as a matter of fact," Collins grinned. "Have you been there?"

"No. I've lived in Kuching all my life. But San Francisco is famous."

Wo Ting rubbed his hands.

"Many Chinese there," he added.

"That's right."

Wo nodded with goodwill. Collins looked out into the street as a breeze rustled through the laundry above.

"Goldahn Gate," Wo continued.

"About your brother," Collins said.

"Ah, my brother," Wo Ting sighed. He was disappointed the conversation had turned back to Wo Sam. "What has happened?"

"We were on the bus this morning from Saratok. We were stopped at the checkpoint below Simanggang, and Wo Sam was arrested."

"That fool."

"But why? He hasn't done anything."

"He's under arrest," Wo Ting said, spitting onto the sidewalk. "That means he's done something wrong."

Wo stood and walked to the curb. A group of people gathered about a Chinese man selling medicine in the street. He had set up a display of photos, of people with ghastly skin diseases: warts, excoriations, boils, and rashes in fading, metallic colors. Collins joined Wo Ting to watch. Wo's assertion had surprised the American. He had expected commiseration and an immediate offer of help. But Wo now stood on the curb absently viewing the sales pitch.

"What do you do in Saratok, Mr. Collins?"

"I'm an engineer. Do you know the Saratok road?"

"Yes," Wo Ting grumbled. "Progress."

"We hope so," Collins replied. "I'm in charge of building it."

Wo Ting turned and sat down again on his stool.

"We must talk to my son," he said.

"Your son? Why?"

"He'll know what to do."

"But we have to do something now. What good will it do to talk to your son?"

Dejected, Wo examined his fingernails, which were brown and cracked.

"Come back tomorrow morning," he said. "My son will be here, Mr. Collins."

"Wo Ting!"

"Come back tomorrow," Wo shouted. He seemed gravely angered by Collins's objection. Reluctantly, the American agreed.

That evening Collins sat in the bar of the Kuching Hotel. The ceiling fans turned about. The plants around the bar rustled in the breezes. The bar was empty, and Collins drank several bottles of Tiger Beer, feeling more and more senseless as the evening wore on.

Collins planned to return to Wo's shop the next morning. But he knew the Australian Army would not respond to Wo Ting's son. Indeed they'd laugh at him. Collins imagined a short, young Chinese man, also in a T-shirt and shorts, counting sacks of rice as they came down a gangplank at the wharf, and he groaned. The heir to the fortune!

"Mr. Collins. My son."

The American turned toward the back of the shop, which had not yet opened for business. Into the room came a tall Chinese man wearing a light, double-breasted Savile Row suit of blue wool, a starched white shirt with black opal cufflinks, and a dark blue tie. His hair was close cut and neat, and his eyeglasses were framed with round, tortoise-shell rims. A white handkerchief pointed up from his breast pocket in three equal peaks. He looked about thirty years old. He extended his hand to Collins, whose surprise was so complete that for a moment he did not return the gesture.

"Mr. Collins, I presume," the man said. "Winston Wo's the name. I understand my uncle Wo Sam is in a spot of trouble."

"Rather!" Collins said. He realized he had employed the British usage, even to the point of extending the second syllable of the word to indicate emphatic agreement. He swore at himself. "That's for sure."

"Doesn't surprise me a bit," Winston continued.

His hand hung in the air a moment longer. Collins's jaw moved about as he ground his teeth in confusion. In his khaki shorts and white shirt—the sleeves rolled up to two different levels—and his soiled, black sandals, he glared at Winston. After a moment he realized he was being rude, and he grasped Winston's hand.

"My pleasure," Collins said.

"All mine, old boy," Winston replied. "As it happens, I was coming over today on business from Singapore, and when my father told me about Wo Sam's troubles, I thought, right, this should be a lark."

Wo Ting surveyed his son's gestures with obvious pride.

"But you seem surprised," Winston continued.

"Well, I am. You see, with *your* father in *this* shop, a local Chinese, untraveled . . . "

"Didn't expect his son to be a chip off the old empire, eh?" Winston grinned. He sat down and crossed his legs. The crease in his pants remained straight.

"Well, I didn't know," Collins said. "But I must say your appearance is—and your English, the accent . . . "

"A doctorate in law. Post doctoral study at the LSE. Quite simple, really."

He explained the conversation to his father. Wo Ting leaned over the table and addressed Collins in Malay.

"Excuse me, Mr. Collins. I was angered by my brother's arrest, and I just forgot. As you can see, Winston is a fine boy. But Wo Sam, I'm sorry to say, has been an idiot all his life."

Winston nodded agreement.

"After the war, you see," Winston said in English, "when the British came back, there was a long period of, well, disagreement between the Chinese and the Malays. And the British colonialists, of course."

"In Malaya," Collins said.

"That's right," Winston said. "As to who would rule the country. The Chinese were frozen out of the government, you might say. Bit of collusion there between the Malays and the Brits. So a lot of the Chinese simply decided not to put up with it, and they fought against it. The Emergency, it was called."

"I've read about it. General Sir Gerald Templar."

"Yes. Many Chinese were put in jail. Many were killed. That cyclone fencing and the checkpoint you see out there on the Simanggang road? It was everywhere in Malaya. For years. A police state, really."

Collins tried to determine what it was about Winston's speech that seemed so odd to him. Surely everything he said was accurate. If anything, Winston spoke English better than Collins. But there was a tinny veneer to his expression that made it sound like a recording. No matter what he said, it sounded depthless and rehearsed, like something from a language class.

Winston took a moment to translate what he had said into Cantonese.

"Our family wanted nothing to do with the Chinese guerrillas," Wo Ting said in Malay. "We're business people. We don't need politics. But my brother insisted on being a revolutionary. Once he called himself the Chinese Sukarno."

Wo Ting grimaced.

"Such an idiot. The Chinese Sukarno!"

He threw his head back and laughed.

"But they put him in jail," he said after a moment.

"How long?"

"Three years."

"When he got out," Winston interjected, "the family insisted he come back here to Sarawak. My father told him he had to go up to Saratok, that we would help him open a cafe there. But he had to stay there, my father said."

"He'd given up the revolution?" Collins asked.

"We forced him to," Wo Ting said. "Wo Sam made us look like fools. He even made me suspect in the minds of the British. Me!"

"What happened?"

Wo Ting looked away. His folded hands quivered on the tabletop.

"My father was put in jail also, Mr. Collins," Winston said.

"For what?"

"Nothing!" Wo Ting said. "For my brother's stupidity."

"How long?"

"Also for three years."

Wo Ting sat silently, very angry.

"My father has little to say about Wo Sam's past," Winston said in English. He laid his glasses on the table.

"But in this case, Wo Sam's innocent," Collins said.

"Oh, no doubt," Winston replied. "And since you've been so kind, I hope you'll permit me to . . . what do you Americans say? Help you out?"

"Yes, please. Help me out."

Winston stood and walked toward the doorway at the front of the shop. He leaned his head out into the light, then returned to the table to sit down. He joined his hands and leaned forward over the table.

"Wouldn't do to have people listening in, would it?"

"I suppose not."

"Have you spoken with anyone else about this, Mr. Collins?"

"No."

"Good. No need to discomfort anyone, what? The way I see it, we have one option."

"What's that?"

"Suleiman bin Yussuf Suleiman."

"Who's he?"

"Rather high up in the Defense Ministry, actually. Liaison between the government and the colonial troops."

Winston paused and then waved a hand before his face.

"I mean our democratic allies. He's quite important. Mucky-muck in the government, to be sure. A man who'll go far, and a friend of mine as well."

"Never heard of him."

"Well, he studied in the States, in fact. And in London, where I met him. When you meet him, you'll come to realize that

Suleiman is a reasonable man. Under the correct circumstances, very reasonable."

Winston broke into a great, broad smile. For the first time Collins saw the resemblance between Winston and his father. The smile was like an exclamation point.

"Meet me here in the morning, and we'll go have a talk with him," Winston said. "He's flexible. A good man."

"Winston, we've got to do something this afternoon! Wo Sam's sitting out there. I don't know what they're doing to him."

Winston peered at the glasses on the table, then removed the handkerchief from his breast pocket.

"Suleiman is the best the Malays have to offer," he said. "But we have to be patient with him."

Collins gathered himself to interrupt, but Winston continued.

"To find how best to negotiate with him, you see."

"I don't see," Collins mumbled.

"You will, Tuan," Winston grinned. He breathed heavily on the lenses.

The next morning, after a long, impatient breakfast, Collins walked with Winston up Merdeka Road to the government buildings. Winston wore a khaki bush suit, short sleeved with epaulettes, a white shirt open at the neck, and dark brown, tasseled loafers. His sunglasses were tinted more darkly in the upper half of the lenses than in the lower half. He carried a slim, leather folder, monogrammed "WW" in gold leaf. Collins wore the same crumpled shorts he had worn to Wo Ting's the day before. He had gone out to buy a new shirt, however, and he had put on a pair of dark gray, cotton socks that made his black, plastic sandals appear more formal. He had carefully shaved, and he had combed his hair.

"Now Suleiman will probably be difficult, because he views himself as a keeper of the flame," Winston said.

"What flame?"

"The flame of Malay independence! Freedom from the colonialist yoke."

"Malay independence!" Collins said. "But that's only part of the story."

"Quite, old boy. You're wondering where the Chinese fit into it, eh?"

The city of Kuching was small, with narrow streets and low buildings. It was saved from being entirely dull by the few hills on which it was situated, by the coconut palm trees that grew everywhere throughout the city, and by the extraordinary mixture of people. On his arrival in Kuching in late 1963, Collins had thought it was a melting pot, so many races mixing so freely. Now he understood that the different peoples stayed rigidly separate in separate neighborhoods, that colors and religions and languages were strictly observed. The street was already filled with people. Malays rode bicycles from which hung plastic sacks, baskets filled with birds, tin cans. There were Tamil women dressed in saris. Some of the dresses were very elegant, with gold-thread brocade, others of stained and ragged cotton. Collins saw a red-skinned, alien British woman, the wife of a government officer, doing her shopping, who stepped aside for a line of abashed Iban tribesmen in loincloths. Straw baskets were slung from their backs. They stared with awe at the woman. Chinese scuttled everywhere from shop to shop. It was a very warm morning, with high clouds white in the sky.

The government office building was new, square, and gray with dark windows and air-conditioning. At six stories, it was the tallest building in town. As they climbed the stairs, Collins's sweat was like ice. Winston appeared unaffected by the change in temperature. Collins marveled at Winston's consistency—always pleasant, always calm.

"Here we are," Winston said as they stepped into an outer office. A view of the Kuching River was obscured by venetian blinds. A large photo of Prime Minister Tengku Abdul Rahman hung above the desk, at which a Chinese secretary sat typing.

"I'm Winston Wo. I'm here with Mr. Daniel Collins, of the U.S. State Department, to see Mr. Suleiman, please."

The secretary excused herself and entered another office. There were some whispers and grunts of surprise.

"Winston Wo?" a man's voice said. "I don't believe it."

After a bustle of movement Suleiman appeared in the doorway.

"Winston!"

He stepped into the office and took each man's hand.

"Suleiman," Winston said. "This is my friend Collins."

"From the States?" Suleiman asked.

"Yes," Collins replied.

Suleiman pumped Collins's hand.

"University of Tennessee," Suleiman said.

"I beg your pardon?"

"London School of Economics."

After a moment's silence Collins looked to Winston for an explanation.

"Did you go to university?" Suleiman asked.

"Yes," Collins said.

There was another pause, during which the American became embarrassed by the Malay's expectant smile.

"Where?" Suleiman asked finally.

"University of California. Berkeley. Class of '50."

"Telegraph Avenue," Suleiman replied. He said nothing about the street. He simply gave the name, as though affixing a stamp to some precise, narrow fact to which both men could clutch.

"I was in Berkeley last winter," Suleiman continued. "Postgraduate seminar. Do you know Ed Travers? Army Corps of Engineers?"

"No, I don't. He lives in Berkeley?"

"You know what I like about the U.S.A.?" Suleiman asked.

"No."

"French fries."

"Really!"

"Yes. And San Francisco, of course."

Suleiman turned from Collins and addressed Winston.

"What a shock to see you!"

Suleiman's face, open and guileless, was very round. His black hair lay across his forehead at an angle, and he frequently ran a hand across it to make sure it remained in place. He had dark skin, and his face contained no lines, so that he appeared very young. He was dressed in a white cotton suit, a white shirt, and a black tie.

"What brings you here?"

He showed the two men into his office. There followed fifteen minutes of small talk, in which Suleiman, between brief questions to the others, explained at length the advances in his career.

"It was by a fluke, really," he said. "There are not many qualified people in the government these days."

"True," Winston said.

"Malays, I mean. The civil service is losing all the British now that Malaysia's no longer a colony. So, really, I fell into this position."

The three men sat in armchairs. Suleiman crossed his legs. His coat remained buttoned.

"Do you know, I am the civilian officer in charge of military relations here in Sarawak? I have rather a lot of clout with the forces."

"Yes, I do know that," Collins replied. His arms were covered with goosebumps from the air-conditioning. "In fact, that's why we're here."

Winston leaned forward. "We have something we'd like to speak with you about." He looked at his watch. "We don't want to take too much of your time."

"You have a Bulova," Suleiman said. "So do I."

He held his right arm out. Surprised, the two men looked on, forced to by Suleiman's enthusiasm.

"I bought it in Hong Kong," he said. "A job like this deserves a gold watch, don't you think?"

"Suleiman, we're here on an important mission," Collins said. "Winston's uncle Wo Sam is being held by the Australians, out at the Simanggang checkpoint."

"No!" Suleiman exclaimed.

"I'm afraid so. It's a mistake, of course. It has to be. We're hoping you'll be able to do something about it."

Suleiman joined his hands and looked up at the ceiling.

"You know the Wo family," Collins continued. "Fine business people. Very honorable."

"Well, yes, I do know that," Suleiman replied. "But I also know about Wo Sam."

"You do?"

"Not about this particular matter. But we do keep tabs on those Chinese who have given us trouble in the past."

Winston stood up and walked toward the window. When he turned back, his eyes were motionless. Sudden anger sounded in his voice.

"Why do you say 'those Chinese?' " he asked.

"Well, you know as well as I that the guerrilla forces are made up of your people. There's no mystery about it, Winston."

"Possibly there's a reason for that," Winston said.

"What? That they're criminals?" Suleiman said.

"No, damn you. You damned Malays have stolen the government."

"Racialist nonsense," Suleiman sniffed.

"Winston. Please," Collins interrupted. He sat helpless, surprised, as the two men began suddenly to argue.

"Half the population is Chinese," Winston continued. "We have almost no high government posts. Chinese aren't even allowed in the army."

"You'd have us arm them as well, Winston?" Suleiman asked.

"Wait, wait," Collins interjected. "We're not here to argue how the government is made up."

"Besides," Suleiman said, "you damned Chinese own everything. What more do you want?"

Winston turned away. Furious, he stood before the window with his back to the others. After a moment Suleiman spoke again.

"Well, there may be some things I can do," he said. His voice rose to a speculative lilt. He surveyed the ends of his fingers. Collins guessed Suleiman was dangling his power before them as a kid would do, and he resented it. However, he thought, if he *can* do something, let him have his way.

"What sorts of things?" Collins asked.

"Oh, I could speak with the Australian command here."

"We'd like you to do that today, Suleiman," Collins said.

Suleiman looked squarely at Winston's back. Collins sensed the advantage Suleiman was taking of Winston's need. There was childishness about it, as though Suleiman were the long-suffering weakling finally in a position of power.

"I've never visited your father's shop, Winston," Suleiman said.

Winston continued looking at the view.

"I understand he's quite wealthy," Suleiman said. "I wonder what sort of price your father would charge."

Winston turned from the window.

"For a watch like this," Suleiman continued.

"What does that matter?" Collins stood and walked to the window. "Watches! We should be concerned about rights, about justice."

"Yes, Mr. Collins, of course," Suleiman replied. "But Winston and I are old friends. This is just a diversion."

"He wouldn't charge you much," Winston said. "Indeed, old boy, I expect he could make you quite a bargain."

Winston removed his own watch and returned to his chair. Collins, left standing by the window, felt the tension ease, for which he was thankful. But the two others now began examining Winston's Bulova.

"Yes. I'm sure a price can be arranged," Winston said.

"May I come for a visit?" Suleiman asked.

"Why not this evening?"

"Winston, this is ridiculous!" Collins interrupted.

He stood with his back to the window. Winston and Suleiman ignored him.

Wo Ting's shop was filled with glass-enclosed counters. Each one contained a shelf covered with red felt, on which gold chains of various lengths and sizes were laid out. There were displays of chain and coins on the felt-covered walls as well, sheltered behind glass. In the candlelight a kind of sepulchral glow flowed from everywhere in the shop. The gold was of a wavering lightness that made it seem to hover in the air above the felt. The light changed moment to moment, and the gold appeared to move back and forth, to disappear, to reappear.

Collins sat alone at a table as Winston rummaged in the back for a bottle of brandy. The meeting with Suleiman that morning had discouraged the American. Collins felt he and Wo Sam were being made fools of. All I do is wait, he thought. That the two men had paid so little attention to Collins's worries irritated him, because he felt they were missing the danger of Wo Sam's situation.

Winston entered the shop and placed a bottle of Courvoisier on the table with three glasses.

"I'm glad my father isn't here," he said. "I'm afraid that, when it comes to Wo Sam, he'd side with the Australians."

A trishaw arrived outside and Winston opened the shop's front door. He beckoned once and Suleiman, nervous and sweating, entered the shop. His watch gleamed in the candlelight as he pulled a handkerchief from his pants pocket. He wore no coat, and the sleeves of his white shirt were rolled up above his elbows. He swabbed his forehead and looked back toward the door, which Winston closed behind him.

"I shouldn't be seen here," Suleiman said.

"Why?" Winston turned back into the shop. "We're respectable citizens."

"Yes, yes. Of course."

"Hello, Suleiman," Collins said. He rose up to shake the Malay's hand, and he realized he had frightened him.

"Mr. Collins," Suleiman whispered. "I'm surprised to see you here."

"I'm just trying to help my friend," Collins replied.

Suleiman sighed. His eyes moved across one wall, pausing at the coins that glimmered most brightly in the candlelight.

"They're beautiful, aren't they?" Winston asked.

The candles lit Suleiman's hair and shoulders. His face was strewn with shadows.

"Let's get on with it, Winston," Collins said.

"Yes. The problem."

Suleiman's head turned about so that he faced both men. He wiped his forehead with the handkerchief.

"The pleasant thing about an evening like this, Mr. Collins, is that we are all reasonable people," Winston nodded. "Don't you agree, Suleiman?"

Suleiman assented. There was a phlegmy, constricted waver in his voice. He sat down.

"Educated. With a feeling for privacy," Winston continued.

"Yes. Yes," Suleiman said.

Winston brought a leather folder up from beneath the table and laid it on the tablecloth. He opened it quickly, and Collins took in a breath of surprise, then of shocked protest. The glow of gold coins broke from the dark leather. Winston laid his fingers on the coins and spread them around. He left the folder open on the table. The coins resembled small pools of flame.

Suleiman's eyes glittered in the light. His hair had become disheveled. He leaned low over the table to look at the coins.

"My uncle Wo Sam has been a child," Winston said. "A disgrace." His voice had a sad tone, as though he were sharing an intimacy with close friends. "But he is no revolutionary."

"What do you want me to do?" Suleiman asked. He took up one of the coins and caressed it with the ends of his fingers.

Collins moved his chair a few inches farther from the table. His hands dropped from the light. He wanted to distance himself from the others as much as he could. A bribe like this could cause terrible problems for him if it were known he had witnessed it — a State Department functionary party to the illegal release of a suspected terrorist. Collins felt the back of his chair digging into his shoulders. He moved to interrupt. But he held himself back. The fact remains, he thought, Wo Sam is not a terrorist. He's an innocent man.

Collins realized a conflict was occurring within Suleiman as well. In the dim amber light and the darkness there was a struggle between the delicate beauty of the gold and Suleiman's sense of himself as an important government officer. Greed burdened his perusal of the folder. But Collins sensed that Suleiman could not simply surrender to it. He had to be helped.

Collins looked toward Winston, whose eyes were bright and black. He seemed unable to speak, and Collins realized he was caught up in his hatred of Suleiman. Of course, Collins thought, Winston planned to bribe Suleiman all along. But now Winston could not give the hint, the nudge, the push that would allow Suleiman to take the gold and get Wo Sam freed. A long silence, fully a minute long, ensued. No one was going to make the move. No one wanted to be responsible for it. Collins lowered his head onto one hand and struggled to calm himself. He hated the silence and the inaction. But he could not speak.

"Arrange Wo Sam's release." The words lurched from Collins's mouth. Suleiman's eyes turned toward him.

"I don't have that kind of authority," he said.

"Yes, you do."

"But what if he's dangerous?"

Collins, embarrassed, addressed the tabletop.

"You can do it, Suleiman," he said. "Wo Sam's done nothing."

After a moment Collins reached across the table and closed the leather folder. He slipped it toward Suleiman.

"It will rectify a terrible wrong," Collins said.

"Here here," Winston whispered.

Suleiman rested a hand on the folder and for a moment fingered the leather strap.

"It's for the good of your new democracy," Collins continued. His voice, its hypocrisy, sickened him. Suleiman pulled the folder toward the edge of the table. "It will ensure Wo Sam gets a a fair shake."

"What's that?" the Malay asked. He dropped the folder onto his lap. "A fair what?"

"Justice," Collins replied. The word sounded like an epithet.

Collins and Winston caught the first bus out of Kuching the next morning. It took three hours to get to the checkpoint, and Collins spent most of it listening to Winston talk. He went on for some time about public transport in rural areas. He chatted about the Earl Grey tea in the café at which the bus stopped for a break. He disliked the sweet coconut cake there, though he thought Collins's iced lychee drink was passable. Winston liked the birds in the forest. He wondered why the Ibans lived in Borneo. Finally he slept.

When they arrived at the checkpoint, Private Perkins and an Iban soldier came up the aisle of the bus checking the passengers' papers. Collins told Perkins he and Winston wished to see the captain, and Perkins escorted them from the bus. They walked through the camp toward Brownly's office. Winston sheltered his head from the sun with a newspaper.

Though there had been rain the night before, the high sun now shone on the tin roofs of the buildings. They were like slabs of blinding snow. The ground was dark red, and sunlight glared from the vast puddles.

"Ghastly place," Winston said as they ascended the stairs to Brownly's office.

Collins knocked on the doorjamb, and Captain Brownly, his forehead resting on one hand as he perused some papers at his desk, looked up at him.

"Good morning," Collins said. "May we come in?"

Brownly's hand remained at his forehead.

"You remember me, I hope," Collins said.

"I do." Brownly surveyed Winston's clothing, which was dotted with perspiration. "Who's he?"

"Wo's the name," Winston said. He extended his hand to the Australian. "Collins here tells me you're responsible for my uncle's release."

"Your uncle, is he?" Brownly replied.

"Well, yes." Winston let his hand drop.

"I don't know how you got away with that, Collins."

Brownly sat back in his chair. The spring that supported the chair-back creaked with his weight. He collected the papers on his desk and tapped them once. The movement, which was quick with irritation, crumpled the bottom half of the papers.

"There was nothing to get away with, Captain," Collins replied evenly. "He's an innocent man."

Brownly laid down the papers on his desk.

"That little bastard is probably a murderer," he said.

"I advise you to keep that opinion to yourself, Captain," Winston interrupted. "It's prejudicial. It would not bear up in a courtroom."

He joined his hands behind him. Winston was so little intimidated by Brownly that the Australian appeared for the moment stymied. He unbuttoned his shirt and adjusted the lapels to let in some air.

"I'm going to give you another opinion, then, Mr. Wo," Brownly said. "When you deal with these kinds of people — guerrillas like these — you don't worry much about evidence."

He gazed out the door a moment.

"Because sometimes the first clue you have about who you're dealing with is your own death."

"Come now," Winston muttered.

"Court of law doesn't mean much out here."

"Where's my uncle?" Winston said.

"That's why we're here." Brownly stood up. "Because those chaps don't give a shit about the law."

"Where's my uncle?"

"That's right. Chaps like him."

Brownly moved from the desk.

"Your uncle is gone," he said.

"Gone!"

"They called us by radio-telephone first thing this morning. He was on the first bus."

"Where to?"

"Saratok. He's there now, I imagine."

Collins and Winston followed Brownly onto the porch. As they descended the steps, Brownly leaned on the wooden railing.

"Listen to me, Collins," he said. "Whatever you did to get that man set free, you made a mistake."

Collins turned away without a response.

As the bus passed through the checkpoint and started up the road again, Winston shook Collins's hand.

"Suleiman came through," he said. He clapped the American's knee. "As I expected he would. Now we go up to Saratok, have a little chat with my uncle the Chinese Sukarno, and be back in Kuching by tomorrow tea."

When they reached Saratok, Collins asked the bus driver to drop them off in front of Wo Sam's café. He noticed that Wo's bicycle shop, usually a center of activity in Saratok because of its pool table, was closed. He stared at the shuttered shop-front as the bus moved through the bazaar. He pointed out the café to the driver. It was closed as well.

Worried, Collins thanked the driver, and the two men descended from the bus. They walked up the steps to the wooden sidewalk. Winston tested the small entry door in the front of the café. He knocked and waited, then knocked again very loudly.

"May I help you, Mr. Collins?" Lew Ling emerged from his shop next door and approached them. A cigarette hung from his mouth. He removed it and flicked it into the road before shaking Collins's hand.

"Yes. Have you seen Wo Sam?" Collins asked.

"He was here this morning. But he didn't stay."

"He didn't? Why not?"

Lew Ling pointed up the road.

"He said he had argued again with his family."

"What was that?" Winston interjected.

"Oh, Wo Sam fought with them many times," Lew Ling said. "I've never met them, of course, but he often said they loved the Tuans a bit too much."

Lew Ling nodded apologetically to Collins.

"Forgive me, Tuan," he said.

"Never mind."

"But he never cared for his family. Cowards, he called them."

"What did he tell you this morning?" Collins asked.

"He said they'd betrayed him again. He told me there was some problem at the Simanggang checkpoint, and that they left him there to rot for a couple of days. 'Me! An innocent man!' he said. 'My own family!' he said. I tried to get him to stay. But he wouldn't. He told me he was going down to the south, into the interior."

Lew Ling shook his head and pulled another cigarette from the pack that was stuck beneath his belt.

"He worries me, Mr. Collins. Wo Sam's argument with his family, it's always been about politics. Always. Now he's going out into the forest, into the mountains."

Lew Ling's match burst into flame. He nodded to Winston.

"Out where they're fighting the war," he said.

10 / The Day Nothing Happened

Raindrops clattered across the palm-leaf roof over Collins's head. The air in the jungle had grown heavier during the night, and now it seemed more difficult to breathe. The storm worried Collins because the Chinese cargo boat for which he was waiting was due in an hour — at seven o'clock in the morning. The river would rise very quickly, and such changes disrupted things. Even so, Collins thought, the boat shouldn't have any trouble making it up here.

Seated on a bench inside the shack's door, he looked out onto the Kanowit River as the storm moved up from the coast. Sibuyoh hunkered next to Collins in the doorway. He was an Iban headman who had accompanied the American to the shack from his longhouse a quarter mile downriver. Collins was glad to see the rains begin. After three months of dry season the roads were bright with hot, yellow dust, and the rivers seemed barely to move. From wrinkled browns and bone-dull greens, the forest now would be shiny and swollen, with blue air visible between the trees. Within a few minutes rain formed a gray, pulpy sheet in the distance. From the shack's roof streams of gathered water fell to the ground, forming a narrow ditch in the mud parallel to the shack's walls. Collins rested his head against the doorjamb and folded his arms. The rain would last this way all day, perhaps several days.

The forest heaved with the first heavy wind. A frond dropped from one of the coconut palms, slid down the roof, and landed on the ground outside the shack. The trees rolled back in the wind. The river was still quite blue, but it was dotted with whitecaps now.

The shack was just a hundred yards below the Antu Kanowit rapids. This stretch of white water was a quarter mile long and descended two hundred feet from the uppermost falls. It could be negotiated only by longboats with very strong engines, and then only during the dry seasons. The rapids were dotted with large boulders. Some stuck up in the air; others were hidden beneath immense surges of water that came down with such violence that spray rose up in clouds the length of the rapids. Now, with the rain, the rapids took on the look of dirty lava, and the noise they made reminded Collins of a long, muffled breath.

The trees cracked and danced against each other. As the ground around the shack turned to mud, the rain seemed to thicken. There was not the sparkle that comes with reflected sunlight. There was no depth to the rain. Collins had heard the Ibans with whom he worked rhapsodizing about the surprises to be found in the monsoon. The tribesmen had myriad words for the rain, each descriptive of a certain rate of fall, of specific colors and intensities. For them, the rain provided mood. It affected the nature of sadness. Its colors conjured up loss or well-being, disruptive spirits in the heavens and in the mud. Occasionally the rain even caused great bravery.

But for Collins, this rain appeared simply to be gray. It got heavier or lighter. Otherwise, gray rain was little different from brown rain. Out here, when it rained, all activity stopped. Like a fire the rain shackled the attention, and people simply watched it from the shelter of the longhouses, from beneath the trees at the river's edge, and from rickety shelters like the one in which Collins stood. Initial fascination gave way after a time to boredom as the rain continued pouring from the sky. It was the boredom that comes when nothing is happening.

Sibuyoh rolled a cigarette between his stubby fingers. A dirty cloth was wrapped about his head. The wrinkles in his golden face were softened by the blue-gray light coming through the doorway. Sibuyoh looked down on the cigarette with an air of interested superiority. His ears were pierced, and the lobes hung down almost to his shoulders. His limbs were very thin, though there was a stringy solidity about them, indicative of the years Sibuyoh had spent clearing the hillsides for dry paddy. He wore a brown loincloth. His thick feet rested flat on the mud floor of the shack.

"We got here just in time," Collins said in Iban.

Sibuyoh did not look up from his cigarette. He had just completed rolling it, and he now examined it to make sure it would hold together.

"Yes. Easy to get wet when it rains like this," he said.

He placed the cigarette in his mouth. He lit it with a Red-Chinese Zippo, then replaced the lighter in the small bag that hung from his loincloth.

"I hope the boat comes, Tuan," he said after a moment. "In the monsoon season the Chinese sometimes give up."

Sibuyoh blew smoke from his mouth and pondered the rain a moment.

"I've seen days when no boat came at all."

He tapped the end of the ash onto the mud floor.

"I've seen weeks like that," he continued.

"Weeks!" Collins groaned. He rested an arm against the jamb and looked at the water running from the roof. Collins's green shirt was unbuttoned to the waist. Its long sleeves were rolled up above his elbows. His left hand clutched the bunched material of his shirt where it ballooned from beneath his belt. His body so filled the doorway that Sibuyoh's small face and shoulders seemed more like a child's than like those of a man of fifty. The American's face was gummy with perspiration. He had five days' growth of beard, not having shaved during his visit to Sibuyoh's longhouse.

"There's nothing you can do, Tuan," Sibuyoh said. "If the Chinese don't come . . . "

He exhaled a puff of smoke, which dispersed in the wind that blew through the doorway.

"No one comes," he concluded.

Collins was due in the town of Sibu the next day for a meeting of development officers from the Malaysian Interior Ministry. They wanted his report on Iban reaction to a proposed road into upriver Kanowit. Sibuyoh's longhouse had been the last stop of an extended trip Collins had made into the interior. He was anxious to make the meeting because Datu Zainal Ibrahim, the Minister of Interior himself, would be there. Zainal, who came from Kuala Lumpur, was on a junket through Borneo, and, amused by the Ibans and other tribes, he claimed to have an interest in their welfare. Collins wanted the road, and even more, the Ibans wanted it. So it was important he attend the meeting.

But the Chinese did not come. By noon the rain had grown monotonously heavy, not changing at all moment to moment. A torpor settled over the shack. Collins's mood grew featureless, so that his thoughts had little variation. He was neither warm nor cold. The waiting made him restless, and he picked at his shirt, tapped the bench with his fingers. The river had come up seven feet. The earth around the shack had turned to sludge. Fronds lay everywhere. Other pieces of wreckage from the storm—shredded deciduous leaves, pieces of torn bark, coconuts, and crushed ferns and flowers—were scattered about, and Collins began to suspect that indeed the boat would not arrive at all.

Sibuyoh sat in the rear of the shack. He pulled a ball of rice, wrapped in a large leaf, from the sack at his waist, opened it, and spread the leaf out between himself and Collins. He offered some of the rice to Collins, who, quite hungry, took a handful of it.

"Does it rain like this in your land?" Sibuyoh asked.

Collins fingered the rice and shoved it into his mouth. A gust of wind blew water into the shack.

"I'm from San Francisco," he said.

"The name of your river?"

"No. Excuse me, Sibuyoh. That's the name of the city I come from. It's a large place, like Singapore. Like Kuching."

"It's in England," Sibuyoh replied.

"No. In the United States."

"I see," Sibuyoh nodded.

"By ship it would be several weeks."

"So that by boat — a boat like mine — you couldn't even get there?"

The longboat in which Sibuyoh had brought Collins to the shack was moored in the river. Sibuyoh had pulled it up on the shore when they had arrived at dawn. Now the boat bobbed in the rising water several feet from the bank. It was held fast by a piece of jute rope. Its outboard engine had been pulled up so that the prop was suspended above the surface of the water.

"No, you couldn't," Collins said.

"There's rain there?" Sibuyoh asked.

Collins took another handful of rice. He reached into his rucksack and took out a packet of Lucky Strikes. He pulled a cigarette from the packet and handed it to Sibuyoh.

"Yes, there's rain," Collins said. "But not like this."

"Heavier?" Sibuyoh asked.

"No. Lighter. And it's much colder. Like the coldest of the rainy season here."

Sibuyoh lit the Lucky Strike, then leaned back against the wall.

"Do people work there?" he asked.

"Oh, yes."

"They have rice, like we do?"

"Some do," Collins replied. "But it's not the same."

"Not the same rice?"

"No. They don't farm it the way the Ibans do."

"Do they have religion?"

"Yes."

"A rice-spirit? A spirit for the harvest?"

Collins grinned and looked out the door. The rain had not changed.

"No," he said. "It's not the same."

"How can the people be happy then?"

Collins shrugged his shoulders. How could he explain to Sibuyoh, he wondered, the exotic humdrum of his life? The Iban would be amazed by the pencils and adding machines and high buildings in San Francisco. He imagined Sibuyoh and himself hunkering on the corner of Broadway and Columbus, sheltered from the rain by an awning. The noise of the place and its sputtering cars, its coffeehouses and baseball and buses — all of it would conspire in a grand mystery to confuse Sibuyoh.

Or a slide rule. The Iban would look over his shoulder while Collins, at his desk figuring a problem, worked the rule back and forth.

"The future, Tuan," he would say.

"Yes, that's right," Collins would reply.

"A people without a rice-spirit can't be living a good life," Sibuyoh concluded now.

"I think you're right," Collins said.

He considered the difficulties of his life here in Sarawak. An American civil engineer, on contract to the Malaysian government from the Agency for International Development. Simple enough. Maybe that explained it all. But as the rain ground against the shack's roof, he felt his mood deteriorating. He was simply biding his time. Building roads? Wonderful endeavor.

"Sometimes I worry I'm not doing anything here," he said in English. The odd-sounding conglomeration made Sibuyoh laugh. He and Collins had known each other only a month, yet the Iban frequently chided Collins for his lapses into that odd language. He had once told Collins that English reminded him of pigs snuffling in the mud.

"What was that?" he asked in Iban.

"Oh, just that I often think these trips I make into the jungle, my visits to the longhouses," Collins replied, "the long discussions with the Ibans about what the Malaysian government wants from them . . . "

Collins turned from the rain. He saw Sibuyoh's eyes, like black stones, staring at him. Collins fell into silence. He had been wandering. He didn't know what to say.

The Iban pushed his spent cigarette into the mud floor. It sizzled a moment, then expired with a last wisp of smoke.

"Pardon me, Tuan," he said, "but I don't understand."

"It's just . . . you see, it's just that I've come to your country from thousands of miles away, Sibuyoh. My people are different from yours. We live differently, in different houses. Strange, cold weather. Machines and customs you can't imagine. And I came all the way here for a reason I don't really comprehend. I sit in the jungle. Listen to the river."

Sibuyoh waited with patience through this reverie. Finally he nodded.

"It's no mystery. We have the same custom," he said. "It's called . . . "

"Bejalai," Collins interrupted.

"Yes, that's right. When the young men go away for years, even. An adventure. I forgot you know the Ibans so well."

"But the Iban knows why he's going," Collins said. "And when he gets there, he knows what he has found, doesn't he?"

"He hopes so. Though it's all a matter of luck. He can't be sure what will happen when he starts out. No one knows what's going to happen, Tuan."

Sibuyoh slapped Collins's knee and broke into laughter.

"Not even the white man," he said. "Although you may think you do."

"Yes, OK."

"When I was a young man, I followed the bejalai far up the Rajang River. Above Belaga. Very interesting up there."

Sibuyoh nodded, affirming his own opinion. The Rajang was the longest river in Sarawak.

"The Ibans there are savages, of course," Sibuyoh continued. "No manners. Don't know how to eat."

Sibuyoh imitated a man slurping his food from a bowl, his fingers spread across his face. The Iban laughed, and his three gold teeth shone in the dull light.

"But very beautiful women, Tuan. Very beautiful."

"What'd you do there?"

"Worked for the Chinese on a boat. Worked for the missionaries."

Sibuyoh nudged the dead cigarette with his toe.

"How long?" Collins asked.

"Nine years."

"Why'd you go? You particularly?"

Collins remembered the kind of longing he had felt in his office in San Francisco, when he had looked out at the bay and thought how he could change everything for himself were he simply to get on an airplane and fly away to a jungle somewhere. He had not been dissatisfied, really. He was not a failure. It was simply that the individuality of the idea had so thrilled him. Then he had actually done it.

"Many do," Sibuyoh replied. "I had no reason, myself. It's a custom."

Collins held his hand out the doorway. Runoff from the roof splashed over it and continued to the ground. The rapids had turned foamy brown. After a long silence, Sibuyoh reached again into his bag and brought out another ball of rice. He handed it to Collins, who unwrapped it and laid it out on top of his rucksack.

And it was true enough, Collins thought, the work he did out here had some importance. The Ibans understood what he was trying to do. Travel in this country was by boat and by foot. The only road outside Kuching, the capital city, was made of gravel and went a hundred miles to the north toward Sibu. New sections were added to it month by month. But they were very small sections, built with great difficulty through jungle, unstable mud, hills, and mountains. Collins's current job was to stump for the road and for arteries to it among the upriver Ibans who would be affected by it. The Ibans were considerably surprised whenever he came to visit because of his ability to speak with them and understand what they wanted. They were not much appreciated by the Malays who ran the government. They loved it when someone important showed an interest in them. Few white men spoke their language. Indeed whenever Collins arrived at a longhouse for a visit, the first thing he heard about was the other white men who could speak Iban. His few years in Sarawak had taught him who those men were, and he had met some of them. It was a small, respected group of people. Collins was gratified to be a member.

Nonetheless, the closer he came to the truth in his understanding of this country, the more cast away he felt within it. The jungle and the mountains surrounded him and convinced him he was simply a stranger. Always a stranger. Even now the air settled about him without motion. He was enveloped by it, and his spirits slowly fell apart. Collins worried that this was the end to which all his work in Sarawak had really come — a missed boat, waiting, a stifling rain.

"Did you come here because you were unhappy?" Sibuyoh asked.

"No. It was to find out what the rest of the world is like, that's all."

"The rest of the world."

Sibuyoh reached up to brush away an insect that had tangled itself in the cloth around his head.

"And so, where we are sitting now, Tuan — this shack — this is the rest of the world?"

He turned from the doorway and laughed. Collins, remaining in the gray, wet light, grinned also. Sibuyoh looked up into the sagging roof, which was hung with cobwebs. To protect against malaria, the government sprayed all the buildings from time to time with DDT. The ridgepole and rafters of the shack, which were crusted with the white residue of the insecticide, looked like bones.

Sibuyoh walked to the rear of the shack, hunkered there and pointed into the dark cobwebs. His laughter grew to a phlegm-ridden outburst. Collins stared into the rain. The river was the color of gray mud.

He watched a cluster of branches and trunks that poised a moment at the top of the rapids. Sibuyoh's laughter blended with the roar of the monsoon in the trees. One day I'll leave, Collins thought. My work will be taken over by some other bureaucrat and I'll be forgotten. The roads he had built would fall away in storms like this. Washed into the rivers.

The trunks appeared to be part of a large clump of river wreckage, trees washed out by the storm. But the wind-torn fronds and branches stuck up into the air. They disappeared into a dark trough as they started down the rapids, then reappeared, turning about and listing. They surged past some boulders and dropped into another trough.

"Sibuyoh," Collins said. He couldn't make out the wreckage for a moment. He beckoned to the Iban to join him at the door.

"What's that?"

Collins pointed to the rapids. The Iban stared a moment into the distance, then took in a breath.

"It's a boat," he replied. "There are people on it."

The boat careened down the rapids. Three men attempted controlling it with paddles. They had put palm fronds upright in the gunnels to act as sails. But the wind had long ago shredded these, and the remaining tattered sticks were what Collins had first noticed. Eight people huddled in the boat. Three others were in the water holding to the boat's gunnels.

"There must have been another boat," Collins said.

"Yes. Capsized. Hit a tree or something."

"We've got to help them," Collins said.

He hurried out the door and, suddenly, the storm battered against him.

"But how, Tuan?" Sibuyoh asked. In the roar of the wind his voice could barely be heard.

"Your boat," Collins yelled. "The engine's good, isn't it?"

"Yes, but it's dangerous out there."

The rain coursed down Collins's back. His shirt became spattered with drops, then was inundated. He walked toward the bank where Sibuyoh's boat was moored, and after a moment Sibuyoh joined him. The rag about the Iban's head was plastered by water to his neck. He stood with his hands on his waist, and his skin, which was tattooed with dark blue designs, gleamed.

"We've got to move quickly," Collins said.

"I won't do it," the Iban replied.

"But we can't let those people drown, Sibuyoh."

"If we go out there, *we'll* drown."

The Iban stepped toward the shack.

"This is stupid, Tuan," he said. He turned toward Collins again. "You don't understand this river."

Collins pulled the boat to the shore and jumped in. He removed the tarp from the engine and pulled the starter cord. The boat floated into the river again, dangling at the end of the rope. When Collins could not get the engine started after several tries, Sibuyoh pulled the boat back to the shore. He untied the rope, turned the boat about and motioned Collins to the bow. Pushing off from the shore, Sibuyoh angrily started the engine and headed the boat into the middle of the river.

Collins's mind rushed wildly. The disabled boat turned about and listed, righted itself, and disappeared in a trough at the bottom of the rapids. It came up again. A spray of brown water hurdled the bow and dispersed into the rain.

"A ghost's taken you," Sibuyoh shouted. He put a hand up to his forehead to shield his eyes from the rain.

"Hurry up, goddamn it," Collins said. The order — in English — got no reply from Sibuyoh, who turned the boat down the full surge of the river.

Water pummeled the sides of the boat and spilled into it. The spray blotched Collins's vision. They could not make headway on the stricken craft. The river flowed so quickly and forcefully and there were so many obstacles that Sibuyoh shouted they might be wrecked just trying to get away from the shore. For a moment the drifting boat disappeared. Collins could see nothing in the squall. Sibuyoh's engine sputtered and quit. He pulled the starter cord several times, then lifted the prop from the water to examine it. They turned about, without direction, until the engine started up again, and Sibuyoh was able to head the boat downriver. Finally they approached the disabled craft, but Sibuyoh could not bring his boat close enough to make contact. The prop had broken on the other boat, which turned in circles down the current. The people on board were all Ibans. Their craft was a single piece of wood carved from a large ironwood trunk. The gunnels were shredded by wear. Moss grew in patches along the sides. The three men struggled to paddle it, but the force of the current was too strong for them. After several minutes Sibuyoh approached the boat from the rear. He came up behind it slowly, and Collins moved to secure the two boats together.

He reached over the side for one of the people in the water — an old, small man, anguished, his undershirt torn to shreds. Collins pulled him up onto the gunnel and reached over to grab his shorts. Sibuyoh's boat lurched as one of the men jumped into it from the other craft. Collins was thrown into the river.

The man clawed at his neck. Collins tried pushing him away, but the man would not let go. They struggled and Collins's mouth filled with water. His throat clogged. He began choking. The old man fought to use Collins's body as a line to the surface. Collins pushed him away.

He gasped as his head broke into the air. The Iban had disappeared. Collins remained quite close to the boats, which were intertwined, people strewn about them like weeds. Sibuyoh tried helping people from one boat into the other. There was a danger Sibuyoh's boat would capsize, and he fought off one of the men to keep his craft steady. The rope between the boats came loose. Sibuyoh grabbed for it. Screaming, he held fast despite the rope's sudden jerking between his hands. One of the others helped him secure the boats again, and Sibuyoh sat down, holding his hands painfully together. As Collins swam toward him, Sibuyoh suddenly pointed back into the river. Collins turned and saw a woman flailing in the water. She was drowning, and Collins swam to her. She reached for him the same way the old man had. Collins fended her off. He swam behind her, a few feet away. Her eyes followed him, and he dived beneath the surface to escape her. Reaching out, he grabbed her legs, pulled her beneath the surface, then wrapped his right arm around her chest. When they came up, the woman sobbed, cries indistinct to Collins, fearful screams. He swam backward toward the boats. Collins panicked as he realized they were moving away from him.

The two craft turned and lurched down the river. Collins held tightly to the woman, who continued fighting him. Suddenly the boats halted, jammed against a large tree trunk beneath the surface. Collins and the woman collided with them. He threw out an arm but could find nothing to hold. Splinters tore at Collins's back. With one of the other men, Sibuyoh took Collins by the shirt and held on long enough for the American to grab the gunnel. The Ibans took the woman into the boat. Collins was hauled up as well. He gasped and flopped into the rear, which was cluttered with muddied, squirming bodies.

The woman lay next to Collins. Her sarong was twisted about her legs. Her stomach rose and fell in spasms, and she cupped her hand over her eyes, protecting them from the rain. One of the children, a girl, stroked the woman's hair, cradling her head in one hand. The girl tried removing pieces of mud from her hair, but there was so much mud that her efforts had little effect. A man sat in the bottom of the boat at Collins's feet. He appeared almost to have died. His face was dark and lined with exhaustion. His hands lay separately in his lap. His shoulders slumped to the left. When Collins turned over, the man dropped a hand onto Collins's ankle.

"Thank you," he said. The voice was a gravelly whisper.

Collins turned away. The vibration of the engine as the boat made its way toward the shore felt warm to him, and he began a kind of daydream in which there were few images, rather washes of liquid warmth that took him over.

Fifteen minutes later Collins stood on the lower bank, three miles below the shack. Rain fell over him in a flood. He attempted wiping the mud from his shirt to no avail. His clothing and his skin were the same yellow-brown. His hair was filled with river silt.

Sibuyoh secured the boats to a tree on the shore. Blood glittered on his palms and he dipped them into a big puddle of rainwater. He winced as he attempted washing them.

Collins turned toward the higher shore, stumbled in the mud so that his arms plunged into the water, then righted himself once more. The Ibans from the boat now sat on the high bank — many of them lying on it — like rubble. There were six adults and four children. They had lost one — the old man. Collins reached for a branch and pulled himself up the bank. He stopped a moment to rest. His back hurt where he had twisted it falling from the boat. He looked down at himself, alarmed by his resemblance to the mud in which he stood.

"You saved them, Tuan," Sibuyoh said. He reached down to help Collins to the bank. At first Collins paid no attention to the Iban's remark. Sibuyoh stood at his side and wrapped his hands in some rags he had brought from the boat.

"We both saved them, Sibuyoh."

"No, Tuan. It was you. You jumped in the river. You pulled them out."

Sibuyoh broke into weary, slow laughter.

"I only pulled one out," Collins said.

"Yes, but if you hadn't insisted, I wouldn't have gone at all."

He shook his head.

"I'm not crazy, Tuan."

He looked into his hands. The rags were stained with engine oil and blood.

"These are poor bandages," he said. He held them out, palms up in the rain.

Collins's legs ached as though they had been beaten with a stick. Water ran down his arms to his hands, then in minute streams from the ends of his fingers to the ground. The stricken Ibans remained scattered in the mud. They were frightened, sodden, broken down. But they were alive. Collins looked up from Sibuyoh's hands into the sky. Rain fell down onto his face as though from a single point, silver and gray lances of water. He felt the storm was trying to blot him out, to erase the memory of what had just happened. He would not allow it. Collins opened his mouth and let the rain fall against his tongue. He felt his own heart beating within the muddy shell of his skin.

11 / A Posthumous Gift

Collins knew the man was dying the moment he saw him lying across the trail. He halted beside an ironwood tree and stared at the twitching body. The man lay on his stomach, a woven straw basket still attached to his back by its black, cloth cinch tied about his forehead. He was an Iban, a small man whose detailed tattoos barely showed on his dark skin. There had been no violence. The only marks on his body were two large scars on one shoulder, years old. Some of his gear — a plastic bottle of cooking oil and five rice-balls wrapped in leaves and tied together with bamboo twine — had fallen out of his basket. The sheath that held his parang knife was twisted across his back, the parang itself still inside.

Collins turned the man over on his side. A billow of lacy spittle passed across his lips. His eyes stared without sight into the sky.

Collins recognized him. Indeed he was the man Collins was traveling to meet. Penghulu Duai was headman at Rumah Batu, politically powerful through upriver Skrang and an opponent of Collins's, and the government's, efforts to put in a road to his region. They had met once previously in Kuching at a meeting of headmen from everywhere in Sarawak. Duai was distinguished at the meeting for being so unsophisticated. The other headmen wore dusty Western suits, shirts, and rubber sandals. Duai arrived in a ceremonial loincloth and bare feet. He was lavishly tattooed with dark blue birds bordered by geometric designs on his chest and stomach. His hair was cut in the traditional Iban manner, straight across the forehead and over the ears, hanging long to the middle of his back.

Duai was well known for his opposition to the government on almost every issue. No national language. No roads. No Chinese. No Malays. Many government people in Kuching laughed at him, considering him a bumpkin. Collins agreed, but Duai nonetheless ran upriver Skrang very well. Normally the long-houses there did not get along well, and many were poor. Duai, a noted diplomat, had helped unite them, making up in cajolery what he lacked in political sophistication. And he had taken many Japanese heads in 1945. He was therefore deeply respected by the Ibans.

"What happened?" Collins asked in Iban. "Please, what happened?"

The man attempted to speak, but the effort was not a reply at all. Simply a mutter, indistinct syllables. Duai was seized by an epilepticlike throe and died, shaking violently a few seconds, his jaw tight and crackling.

Collins lay him to the ground. His shadow formed a dark frame around the Iban. He checked the small, cotton pouch attached to Duai's loincloth. There were some coins plus a tin of Chinese tobacco and some yellow rolling papers. Inside the basket was more food — a sack of sugar, a block of salt wrapped in plastic, some cilantro and other spices, plus more tins of tobacco. Duai had not been robbed, not murdered. Who would murder him out here anyway? Collins wondered. Rumah Batu was twenty-three miles away.

Collins turned Duai over once more. He expected him to move, to grunt, to show surprise that his sleep and his privacy were being invaded. But Duai simply turned over with Collins's effort, like a mattress. The Iban's skin felt like submerged leather, and Collins let go of him, repulsed. The body fell back to the ground. Where his head hit the earth, a flat cloud of dust whirled into the air and very slowly dispersed.

Collins stood, removed his rucksack and laid it on the ground. What could he possibly do with Duai? He had come along so haplessly at the moment of the man's death that it seemed Duai must have been ambushed for Collins's benefit. He wiped the sweat from his face. He looked into the trees. Sweat ran into his eyes, and the sun, already slivered by palm fronds, melted into liquid. The singing of birds in the forest was underscored by the bass chatter of orangutans far upriver. The noise of their yelling and their passage through the trees broke into the simplicity of Collins's fear. He cursed himself for being in the forest at all.

He noticed a trickle of fresh blood running from a cut on the Iban's ankle. Kneeling and looking carefully at the blood, Collins discovered a small hole torn open at one side. Duai had surprised a krait, probably sunning itself on the trail. The snake, its black and yellow stripes blending into the dead leaves on the trail, had attacked him. There had been no time for a tourniquet. The man had died in minutes.

Collins looked about for the snake. For a moment he wished the body would disappear somehow, that it would go away. Then he swore at himself for the cruelty of his complaints. His own misfortune was nonexistent compared to that of the Iban. Misfortune was hardly the word for it. Rather, a grave disaster, killed on a trail far from anywhere, without a witness, to be discovered by a Tuan who had no idea what to do.

I've got to pack him out of here, Collins abruptly decided. But as far as he was from the nearest village, with some very rugged terrain on the way, the task was enormous. I can't leave him out here to molder, Collins thought. It would be like abandoning him to die. Collins snickered at the irony of this thought. But it was unthinkable just to desert the man. Duai was too important to be resigned to the jungle. Collins decided it was absolutely necessary to take him back to Rumah Batu. A cynical idea, he thought, but the truth anyway. Collins had been going there to meet with Duai and several other headmen, one of many trips in Ulu Skrang to lobby for the road. Duai was the central figure.

The American had been walking only a half hour from the riverbank where the Chinese cargo boat had left him. There would not be another boat for three days. This was the kind of trip he normally loved — walking far upriver and disappearing for a time into the villages. Though he still had difficulties with the bad food, the filth, and the sickness among the Ibans, Collins much preferred traveling out here to sitting in his office in Kuching. There, his work was like the work he had done in California years before, with paper and engineering plans and T-squares. Out here, he could talk and laugh. Here there was sweat. There were the rain and the dark forests.

Collins opened his rucksack and removed his sunglasses, two bananas, and his San Francisco Giants cap. He placed the bananas in a pocket of his shorts and secured the cap on his head. Slipping the glasses into his shirt pocket, he knelt once more over Duai. The spittle had begun running from either side of the Iban's mouth, and Collins wiped it away. With considerable difficulty Collins removed Duai's basket and cloth harness and lay them aside. He was able to pull the Iban to a sitting position. He reached under his arms from behind and dragged him to a tree. Duai's feet leaned evenly to the right, and one of his rubber thongs fell off. Collins leaned him against the tree, then took up the harness and tied the man's hands together at the wrists. Duai's eyes were glassed behind the thin, open slits of his lids. His mouth hung open. He looked sleepily violent, as though he were about to awake from a dream to attack Collins. Collins knelt before him and laid the dead man's arms over his own head, so that the two men faced each other in an embrace. He turned about onto his knees and leaned forward. The body fell against his back like a sack of dirt, knocking Collins to the ground. He sprawled on the trail, and the baseball cap fell into the underbrush beyond his reach. He got up to his hands and knees. He reached out for the cap, but Duai's weight and the cumbersome swinging of his arms and legs made it difficult for Collins to balance himself. To hell with it, Collins whispered, and he steadied himself and stood, taking Duai's legs into each of his arms. He clasped his hands together to steady the legs against his sides. Staggering at first beneath the weight, Collins cursed and started up the trail.

He walked for an hour through the low hills, down a loose section of cliff slippery with shale along the bank of the river.

The sunlight against his neck felt like an iron against a sheet. He was sweating so much that Duai's legs slid about Collins's trunk.

Collins recalled the day four and a half years earlier, in Washington, when he and several others had gathered for an orientation meeting. "The Agency for International Development is just that, gentlemen," the State Department representative had said. He had had a white, short-sleeved shirt and short hair done in the Kennedy style, which reminded Collins of an exploded cigar blooming from his forehead. "We're out there to bring those people into the twentieth century — through development. Now some of our people are in risky situations. As you know, we operate in some war zones, and there are always guerrillas to worry about, anti-Americans and so on. So you have to be ready for all kinds of . . . " — the man allowed a tiny smile to appear on his face — ". . . contingencies," he concluded. I wish that fellow were here now, Collins thought.

He stepped over a wet log that had fallen across the trail. The weight shifted to one side. Stumbling, Collins put out a hand against a tree. It occurred to him that simple blind responsibility forced him to do this. It had not been a rational decision. No decision at all, in fact. But the sliding sweat, the odor, which had now become very strong, and Collins's aching shoulders and hips called his sense of duty to question. What do I owe this Iban? he wondered. The answer curled through Collins's brain again and again. A great deal, Collins thought. A posthumous gift. You'll be a hero!

Duai had argued that other rivers had been ruined by the arrival of the Tuans and their machines. Not that the roads were useless. Indeed the roads provided the way for people to stream from the longhouses, so that in effect the forests were being emptied by the government. That meant the end to opposition in Sarawak. "No roads, no roads," Duai had shouted in Kuching, his tattoos quivering on his upper arms. The Malay bureaucrats, attempting conciliation, barely stifled their laughter. Collins had been furious with the waste of his time, but in fact there still was no road. That Duai could now save the project seemed ludicrous to Collins. He'll roll in his damned grave, the American thought as he gasped up the trail.

The path entered more thick forest, wet with residue from the previous night. The broad leaves of the ferns appeared laden with oil. Because of the shade cast by the trees, the mist remained close to the leaves. They brushed against him as he passed and left swatches of cold water on his arms and shoulders. His legs quivered with the body's weight.

After two and a half hours of steady hiking, Collins lowered the body to a dirt bank beneath some ironwood trees. Collins leaned back against the spread-eagled Iban. The thought crossed his mind that they must look like tobogganers transported to a snowless, deserted jungle. He reached up, took Duai's hands in his, slid them over his head, and let the man fall back to the ground.

The heat had begun to swell Duai's face. The body gave off a smell like that of a locked, flooded cellar. The disgust Collins felt increased his determination to carry on. He had fourteen miles to go to Rumah Batu. Collins sat down across the trail from Duai. The Iban's head was thrown back against the bank. His mouth hung open, and he stared at the trees. Collins, still frightened by him, expected him to turn about and say something. That he remained absolutely still, his head at a discomforting angle to his shoulders, intimidated Collins. He picked the man up again and started up the trail.

Collins climbed through the forest until the trail came out a few hundred feet above the Skrang River. Gray-blue clouds upriver formed smears of rain against the hills. Collins's plastic sandals slipped when he tried negotiating the mud and shale along the path. His thoughts had scattered, and he realized he was growing dehydrated and that each step drained him more and more of his own strength. Duai's weight had so strained Collins's back that the rest-stops gave him no relief at all.

He stumbled as he skirted the side of a cliff above the water. He swore at the body and let the legs drop, intending to punish it for its treatment of him. The dead man's arms pulled at Collins's throat. Collins, unbalanced, staggered about the trail and, falling to his knees, rolled with Duai into the underbrush. He broke his fall, then slid with Duai deeper into it, head first, tangling himself within the man's legs and the knotted creepers and vines down the embankment.

When they stopped, Collins was too fatigued for the moment to move. He thought he'd like to kill this son of a bitch. He elbowed the man in the throat, took his arm, and shook it as though to wake him up. The distaste Collins had felt on the trail blossomed to a morbid conviction, mindless and without direction, that he had been betrayed. His efforts to be rational failed him. It occurred to him again that the poor man was dead, emptied of his life by a small, striped snake. The man had borne no malice; he was an innocent in the woods like Collins himself.

"But you're a shit anyway," he said as he painfully extracted himself from Duai's grasp and began pulling him back from the underbrush to the trail.

When they came down the trail, they approached a bridge across the Skrang, a single tree trunk forty feet long, laid across the river between its two high banks. It was slick with moisture. Collins set the body up against a tree and went to the log to test his footing. The Ibans ran across these rivers with short, level steps, their forward momentum carrying them along. Collins had witnessed old men carrying sixty-pound bundles of wood on their backs, racing across these bridges in monsoon rainstorms without incident. Collins himself was not so confident. Though he had imitated the walk and had had few accidents, he had never mastered it.

It began raining heavily. Collins imagined himself dropping from the bridge, falling twenty feet to the water's surface, pulled by Duai into the river to his own death by drowning. No one to witness it. A silent killing in the jungle, murdered by a dead man.

I'm not going to do that, Collins thought. He turned away from the river. Rainwater dropped freely from the ends of his fingers as he walked through the mud toward Duai. Collins appeared to be inundated with water himself, the storm blowing through him to the ground.

"Not going to do that at all," he muttered.

Collins hitched Duai up beneath the arms, and pulled the man toward the bank. By now Duai was badly swollen, cumbersome in his crouched position. He was a ghastly burden, and Collins hurried to rid himself of it. He propped the body up on the edge of the bank, took a breath and held it a moment, confused by the mix of fear and relief that cluttered his mind. He imagined Duai's body skittering down the bank, winced with each blow Duai would take from his rough fall as he bounced from a tree trunk, slithered down a mud face, and rolled over the single boulder at the base of the embankment into the river.

Crouching on one knee, Collins himself was discolored by wet mud. His shirt was open to his waist. His hair hung down before his eyes, and water ran from it down his mud-spattered face. His failure to bring Duai to Rumah Batu caused a loathing for himself he could not control. How can you abandon him? How can you let him go? Collins surveyed the water's surface. As Duai swirled and rolled beneath the log bridge, you'd look away? Is that it? Or watch his body tumble through the riffles downriver and disappear?

He lay the body back once more and stared at the bridge. After a moment he took Duai up onto his back. He stood and secured Duai's legs. The rain, so heavy now that it obscured the surface of the river, appeared itself to have turned brown. The trees on both banks blew about, gray and sodden in the gusty wind. Collins decided simply to run across the log bridge, as he had so often seen the Ibans do it. The better the plan, he thought bitterly, the more certain he was he would fall. No. Abandon was the only way.

He plodded through the mud along the edge of the bank, making sure the Iban was steady in his grasp and clasping him tightly. He then turned quickly onto the log bridge. To his surprise, the footing was good. He hurried the length of half the log, his feet splayed to either side, his knees bowed like saplings. He did not dare look down at the water, up into the rain, or to either side. His momentum carried him, but he was disoriented and ridden with fear. He ran to the far side, and as he approached the bank, his left foot skittered across a piece of slick moss and he fell. He landed chest first on the log, and for a few moments he was knocked out of breath. Duai's head jerked about, hung from its neck. His face lay directly next to Collins's, and their cheeks nestled against one another. The Iban's distended skin seemed about to pop from the force of the swelling. His body lay on Collins's, a precarious burden, and Collins was sickened by it. He waited a moment, his legs to either side of the log. He had bruised his ribs. He found it difficult to move at all. His chest ached.

Large drops of rain ricocheted from his skin. They sounded like gravel tossed against a wall. Collins was five feet from the far bank. He lifted his feet and curled them about the top of the log. He would have to shinny to the bank, careful to maintain the balance that weighed him down. The river surged beneath him. He pulled himself forward. He hated the Iban. Such a fool, he thought. Should know the terrain out here. Collins reached for a vine, gnarled and embedded in the mud, on the edge of the bank. As he pulled himself forward, the vine came away in his hand. He rolled to his left with the force of Duai's body and felt himself sliding from the log. He screamed. Collins's legs swung like a pendulum below him before he lost his grip and fell.

They landed on the bank, several feet below its edge. Duai's body cushioned Collins's fall, and the two men rolled down the bank. Collins threw out his arms, to stop their fall toward the river. They became tangled in the underbrush and finally stopped there. Collins looked over his shoulder at the river below him. Terrified, he scrambled up the bank, pulling himself and Duai inch by inch through the mud.

When he reached the top of the bank, he rolled over on his side, exhausted, and with Duai beside him, lay there awash with water and mud. The forest around them blew messily in the wind, and rain pressed through the trees. Collins imagined the turning of their two bodies in the water, Collins and Duai head over heels downriver, lost forever. He stood and struggled several yards up the trail, stopped to rest, walked again and stopped. Duai's body felt glued to his back. It was a stiff sack of bones and ended hopes. Collins sensed that in its decay the body was struggling to hold on to him. The chest pinned to his back seemed to gel with his own skin and to form a mess of blood and ooze that entered into him. The mud thickened beneath Collins's sandals and sucked them down. He fell once on the path and attempted standing again. Finally Collins dropped Duai, a hunched, swollen mannequin, by the side of the trail.

Collins crawled a few feet away. He sat up against a tree trunk and rested his arms on his raised knees. He watched Duai a while, then closed his eyes and dozed. Collins worried he and Duai were completely isolated now and lost. Collins could not guess how long the storm would last.

Laughter came from the rain. It sounded like delirium. He awakened abruptly, certain Duai had returned from the dead, that it was a dream, a joke. But soon he saw two Iban children and a man walking down the trail, sheltering themselves from the rain with giant, green philodendron leaves. When they spotted Duai, the children yelled with alarm. The man appeared as frightened as the children. He raised the leaf far above his head and peered at Duai's body. The Ibans had not seen Collins, so that when he listlessly waved at them, they were startled and retreated behind some ferns, shouting there was a ghost on the trail, there were bad ghosts, bad, bad ghosts.

A half hour later the Ibans brought Collins to the longhouse Rumah Batu. They helped him bathe and gave him a cotton sarong to wear. Collins recovered on the long inside porch. Duai's brother, a younger, skinny man whose name was Tulit, thanked him profusely for what he had done.

"We are very grateful, Tuan," Tulit said as he offered Collins a Rothman's cigarette. The two men sat on a rattan mat. Collins had propped himself against a wall and was encircled by several of the longhouse's occupants. He accepted the cigarette, realizing it was a special gift. Rain battered the thatched roof and made it necessary for Collins to lean close to Tulit, who spoke very softly and quite respectfully. "Duai will not travel alone now, because you have brought him back to us. His soul is happy."

Collins was less enthused, but he understood the Iban's sincerity.

"Thank you," Collins replied. His voice sounded distant, even removed from him. He was too tired to speak, but he made the effort anyway. Several children and women crowded about him, and Tulit's wife placed an aluminum teapot and two glasses on the mat between the men. "It is our custom to help those in distress," Collins continued. "We fear for dead souls. They must be protected."

Tulit lit Collins's cigarette and poured him a cup of tea. His face was taut with concern, and as he spoke, Collins understood how grateful the man really was. His own fatigue and the conviction that willfully, and hypocritically, he had made a fool of himself began to lessen.

"We will celebrate your kindness," Tulit said. Collins, sipping his tea, did not respond. He noticed Tulit's wife again, this time holding a green, glass bottle filled with tuak.

"The people of the house want to thank you, Tuan," Tulit continued. He gestured toward the far end of the porch. Collins, with dismay, realized there was going to be a speech, maybe a dance. He sipped once more from his tea and stood up. His chest ached, and he sighed as he followed Tulit through the crowd, past the many villagers who reached out to touch his arms.

A small gamelan had been set up, and three players now began the leaden, dirgelike music. Many children had gathered about the musicians, and, as he approached them, Collins saw one of the villagers dressed in a ragged costume of feathers lying heavily along his shoulders and arms, with a large headdress that resembled a bird's beak. He was to be entertained by a dance of the spirit, a portrayal of the fierce bird Lang in flight. Collins knew he would simply nod and struggle through the entertainment, dumbfounded by fatigue. But the dancer had begun already. His bedraggled costume, years old, seemed to disintegrate even while he danced. As Collins sat down next to Tulit, he noticed how finely the dancer moved, how his grace actually enlivened the wings he wore. Their age did not matter. Nor did their tattered condition. In the candlelit gloom of the long porch, the deep bass gong sending a shiver along the bamboo floor, Collins was moved.

He recalled the ghastliness and the mud of Duai's death, the decay of his body in the wet heat. But as the dancer swirled about, Collins felt his own spirits rise, as suddenly as they had fallen into horror on the trail. The dance provoked him to the knowledge that he had done something of great value despite all his complaining. He had saved the Iban's soul. Collins folded his hands in his lap and stared at them, then up at the retreating dancer who moved slowly in a circle, his arms still graceful beneath the burden of his wings.

12 / The King

"We're just damned glad to have him," Collins beamed.

"You're forunate," Joe Salt said. "A fellow like Eddie . . . as good as he is . . . in a situation like that, you couldn't have a better man."

Salt fingered the glass of Tiger Beer on the table before him. At the rear of the café the Chinese chef stirred a mixture of shredded pork and green beans, tossing it quickly from his wok onto a white crockery dish. He moved so rapidly from order to order that he appeared automated. He shouted at the two waiters. The rattle of his voice underscored the fervor of his cooking.

"Eddie's really the best I've ever seen out here," Salt grinned. The photographer was of medium height, thin, with very defined musculature and extremely curly hair. He was dressed in a green T-shirt, khaki shorts, and sandals. He had been visiting on assignment from the *National Geographic,* and his article about the new nation of Malaysia, with the state of Sarawak as its centerpiece, had almost written itself, he had said. Eddie Gould had provided the impulse for the last section of the piece, about the Peace Corps, the Agency for International Development, and other examples of American largesse and how they were bringing light to the jungles of Borneo.

"You ought to go up and see him," Salt said. "It'd be a treat."

Collins was inclined to do so. In Sarawak, where the Peace Corps had a large presence, his own associates, the AID people,

205

who were far more professional and capable, but more secretive, had received short shrift. They didn't bring publicity down upon themselves as the Peace Corps people did. He sipped his beer as the waiter placed the pork dish before them.

"I think I will," Collins said. "It's a pleasure to hear about people like Eddie. Doesn't happen too often."

Salt laid his chopsticks on the table. His eyebrows rose in quizzical uncertainty.

"I mean, you put people out there by themselves," Collins explained, "and it sometimes results in a kind of . . . well, disintegration. Nothing serious, of course. Sometimes it's a retreat. They read books all day instead of doing what they're supposed to do. Or they don't do *anything* instead of doing what they're supposed to do."

Collins looked out to the sidewalk. A crowd of Malay students passed up the street. They were dressed in white shirts, dark blue shorts, and sandals — their school uniform. There was a languid pleasure about their passing. Their dark skin and black hair gave soft contrast to the noise of traffic and bustle from the potholed street.

"Most of our people, of course, do better than that," Collins continued. He spooned a pile of meat from the bowl and laid it next to the white rice on his plate. "You say you've finished your article?"

"That's right," Salt replied. He pulled his canvas bag from the floor and set it on the table beside his plate of rice. "And I've got the film right here."

Salt smiled broadly. His curly hair appeared electrified against the water-stained wall behind him.

"I'm going to try to get him on the cover, and if I do that," he grinned, "Eddie'll be famous."

After three and a half days' travel on the Baleh River, Collins's boat reached the first of the river's extensive system of rapids. The ironwood trees that grew out over the water were held together by the mesh of ferns and deciduous plants that formed a gigantic cliff on each shore. A hundred yards farther there were several very steep rapids through which the boat would have to pass. The boatdriver shouted at the guide in the prow, who pointed the way through each plateau of rocks.

The river narrowed considerably, and the forest grew darker. The trees here were very thick; their variegated roots gripped the banks like broken hands. There were fewer people, but, if anything, the atmosphere was friendlier with the wet odors of fruit and fallen green. The river now was very clear. The forest formed a long, sun-dappled cavern about the American's boat. Collins was certain they would make the upper rapids at Rumah Bintang before noon, and indeed within half an hour he heard the approaching roar of the falls.

The boat progressed another half mile up the river. As it slowed at the foot of the rapids, Collins pondered Eddie's peculiar success. There was so little to fall back on as a bureaucrat in a jungle like this. True, there was the government, the system he and Eddie represented and the employer who paid them. But Washington was fifteen thousand miles away. Its moral pull was therefore weak. As if to underscore the fact, Eddie, trained in Washington, filled up with a battery of State Department certitudes, had come out here and abandoned that training immediately.

Eddie's initial assignment had been to supervise the building of a new runway at the Kuching airport. With very little hesitation he had turned it down in favor of going far, far into the outback. Collins, recently promoted to run the AID program in Sarawak, remembered his own reluctance to let Eddie do it—a reluctance strengthened by Eddie's youthful arrogance. The man was twenty-seven but appeared eighteen. He seemed to have no consideration for himself. He didn't care that he was a dignitary. In support of his petition for a post in the jungle, he had argued that if everyone were aware of the consequences of their actions, no one would do anything. So, finally, Eddie ascended the Baleh River much farther than even the Malaysian government had thought advisable. So few Ibans lived in Bintang it was unthinkable that any foreigner would wish to go there. None ever had. But Eddie seemed to feel there was no reason to do *any* of this if he did not immerse himself in it totally. After he had gone up the

river, there had been no word from him for six months. He was
supposed to be mapping the uncharted tributaries of the Baleh,
and Collins had assumed that was happening. When Eddie had
finally come down to the district capital of Kanowit to pick up his
mail, Collins had gone there to see him. Reassured that Eddie
was merely a fervid civil servant, not harmful or nuts, in fact one
of the best, he had let him return upriver.

Now the boat ascended the rapids slowly. These were quite
extensive, a barrier to most travel farther upriver. The boat paused
periodically in its ascent, then turned and scurried loudly
through each portal of white water. At the top, on the right bank
opposite two large boulders through which the entire river
passed in a violent falls, the longhouse Rumah Bintang jutted
from the forest. The driver moored the boat opposite the falls,
and Collins walked up a path toward the longhouse. Several
hundred Ibans had gathered on the boulders overlooking the
river. They now descended to the bank, and Collins saw there
was a long gauntlet of women leading to the longhouse, each
holding a palm frond extended into the air. The pathway between
the women led to a notched log, which formed the stairway to
the house's entrance. A middle-aged Iban man, grizzled and
brown in a black loincloth, his mouth obscured by an enormous
homemade cigar, walked down from the house with three other
Ibans and greeted Collins. The Iban had to shout to be heard
over the roar of the falls.

"Good afternoon, Tuan. Thank you for coming. I am Headman Lupit."

He stepped forward and ponderously shook Collins's hand,
once.

"We're honored by your visit," he said.

Lupit gestured to the other men, who Collins realized were
chiefs of other houses farther upriver. They offered him cigarettes and a small glass of tuak. Collins quickly downed it. He
looked toward the longhouse.

"May I speak with Eddie?" he asked.

Lupit gestured toward the women. Collins walked up the path
beneath the raised fronds. There were expressions of wonder.

Collins's appearance this deep in the jungle proved Tuan Eddie was a weighty personage, very important to the White Man's Way. Surely their forest was now blessed. The crop would do well. Great fortune had come upon them.

Several children broke from the surrounding crowd to scurry toward the longhouse. But their clamor, each child vying to enter the house first, was interrupted by the appearance in the door-way—a great bird, Collins thought, a mannered, gorgeous appa-rition—of Tuan Eddie himself.

He was dressed in a black loincloth. His body was tattooed, everywhere, in geometric designs and figures of birds and snakes. The tattoos were similar to those Collins had seen on numerous chieftains up and down the rivers. But these were far more stylized and fluid. Collins realized the tattoos were of Eddie's own design. There was writing on some of them, as well. "Get off my cloud," in blue, etched across one shoulder. "I can't get no satisfaction" on one leg. Collins saw they were made from charcoal and local dyes, and were therefore temporary. The beak of one bird's head, drawn across his throat, was smeared

Eddie's white skin was incongruous in the costume. It made him resemble an emaciated ghost, done up artfully. His horn-rimmed glasses gave him a comic, priestly look. They were askew on his face. One lens was cracked, and a stem was held to the rest of the frame with soiled, white adhesive tape.

Eddie's headdress simply alarmed Collins. Numerous long feathers, blue and green, appeared to leap from the band that held them to his head. As he lowered himself step by step, the feathers jostled each other in the air. The headdress was not a traditional one. Collins had never seen one like it, and he guessed it too had been made by Tuan Eddie. The feathers were like small leaves rustling against one another, a delicacy within the rugged noise from the river.

"Hello, Dan," Eddie said. He extended his hand. His face was barely lined. The small patches of fluff that appeared on Eddie's chin had been there several weeks, Collins guessed, but they were not yet a beard.

"What the hell is all this?" Collins asked.

"All what?"

"This play-act. The feathers. What are you doing up here?"

Eddie remained silent a moment. At first he appeared confused.

"What's going on, Eddie?" Collins asked.

Eddie looked down at the tattoos on his body.

"Nothing's going on. I thought you'd like all this stuff. That's why I wore it."

The crowd of Ibans had gathered around them. Each of the men wore a loincloth similar to Eddie's, and their bodies were tattooed in dark blue. The men wore their hair quite long in a traditional cut that exposed their ears. Many of them had long, pierced earlobes, which extended below their jaws. The women wore black, cotton sarongs about their waists and were bare-breasted. One of them stood to one side behind Eddie, young and very shy. She's not more than thirteen, Collins thought. She stared at the ground, then glanced at the two white men. There was a smile on her lips. Her hands and feet had the same thickness as those of the other women, which came from the difficult work they did, the exposure to sun and mud. But she was the daughter of a wealthy tribesman, Collins thought, judging from the heavy brass rings that hung from each earlobe. The rings were a fashionable jewelry that Collins found very attractive in the Iban women. The balance required to keep them from swinging about gave the women a very correct posture and a careful step. So small, they walked with extreme delicacy, in contrast to the obvious difficulties they faced in their lives in the forest.

Eddie noticed Collins's interest.

"This is Lama," he said. "She's my wife."

"We've heard quite a bit about you downriver, Eddie," Collins continued. The news of Eddie's wife dismayed him. "And I want to talk to you about it . . . in private."

Eddie laughed.

"But nobody here can speak English, Dan," he replied.

Collins looked about at the Ibans. The Americans, white-skinned and fleshy, were a foot taller than any of the natives. The

Ibans, grubby and dignified, stood very respectfully at a distance. A pall of smoke from their homemade cigarettes hung over the group.

"I want to be alone anyway," Collins said.

"Oh all right,"Eddie replied. "Come on, we'll take a walk up the river."

He asked the Ibans to leave them alone a while. Collins, sensing Lupit could be offended, addressed him.

"Excuse us," he said in Iban. "I'm honored to be here, and thank you for your kindness. We are old friends and wish just a moment of privacy."

The headman nodded and turned away, gesturing the others back to the longhouse.

The two Americans walked along the riverbank above the falls. They entered a shady area beneath several large trees. Collins leaned against one of the trees and folded his arms. Eddie, his feathers waffling about on a breeze, hunkered down like an Iban tribesman, hands hanging listlessly about his knees. The posture seemed to Collins phony, mannered, as though Eddie wished to show some kind of cultural superiority to the other American.

"So you put on this outfit just for me?" Collins asked.

"Well, no," Eddie smiled. "I dress this way, actually, all the time."

Collins closed his eyes and remained silent a moment.

"Why, Eddie?"

"Because *they* do."

Eddie picked up a pebble from the ground and tossed it listlessly toward a tree several feet away. Collins became outraged.

"I want you out of here," he said.

"But why?" Eddie replied. He wiped his shoulder, and a portion of the tattoo smeared beneath his hand.

"We're in a delicate position, Eddie. You represent the U.S. State Department, you know, and as such . . . "

"Well, that's right," Eddie interrupted. "That's the way *I* feel about it."

Collins sighed. He seemed anxious to say everything he could as quickly as possible. The weight of his task, so large after so few minutes to consider it, seemed to blurt from him all at once. Eddie had sold himself into a primitive, irrational debauchery, and he proved it with his tattoos, with the grandiose idiocy of his feathers.

"I do!" Eddie continued. "I came up here and did what I was supposed to do."

"What? Become an Iban?"

Eddie looked down at his feet.

"No. I've taught these people how to grow green beans. You know what that means? They've got greens in their diet. First time ever. That's what I'm talking about. And we got them some chickens."

"Oh I know about all that," Collins interrupted. "Don't talk to me about chickens."

"But that's what I'm supposed to do, isn't it, Dan?"

"What?"

"Help out. I was trained to come out here and do this. I was trained! By you!"

Eddie pursed his lips and his eyes tightened, as if he were caught in a deception.

"To befriend the people. That's what you told us to do. Show them how good the Americans are."

"But not like this!" Collins shouted. His exasperation startled Eddie, who actually began to pout. His headdress fluttered in a warm breeze. Collins noticed the group of Ibans far below and was surprised by the number that remained outside the long-house. Virtually the entire village stood before the house, watching the Americans with marked intent. There was a stoical mournfulness about them. A white parabola of mist rose up through the forest. Inundated with water, the ground glistened. The forest itself seemed gloomy, heavy, yet it was speckled with wild fruits and orchids. Collins felt a kind of enveloping comfort from it. It was obscure, yet at the same moment it had a lilt, a darkness of exceeding beauty. It carried an atmosphere of sweat. Collins imagined his own enjoyment of the place, living in such forceful fruition.

"Do you know what this is going to look like?" Collins asked. "How the people in Washington are going to feel about this?"

"Who cares? How are they going . . . "

"You're going to be famous, Eddie." Collins's repetition of Joe Salt's words caused him to shudder. He imagined the State Department . . . Dean Rusk himself, probably, thumbing through the latest issue of the *National Geographic,* coming across Eddie as he hunkered in the longhouse porch polishing his blowgun or weaving a basket or some other damned thing. "Who runs that show out there?" Rusk would ask, and the assistant would find out that it was Dan Collins who ran that show.

"Famous?" Eddie asked.

"Yes. That *Geographic* article."

Eddie grimaced. "Dan. Pardon me," he said. "But I think you're being foolish."

Collins moved a few feet away from the tree. He looked down at Eddie, who remained squatting on the ground. The look on Eddie's face, a kind of lackadaisical pity, caused Collins to want to knock the feathers from his head.

"Goddamn you . . . "

"Look, I'm going down to the longhouse to ask my wife to make us some lunch," Eddie said. He stood and turned down the trail. As Eddie jumped over a large root, Collins noticed the soles of his feet had hardened and cracked, and that they appeared to have spread out, like those of the Ibans themselves.

"Secure your boat," Eddie said as he retreated, "and come have something to eat. We can settle this pretty easily."

A half hour later Collins entered the longhouse and walked the length of the porch toward Eddie's room. The floor was made of bamboo slats, and his passage caused a clatter that startled the animals below. The house had seventy-five rooms side by side, each of which fronted on the porch. Collins acknowledged the greetings offered by the Ibans who worked there. Though it was still daytime, the light that entered through the doors from the outer porch did little to push back the gloom. Collins paused a moment to speak with a woman who wove a large rice basket. She sat in a swatch of sun near a door. Her thick fingers pushed the rattan straw in and out of the basket frame. Her hair, which was graying, was pulled back into a tight bun. She wore a sarong about her waist. Her left foot lay on its side where it extended from beneath the sarong.

"How long does a basket like this last?" Collins asked.

The woman did not look up at him and replied with an indifferent tone that sounded insulting. Collins knew, however, from his own work with the Ibans that she was simply reticent and shy. She continued the work as she spoke.

"Many years, Tuan. The only problem is that we can't keep the rats away."

"The basket's very large," Collins said.

"Yes," she replied. "A year's worth of rice. The rats can eat a month's worth, so it's important we keep them out."

Collins smiled and pointed toward the far end of the house.

"Is Tuan Eddie's room down there?"

"Yes, it's the next to last, next to the headman's."

Collins thanked her. When he entered the room, he saw Eddie seated at the rear next to the folded mat that served as his bed. He was repairing a basket himself, and as Collins approached, he gestured toward a mat next to him.

"Looks like you're enjoying yourself up here, Eddie."

Eddie's face retained a childish puffiness, though Collins realized he had lost quite a bit of weight. He wondered if Eddie were not enacting a youthful ideal — that he'd become, through some insanity, an innocent in the forest. In other cases like this of which he had heard, Collins suspected something destructive — that the person was involved in escape, that the isolation and the jungle became, bad as they were, preferable to whatever the person had left. Such people went native with a scowl and made of their effort a self-righteous cause. But Eddie seemed gewgawed, humorous. He's like a kid, Collins thought. Can't judge. His innocence has put him in this damned loincloth. He'll be insulted when I tell him to put on his pants.

"I'm interested in the tattoos, Eddie."

"You like them? I made them myself," Eddie said as he surveyed the bird on his chest. "They're like Lupit's."

"A little more stylized . . . "

"He's my father-in-law, Dan." Eddie chuckled a moment. "I should tell you," he continued. "I've become . . . well, a kind of prime minister to him. Vice-chief, I guess."

"What do you mean, you're a king or something?"

"No, no. Just, well, second in command, I suppose. Incognito, though. Incognito."

Collins looked over the tattoos on Eddie's arm. Now they were badly smeared, and when he touched one of them, the dye came off on his fingers. A tin pot fell to the floor of the cubicle at the rear of the room, and a woman peered around the bamboo partition. It was Lama, who giggled as she walked into the room.

"Excuse me," she said. "The fire is hot."

Lama spoke with a very fine accent. Her face, which carried little worry, appeared so fresh that she made Collins smile.

"So, what do you think these people are?" Eddie blurted as he pushed the steel needle through the basket. Lama, embarrassed and pleased by Collins's visit, returned to the kitchen. "Why do they frighten you?"

"They don't frighten me," Collins replied.

"Then what do you have against tattoos or loincloths? Or my feathers?"

As he asked these questions, Eddie became noticeably angry. He hunched his shoulders forward to listen.

"But Eddie, it's not *their* customs I'm against. It's yours!"

Eddie set the basket and the needle down.

"For what reason could you be offended by them?" he asked.

Collins wondered whether Eddie were not having considerable fun with this. The drama of the conversation seemed to enliven him, while it merely irritated Collins. He felt there really should be no question of the impropriety of Eddie's actions.

"Here's the issue, Eddie. We have rules. I mean, the State Department has. It causes political problems when our people decide to go native. Malaysian government doesn't like it. It looks bad for them because they have to admit they *have* natives."

Collins grinned.

"Our government doesn't like it because . . . well, we represent the way it's supposed to be, you know. Technology, progress . . . "

Eddie leaned back against the wall. He raised his knees and let his hands rest on them. The fingers were quite soiled, the nails cracked.

"Look," Collins continued. "No matter what happens to our people out here, no matter how . . . democratic you may feel, there's one thing you can't do."

"What's that?"

"Become one of *them*. You know, an Iban. Or a Swahili. Or an Untouchable. Doesn't matter who the host population is."

"The natives, you mean."

"Right, dammit. The natives. It doesn't matter what else you do. You just don't do that. State Department rule number one."

"Why not?" Eddie asked.

"The governments are offended. And if you have a government that's offended . . . "

"Oh fuck your governments."

Collins did not finish. He now imagined the Minister of the Interior for Malaysia, Datu Zainal Ibrahim, who spoke perfect Oxford English, chiding him for the unseemly spectacle of an American living like, well, like Tarzan, Mr. Collins. Altogether unacceptable. And in the pages of an international magazine. Awful, Mr. Collins. Really quite awful.

"I've got to implore you, Eddie. Give this up. Come back downriver with me. This here . . . "

Collins gestured toward the longhouse porch and the jungle beyond.

"You can't do this."

He stood and moved toward the door. Lama looked around the edge of the partition. When she saw Collins was leaving, she glanced at Eddie, who remained seated on the floor silently.

"You're not staying?" she asked.

Collins attempted a smile, then shook his head. He addressed Eddie in English.

"I don't see how I can stay, Eddie. I'm proposing something to you that you obviously don't want to do. I guess I'm the enemy, really."

"Sure, if you wish," Eddie replied. "But you're my guest. Lama's made a dinner for us."

Collins opened the door. He was struck by the sad surprise on Lama's face.

"I'm sorry, Eddie. We've got to go tomorrow. I want you to go with me."

He closed the door behind him and walked from the longhouse.

Headman Lupit asked Collins to spend the night in his room and, after an embarrassing festival on the porch, at which Collins was congratulated for being such a fine man, and was told that Eddie was more than just a white man, rather an orang pandai — a wise man of great judgment, kindness, and conciliation — Collins had slipped away and gone to bed. In Lupit's bed, as it happened. The headman himself and his wife slept on the floor. It began raining, and soon the forest was awash with the storm. The roof-thatch absorbed the sound of the rain and deepened it, so that as Collins fell into his uncomfortable sleep, came out of it, and returned, the rain intruded on him like waves up and back on a black beach. He rose once and looked out the open window behind the kitchen. The trees blew about with abandon, slick with dark water.

The next morning Collins arranged his gear in the boat. The sun had risen from a gray mist that dispersed into the forest. It was exceedingly warm, and Collins's efforts were listless, without spirit. He sat on the bank watching the falls as it coursed between the two boulders above. The mist ascended into the trees and enveloped the lower branches.

Eddie walked down from the house, gesturing at the children who attempted following him. They returned to the overlook above, where Collins noticed all the villagers were standing. Eddie's tattoos were now badly smeared, though he still wore his headdress. Collins saw he had not slept. His eyes were blotched red and unfocused.

"Dan, I'm not leaving," he said.

"Why not?"

"My whole family's here. This is what I want. It's too important."

Collins tossed a rock into the river. He did not want to look at Eddie. The intensity of the man's distress deterred him, and finally he spoke with abrupt rudeness.

"Eddie, get your gear. Now. We're leaving in half an hour."

Eddie swore and turned toward the longhouse. He approached Lupit and Lama and spoke with them a moment. There was a long conversation, during which the Ibans grew very agitated. They began yelling, gesturing angrily at Collins. Eddie appeared surprised by their response. He shook his head and held his hands out toward them. They pushed him aside and moved down the bank toward Collins.

They looked ready for a battle. Their voices were garbled. They raged through the forest. At first Collins laughed. The matter seemed still to be private, something between the two Americans alone. But then he realized that neither he nor Eddie had seriously enquired about their interests. Suddenly he noticed one of them was carrying a shotgun. A few were even armed with ancient blowguns. Collins could not imagine them using the weapons. The Ibans were no longer fierce. The last heads had been taken in 1945, and those from the Japanese, true enemies, hardly nervous bureaucrats like Collins himself.

His fear worsened as he imagined his own head, with a grimacing smile, hilarious, hanging in a basket from the ridgepole of the longhouse.

The forest gathered up behind the Ibans, beyond the long reach of the longhouse, into a kind of gargantuan wall. Such light as there was was muted and gray. The natives now began running toward Collins. Spittle turned acrid in his mouth. He hated his own sense of duty, the cavalier authority he had felt over Eddie's life. Now I'm going to get killed for it, he thought.

Collins spotted Eddie at the rear of the crowd of Ibans. His feathers jounced about his head. He stumbled behind them, shouting. The Ibans approached and began a chant, translated approximately, Collins noticed, as "Yankee Go Home," over and over again. They waved their blowguns in the air, menaced the American with machetes. Eddie pushed through the crowd. He glowered at Collins as he spoke in Iban.

"Look, you've got to get out of here," he said.

"I know it, but . . . "

"Do it somehow. I'm sorry this has happened, Dan."

Eddie turned to the Ibans.

"Please, my friends. Thank you for helping me. Go back to the longhouse, please."

He turned again to Collins.

"They're angry, Dan," Eddie said in English. "I don't think we *can* get out of here, no matter what."

Collins, his voice fluttering, pursed his lips.

"Got to, Eddie."

"Oh, Christ!" Eddie yelled. "Give this up, would you?"

"Now, Eddie. Get your gear now. Take them back to the longhouse with you, and don't bring them back."

"Dan!" Eddie shouted. It was not an order, nor was it defiance. Collins heard, for the first time, anguish in Eddie's voice. His soiled skin and the feathers, wavering above the glasses that sat askew on his nose, now became a picture of exceeding sadness. Collins spoke up quickly.

"This is important," he yelled. "Just get your clothes, your books, whatever. You're getting out of here."

He turned angrily and walked up the bank, directly below the falls. He sat down on a large boulder shaded by the forest and watched Eddie, followed by the still smoldering crowd of Ibans, as he returned to the longhouse.

Collins knew Eddie was merely in love—in love with his young wife, with the people on upriver Bintang, the forest itself. Eddie *had* lost his mind. Even so Collins grudgingly admired the loss. Eddie was a fool. He was a kind of traitor. But the foolishness and treason had been matters of profound feeling, of an admirable sensitivity to beauty, to flesh and fine mud, to the forest. The dilapidated longhouse that seemed always to tilt no matter the perspective, the poverty of the Ibans . . . all this simply added to the eeriness of this place. Collins could come up with nothing to explain it away. Narrowed by his own task, blind to such romantic gush, he realized nonetheless he was now destroying Eddie's new life, all for the sake of the bureaucracy and of what was expected of him by Washington. So Collins found he resented his own task. He had brought great power to bear against the powerless. Eddie was right, he thought. You are just an intruder.

As he glanced again toward the falls, he saw Lama ascending the path from the longhouse. She walked very carefully, upright. Her negotiation of the rocks, over which she tiptoed while supporting her heavy earrings in the palms of her hands, was quite careful. She glanced at Collins with annoyance, he thought. After a moment he realized she was mortified. She approached him, and, very nervous, he stood to greet her.

"I'm sorry, Lama," he said.

"Excuse me, Tuan, I shouldn't do this, but may I plead for Eddie?"

"Plead?"

"Yes," Lama continued. "Please don't take him away. This is very bad. He's my husband and I love him."

"Oh yes, I . . . "

"I'll die, Tuan."

"What do you mean?"

"My people will reject me if he goes. I can't go with him, and I'll be alone. They'll laugh at me. 'Tuan's wife,' they'll call me. Butterfly. Make fun of me."

Collins knew there were many Iban women her age who had already had children of their own. But Lama's appearance defied that possibility. She was tiny. Her eyes glistened. The skin of her shoulders and torso was quite smooth, very dark, with no tattoos, and then gave way at her hands to cracks and work-thickened fingers. But she looked contrite.

"You know I can't do that," Collins replied.

"My father will suffer as well." Lama pointed toward the longhouse. "Eddie is his son. He has taught Eddie."

She began weeping. Her tears, heavy and invasive, immediately ruined Collins's protest. He was confused, unable to move.

"What harm is he doing?" Lama suddenly asked. Her voice, without control, had risen to a shout.

There was noise from the longhouse. Eddie, dressed in a pair of shorts and a white T-shirt, carried a military duffel on one shoulder. He remained barefoot. He had washed the tattoos from his arms and shoulders, and Collins saw the dyes had not come away completely. He was followed by a crowd of two hundred Ibans. The talk was chaotic, a rubble of confused protest.

"This is a terrible mistake," Lama muttered.

She turned toward Eddie. Her face was smirched by her tears. When Eddie saw her, he gripped the duffel tightly. He appeared threatened by her grief. He was embarrassed the way a teenager at a prom would be. There was no embrace. Lupit had led the way before the other Ibans. He walked with a kind of ceremonial heaviness, and Collins realized Lupit was shielding his own unhappiness behind his stoical passage up the pathway. The old man barely looked at Collins, who now turned down the trail toward the boat. Collins did not speak. His descent to the river held no sense of victory for him.

Eddie walked down to the boat and threw his duffel into the prow. He did not look back at the bank. He began climbing into it when Collins took his arm to pull him back onto the muddy bank.

"Look, I can't stand doing it this way, Eddie," he said.

"I'm sorry?"

"I think it's a dereliction," Collins continued, "the worst sort of dereliction."

He glanced at Eddie, then placed his hands in his pockets and glared at the mud below.

"But you're staying," he said.

Eddie, distracted by his effort to get into the boat, did not hear. He continued protesting, until Collins descended into the boat himself.

"I said you're not leaving."

Eddie's face maintained a kind of blank misunderstanding.

"Get your gear out of the boat," Collins said.

"But, Dan . . . "

"Please," Collins insisted. "Now. And no explanations. No questions."

Confused, Eddie grabbed his duffel and passed it up to the bank. He climbed the bank himself, then stood to watch Collins. Irritated by his own fecklessness, Collins sensed a smile on Eddie's face.

"Three days up here," Collins muttered grumpily. "Just to find out you're doing the right thing. And now three days back."

He motioned to the driver, who engaged the engine. The boat turned about before the falls. Eddie walked up the bank and spoke with Lupit, after which the Ibans broke into immediate raucous noise. Collins could hear none of the celebration because of the roar of the water. Several Ibans ran across the rocks shouting at the boat. Caught a moment in a large riffle before the falls, Collins barely noticed them. They appeared shrouded in the spray up above. After a moment he saw Lupit walking rapidly down the pathway to the edge of the pool. Collins ordered the driver to return to the bank. As they approached him, Lupit raised his hand into the air. In the sunlit mist his body looked shrunken, like old wood. There was a flurry of color in his hand, Eddie's feathers. When the boat nudged the shore, Lupit waded into the pool and handed the feathers to Collins.

"Thank you, Tuan," he said. "Please, take them as a gift. For your kindness."

His face, shining with water, appeared flushed. Collins himself was quite wet, and Lupit placed a hand on his shoulder.

"It's a gift," Lupit shouted.

"For what? For Eddie?"

Lupit did not answer. Rather he thrust the feathers onto Collins's head. Collins, disgruntled, adjusted the headdress. Lupit clapped him again on the shoulder.

"Feel damned stupid," Collins grumbled in English.

The boat pulled away from the shore. Caught in the rush of air from the waterfall, the feathers battered Collins's face. He wondered how he would report this to the AID people in Kuala Lumpur. Well, he didn't *have* to report it. But then there was the article. What'll they do when Salt's article — goddamned Joe Salt, he muttered — comes out? Eddie gone native. Eddie tattooed. Eddie a headhunter. Collins allowed his fears to overtake him entirely, and he slouched against his gear. The boat was lost a moment in the sun-dazzled mist, then moved farther downriver toward the protective isolation of the rapids. Collins sat up and turned to look once again at the Ibans. He glowered at them as they stood on the banks waving. Then he glowered at Eddie who, followed by his wife, shouldered his duffel happily up the log into the longhouse, and finally at Lupit, grateful and stoic on the lower shore. Collins leaned far back against his gear and surveyed the forest as it passed above the boat. The feathers obscured his sight. Maybe he'd wear them, he chuckled, when he submitted his report to the people in Kuala Lumpur. He laced his fingers behind his head and sighed in the dappled light. He knew the feathers looked ridiculous on him. Yet, for the moment, he felt they must adorn him, too, as they would a king.

MALAYSIA

Malaya

Brunei

Singapore

Sarawak

Sabah

Indonesian
Borneo

SARAWAK

SIBU

KANOW

SARATOK

KUCHING

SIMANGGANG